Also by TJ Whittle

Without Your Courage

AN EMPTY STOOL

An Empty Stool

By

TJ Whittle

Desert Palm Press

An Empty Stool

by TJ Whittle

© 2017 by TJ Whittle

(trade) ISBN: 9781942976332
(ebook) ISBN: 9781942976349
(pdf) ISBN: 9781942976356

Desert Palm Press
1961 Main Street, Suite 220
Watsonville, California 95076
www.desertpalmpress.com

Editor: CK King (https://www.facebook.com/RavensEyeEditing)
Cover Design: TreeHouse Studio, Winston-Salem, NC

Printed in the United States of America
First Edition May/2017

Acknowledgements

Thanks to the love and support of my wife, I continue to grow as both an author and a person. Thank you for the love you provide that allows this to happen. You encourage me to write, to be all I can, do all that makes me happy. Then we move on and you become my editor. During this stage, you push me a little more and then a little more again, challenging me the entire way.

Kerry Keohane Debrah, thank you for being my straight wife. You get me, you accept me, and you love me. Thank you for all your support. You are a strong woman who I am proud to know and love.

To all our children and grandchildren, thank you for the joy and laughter you bring to our world. We love each and every one of you. You bring so much pride and joy.

.

Dedication

This book is dedicated to all those who give of themselves day in and day out to help keep those without a voice safe. Our children are our future, and every one of them deserve to be loved and nurtured. Every one of them should know they are unique and important.

I'd like to say a special thank you to Helene Greening Mahros. Thanks for the help you gave me with this story, and thank you for all you have done over the years to keep so many children safe. You are a very special woman.

Prologue

AN ORANGEY-BROWN POWDER *covered the tips of her small fingers, the metal cool to her touch. "Two times one equals two." Her voice was barely a whisper. The last thing she wanted was to alert them to where she was.*

"Two times three equals—"

Bang. A slamming door silenced her. She rested her head on the pillow she'd managed to bring with her and lay still, the dusty wooden planks cold against her skin. Her shorts and t-shirt gave little protection from the crisp night air.

The two distinctive voices again began yelling at one another from the kitchen below her. Knowing it was safe, she continued with her ritual.

"Two times four equals eight."

When the rumbling began, she knew she could count on the springs. Tonight, as the yelling got louder, the coils were again there for her. They'd never let her down. They allowed her to stay there for as long as she needed.

"Fifteen times four equals sixty."

Sleep was calling to her. The yelling was loud but had become nothing more than white noise as her eyelids gave up their battle, the room now in darkness. Suddenly, her eyes flew open. She didn't know what was happening. Something had her leg, and she was being dragged from her precious springs. The safety she'd felt earlier was now replaced with terror. The darkness that had surrounded her like a blanket was now invaded by a bright light as she was yanked out from under her bed.

Her eyes worked to adjust to the sudden change. A searing pain spread through her head, again and again. What was it? She didn't know. It was matched by sharp jolts in her back. Panic flooded her veins. She became aware of something familiar. The voice of her mother. What was she saying? Telling herself to focus, she listened carefully to the words that were all a blur, blending into one another.

"It's all your fault. If it wasn't for you we'd be happy. You ruined everything."

Whose fault? What was ruined? Who made her mother unhappy? And why was that piercing pain still ripping through her head?

She recognised where she was. Her eyes adjusted to the light, and she could see the broken banisters along the stairs. Her head came down hard on each step, as she was pulled down them on her back. What was going on? Why was this happening?

The hand gripping her leg pulled harder. She was now next to the cupboards in the kitchen. Two of the rickety chairs were tipped over beside the table, a broken beer bottle beneath one. The floor beneath her was cold and wet, the broken lino scratched her bare arms. The rumble surrounded her now. It was loud. Her head felt like it was being squeezed and there was a buzzing in her ears. She had to concentrate to make out the words. They all tangled together in a mumbled haze, but if she really listened, she could make them out.

"Yeah, it's all her fault. We'd be having fun if it wasn't for her. All the money we waste feeding the ungrateful brat. And the clothes she just keeps getting too big for."

Then it was her mother's turn, "Yeah, selfish cow. She needs to be taught a lesson."

"That's what I'm gonna do," the deeper, gravelly voice of her father answered.

What were they talking about? Who was going to be punished? She felt a sudden pain bite into her arm, going deeper and deeper. Not stopping. Then another. And another. What was that? Was she being stung? She didn't know, but she needed it to stop. She tried to move away but couldn't. Something was trapping her there, unable to escape. What was pinning her down?

She looked up. Her mother was holding her to the floor, a strange smile over her face. One she'd never seen before. A smile should be friendly, so why was this one scaring her, and what was her mother now laughing at? As she tried to work it out, another bout of pain began. She turned to look at her arm. The bright-red tip of a cigarette was slowly being pressed into her skin. That smell. She didn't know what it was, but it was awful. It got into her nostrils and made her think she was going to throw up. Suddenly everything went dark. The deep scratchy voice melded with the higher, witchy shrieks of her mother before fading away.

***

Jo bolted upright, sweat pouring from her. She struggled to breathe in deeply, slowly allowing air to inflate her lungs to their full capacity before releasing it again. As her pulse began to slow, she turned the bedside lamp on. Jo looked to her hands. They lay trembling in her lap, resting above the covers. The nightmares that enjoyed disturbing her sleep so often were more intense lately, and she wondered why.

Her eyes tentatively made their way up her arm to her bicep. The soft flesh that was normally covered, out of view of others, was now exposed. Crimson spots of scarred skin looked back at her, as angry as ever.

Allowing her eyes to continue on the path she knew they needed to take, Jo cautiously lifted the bottom of her singlet up higher, toward her breasts, revealing the many crisscrossed lines that climbed upward from her navel to her breasts. There were too many to count, all layered one over the other. The anger in them had died down over the years, and Jo had become very good at ignoring their existence. If she simply kept her head up and stayed away from mirrors, it was easy.

She knew she had to acknowledge them, here in the safety of her room, letting them have their say, allowing her to never forget. On occasion, when the child she'd once been asked to be remembered, she'd listen. She wouldn't deny the small girl, she couldn't. So much had been taken from her already. To take this right, this need to be heard, would be unfair. Jo refused to do that to her.

Jo lifted the singlet over her head, letting her gaze fall to her chest. The scars ended their path just above her nipples. The underside of her breasts both hid multiple marks, all blending into the others that covered her stomach. Her nipples had been saved, as had her upper chest and neck. He knew people would notice wounds if they were placed that high. He left that area untouched. The bile was rising in her throat and Jo needed to move quickly.

"Shit, shit, shit." Speaking through clenched teeth, she hoped the words would buy her some time.

Jo threw the covers back. Naked feet collided with cold wooden floorboards. Covering her mouth, she ran. The first waves rose from her stomach. Leaning over the toilet, she collapsed to her knees. The heaving refused to subside until she had nothing else to give. A cold sheen covered her forehead, as she lay on the bathroom floor mustering the strength to get up. Finally, able to drag herself to her feet, Jo stumbled to the old wooden crates that stored her meagre belongings.

In the dim light, Jo dug in the boxes that substituted for drawers until she located a pair of socks and a sweatshirt. She tugged them on before slipping beneath the sheets she knew would be damp and cool. Trying to avoid the remnants of her sweat-ravaged nightmare, she pulled her covers over her head, blocking out the musty odour that filled her dingy flat. Exhaustion claimed her.

Chapter One

"TO BUMP," HOPE RAISED her glass out in front.

"Here's hoping he, or she, makes an appearance soon."

Hope shook her head. "I still can't believe you worked up to your due date. I was half expecting to have to deliver Bump on the bar."

"Oh, my God," Andy half squealed half choked, his face screwed up. "You'd have been on your own with that one." Leaning in, he hugged a puffy-faced Jane and patted her tummy. "I love you both, but seriously, can you imagine me delivering a baby?"

"There'd be a lot of screaming involved and not from Jane," Hope kidded.

"Oh, you could count on it," Andy said, as they all laughed.

"There's always a place here for you, Jane. I couldn't have made it through the past year without all the support you and Andy have given me."

"Thanks, Hope. Working for you has given me so much more than simply a job. Bump and I have family here now and that feels so good."

"We all gained that." Andy spoke over the rim of his glass.

"Actually, it's you we have to thank, really." Hope pointed a finger in Andy's direction.

Lifted eyebrows topped the look of innocence plastered over Andy's features. "Me?"

Hope and Jane laughed. Both knew him well enough to know the look may say sweet and innocent, but looks could be so deceiving.

"Yes you, but in this instance, you did something good. Remember that first night you took me out with you, not long after I hired you?"

Andy nodded. "Yep, I thought it would be a good chance for you to meet new people, though I really hadn't thought it through beforehand. It's a good thing I didn't. If I had, I probably wouldn't have asked you to come."

Jane looked at Andy, lines creasing her forehead. "Why?"

Andy pushed his glass toward Hope. "This story may require a top up."

Hope rolled her eyes. "Any excuse for more wine."

Andy looked to his left, then right, before leaning in. He spoke in an exaggerated whisper. "Shh, don't give away my secrets."

The group laughed again. The place was almost empty. An older couple sat at the windows, enjoying the sun while they took their time over coffee. Most afternoons they had a slow stream of people in need of a caffeine fix and snacks, but the place would remain quiet now until closer to dinner time when it would fill up again. Hope placed a full glass in front of Andy, and he began his story again.

"I went out all the time, either on my own and happy to meet up with whomever, or with a few other guys. Most of the time, a night out would be for one of two things. Either I was set to dance all night at a rave where talking was not on the menu, or I was on the prowl for a quick fuck. Again, not much talking involved. The bars and clubs I went to catered to the gay males of this fine city, but I'd never really considered where the lesbians might go or what they did."

Jane shook her head but laughed at the same time. "So where did you go?"

"He took me to his usual spots. We went into this bar and, other than two fag bangles, I was the only other woman. When we walked in, all eyes followed me. I was the vampire deciding who I might like to bite, and they were all worried it might be them."

Jane's eyes grew wide. "Really?"

Hope nodded. "Really."

Jane looked from Hope to Andy and back again. "I have a question."

"Sure, what is it?" Hope took a sip of her water.

"What on earth is a fag bangle?"

"A fag bangle is a straight girl who likes to hang off her gay friend's arm," Hope said.

"Okay, so they were accepted amongst the crowd at the bar, but you were looked at strangely?"

"Yeah, strange concept, isn't it? You'd think with all the discrimination that's been dished out to the gay community there'd be more support within. I was actually blown away to see how segregated gays and lesbians were when I got home."

"See, for me, I never knew anything but that," Andy added. "From the time I came out, there were always places I could go, but they were really only visited by other gay guys. The sole reason for existing was to provide a safe place to hook up."

"I think that's kind of sad, really." Jane frowned, and Hope nodded her agreement.

"I think so too," Andy shrugged, "now that I know better."

"Okay, back to the story." Hope sat up in her seat. "We had a few drinks there with me feeling like all the conversation was being monitored in case someone let out some top-secret codes around me."

"Because I've got friends who are gay and straight, both men and women, I figured everyone did. Until that night. It was an eye-opener for both of us," Andy admitted.

"I understand. For many years, gay men had to keep their meetings very secret. Getting caught could mean losing so much—families, jobs, freedom. It's all too easy to forget that it wasn't that many years ago, when homosexuality was illegal. People were imprisoned and locked up in mental institutions. They were put through electric shock treatment, lobotomies, chemical sterilisation, and beatings." Hope stared into her water for a moment, silently thanking those who went before her, those who had sacrificed so much.

"Sadly, most of my generation and younger never think of that. They take their freedom for granted, never considering others may not have had the same." Andy raised his wine. "I think a toast is due." He waited for Jane and Hope to raise their drinks. "To those who were brave enough to make the changes that allow us so much more freedom."

Three glasses clinked together, and the friends all took sips.

"Now, back to how *I* was brilliant enough to bring about all of this." Andy's arms opened in a flamboyant sweep of the room, ending with a fluid turn of his hands.

"Well, we went dancing." Hope recalled. "I was, again, one of very few women in the club and, once more, all eyes followed me. Though I must say, once I started dancing everyone seemed to forget that I was a woman. They were all in their own worlds and happy to be there."

"It helped that you can dance." Andy grinned.

"That I owe to a flatmate who loved to watch all the music videos and attempted to copy the dance moves. She ended up getting me and our other flatmate to join in for fitness. Seriously, if her upper-class English parents had seen those sessions, they would've keeled over."

"I wish I'd been a fly on the wall for that," Jane teased.

"Maybe we could re-enact those workouts one day." Andy jumped up, thrusting his hips back and forth before shimmying his top half.

Feeling her face redden, Hope shook her head vigorously. "Not on your life, mate. Now, let's get back on track. After I got home from dancing with Andy, I lay in bed and started to think how it would be nice to have somewhere to go that allowed people to have a few drinks, maybe a light meal, as well as somewhere to dance. Not rave music, just sounds that have a good beat that you want to sing and dance to with friends, in between drinks and conversation, a place where men and women, gay and straight, could mix and mingle. Then I wondered, why not here? The more I thought about it, the more I liked the idea. The best part was that I could keep the café style during the day, honouring Aunt Em and all that this place meant to her, as well as it becoming a place in the evenings that I could enjoy developing. Out of all that came Jem's."

"I'm so happy you decided to take the risk, Hope," Jane smiled broadly. "If you hadn't, then you wouldn't have needed more staff, and I'd never have met you guys. I'm going to miss not seeing you both every day."

Andy moved closer and wrapped his arm around Jane. "We're going to miss you too, but you've got the most important job of all now. Being a mum."

Jane rubbed her belly. "I know, and it scares the shit out of me. Being a mum was never part of my plan."

"You'll be a great mum," Hope assured her. "I think you'll surprise yourself."

A hint of tears welled in the corners of Jane's eyes. "Thanks guys."

Hope rubbed her friend's shoulder. "Now I have to try and fill your shoes on the lunch shift till we hire a replacement. I think I've got a pretty big task ahead of me."

"Don't worry," Andy soothed. "I'll be here to show you how it's done."

The three friends shared stories for a further hour, before Hope noticed Jane beginning to tire. She admitted her back was aching, and she was ready to head home for a long soak in a hot bath. Hope threw Andy her car keys. "Why don't you make sure Jane gets home safe and sound. I won't need my car tonight, so you can take it home and just bring it back in the morning.

"Thanks Hope, my feet feel like they could explode at any minute."

Scrunching his face up, Andy stood. "Let's get you home before that happens."

Evening was fast approaching and Hope needed to complete her regular afternoon chores. She made sure there were enough drinks in the fridges, the register had sufficient float, and the tables were in place for the evening crowd.

Her cloth swept over the shiny beer taps, wiping away the condensation that would be replaced within minutes. She threw the now wet cloth in a bucket under the bar with the dirty aprons and bar runners. She ran her fingers over the smooth, varnished surface of the wood.

This honey-coloured rimu had once been Aunt Em's serving counter. Hope had spent many afternoons sitting at the counter doing her homework and enjoying her aunt's homemade cookies and cakes. When it was time to renovate, the one thing Hope was certain of was this wood needed to have a home in the new bar. Hope needed Aunt Em with her.

I hope you like what I've done with the place, Aunt Em. Your regulars still come and visit me. I think they're checking up on me for you. We still chat and laugh. I hear you sometimes, when I'm here on my own. I miss you so much. Hope followed a darker grain the length of the bar, stopping at the end and smiling, before she undertook the endless paperwork that awaited her.

Chapter Two

"COME ON YOU TWO, let's go outside for a little fresh air." The instant Jo walked into the room, her two companions were on their feet, waiting on her every move. She headed for the door, and both ran to her side. Before Jo could get the door half open, they were gone in a flurry, leaping at one another, taking each other out at the feet, and running around in circles. Jo never tired of watching this ritual.

Ruby and Oscar were the best. Since the day she got them, they'd been so much fun, utterly full of life and such great company. She'd never had a pet before, or even thought of having one, until that Sunday, almost a year ago.

Jo had been shooting photos. Sundays were always a time Jo looked forward to. She'd head out with her camera to the local parks and playgrounds where she got to see kids at ease, having fun with their parents. She got the chance to see mums and dads watching their babies explore the world around them. Adults made time to relax, taking pleasure in being together over a coffee, sometimes becoming carefree again, just as they were when they were kids. Jo loved to see a dad on the swings or a mum kicking a soccer ball, but what she loved the most was watching the smiles and hearing the laughter. She sat on a park bench, watching a family fly their kites.

The older lady sitting next to her leaned over to speak. "The laughter is contagious, isn't it?"

"It's what brings me back most weekends," Jo agreed.

Sitting between them was the cutest dog Jo had ever seen. She was small and a little scruffy. Patches of ginger blotted the white fur over her head and back.

"She's so cute. What's her name? That is, if she is a she." Jo laughed. "I'm not very good at guessing when it comes to dogs."

The lady laughed with Jo. "Well, you got it right this time; her name's Angel." The woman gently stroked Angel's head. "She isn't as cute as usual. I'm afraid she's looking more like a haggard mother who's sleep deprived." She bent down to give Angel a little kiss to the top of her head. "I've brought her out for a little time to herself. She had pups a few weeks ago and really needed a break from them. I thought this would be nice for both of us." The older woman extended her hand. "I'm Olivia."

Jo framed the woman's much finer hand with her own. "Pleased to meet you, Olivia. I'm Jo."

The two talked easily, as they watched the comings and goings around them. Angel began nudging Jo, trying to encourage a pat. "She usually isn't very interested in other people. She's a bit of a mummy's girl. You must be a very special person, Jo."

Petting the little dog, Jo shook her head. "That's nice of you to say, but I can assure you, there's nothing special about me. I'm very regular. If anything, I'd fit more into the boring, dull category."

"Angel seems to think differently. Since she hasn't steered me wrong in the three years we've been together, I think I might just trust her on this one."

"Did you get Angel as a puppy?"

"Yes. I was lonely after my husband, Daniel, passed away." Olivia stared at the clear blue sky above them, a little lost in thought for a moment. "Sadly, we never had any children. For many years, we hoped we'd be blessed with a child, but it wasn't to be. When we came to accept that, we moved on and had a very full life together." She turned back to Jo. "Daniel passed away a little over three years ago."

"I'm sorry for your loss, Olivia."

A smile crinkled the corners of old eyes. "I was lost without Daniel for a while there. He was my world and it hurt so much to be without him, but I'd go through it all again if I were given the chance. True love is one of the greatest gifts you could ever receive. If you're ever offered the chance, please my dear, grab on to it with both hands."

Olivia looked at her watch. "I've enjoyed your company, Jo, thank you. I'd better get Angel back to her babies now; they'll be pining for her and ready for more milk." Jo smiled, but before she could answer, Olivia continued, "You should come visit and meet the puppies if you have time. We live just around the corner."

"Really? I'd love to see them."

Jo was on her feet in a flash, her hands clasped tightly in front of her to stop herself from clapping them together in her excitement. The three new friends set off. As they rounded a corner, entering a no-exit street, Jo instantly felt a sense of calm. She'd been past the end of this road many times, when out and about on her bike rides, yet had never bothered to look down the quaint little cul-de-sac.

Large maple trees, tall and sturdy, shadowed the road for as far as Jo could see. Full of life, their dense roots lifted the footpath. Jo gazed up at the branches covered with leaves representing every shade of green she could imagine. The sun, working hard to force its rays through the vegetation, cast a pattern of shadows on Jo's face as she tilted her head to the sky.

"The trees are beautiful. I love the way their limbs have twisted around one another. They have so much character." Drawing her eyes back to the woman walking beside her, Jo received her warm smile. "If these trees could talk, imagine the tales they could share."

Olivia nodded. "They could definitely tell many a story, I'm sure. They've been here through generations and have seen a great deal of change in their time."

Jo grew quiet as she walked beside Olivia and Angel, taking in the peace she felt as she wove in and out of the mix of sunlight and shade. At the end of the serene street, Olivia led them to a side gate. The sight of the house beyond brought Jo to a standstill. The two-storey villa must have been almost as old as the trees lining the street and was, without a doubt, one of the biggest houses Jo had ever seen. It towered over the other homes nestled into the neighbourhood.

Olivia beckoned with her hand. "Come on, I'll get us something to drink. You must be thirsty."

"That'd be great. I could do with a drink now."

Olivia climbed the stairs in front of them, and Jo guessed the house to have been built in the early 1900s. In amazing condition, the residence was obviously well loved. Painted white with smoky grey trim, the home, like the street it resided on, surrounded Jo with a warm welcoming feel. Ascending the front stairs behind her new friends, Jo followed Olivia who was now inside holding the door open for her.

"Please, come in."

Jo entered the wide, open entranceway and immediately heard the sounds of puppies wanting their mother. Angel, recognising her babies' squeaks and squeals, raced down the hallway then off into a side room.

Olivia closed the door behind Jo, laughing lightly. "If you follow Angel, she'll be proud to introduce you to her little ones. A break from them is important, but now she'll be pleased to be back with them."

Jo waited for Olivia to walk ahead. The second Jo entered the room, Angel made a mad dash for her, seeming to encourage Jo to come and see the squirmy little canines. Jo forgot her manners and moved past Olivia. At the sight of the furry puppies, who were now all feeding from their mother, Jo knelt beside the enclosure that held Angel and her pups.

The wire pen was up against a couch. Jo figured it had been placed there to enable Angel the freedom to get herself in and out, while at the same time providing the newborns a safe environment. The sight of all four babies lying on top of one another, suckling from their mother, made Jo melt.

Olivia rested a gentle hand on Jo's shoulder. "I'll be back in just a minute. I'm going to switch the jug on."

Jo fell in love with the small balls of fluff. Slowly, one by one, they finished feeding from Angel and began to move around. The fullness of their bellies limited their movement, and Jo started giggling.

Two pups had mismatched eyes, each with one brown and one blue. Jo had never seen this in animals before and found the contrast fascinating. These two were more mischievous than the others. They tried getting the two quieter pups to play, but this was a wasted effort. They moved on to grabbing Angel by her ears. Finding them too adorable to resist, Jo scooped them up. Both decided it was fun to chew on Jo's nose, their breath still sweet with the smell of milk. As neither had teeth yet, their gummy bites managed to evoke a fresh round of giggles.

Jo gave the babies back to their mother and sat on the floor to watch the little family. She noticed the faint smell of mothballs mingled with something sweet. She couldn't name the scent but knew it made the house feel warm and enticing.

Olivia returned with a tray that she laid on a small table that divided two large, wingback chairs. She sat in one, gesturing to Jo to take her place in the other. "Please, take a seat. The chair is a lot more comfortable than the floor."

The tray between them contained drinks accompanied by what looked to be freshly baked biscuits. Jo smiled at the source of the sweet smell.

"Thanks for inviting me back to see Angel's babies, Olivia. They're gorgeous."

"Thank you for coming and for talking with me at the park. I've loved the conversation. It's so nice to have company. I rattle around this huge house all on my own, and as much as I'm grateful to have such a lovely home, I do get lonely."

Jo looked into Olivia's eyes and could see the loneliness there. She felt for the older woman. Of all people, Jo knew what it was to be lonely.

"I've loved your company Olivia. I spend a lot of time on my own as well. Maybe we could spend more time together."

A full smile lit up Olivia's features, and Jo felt as though she'd just won a major prize. "I'd love that. Please, come and visit me as often as you like. I don't go out much, only to get groceries or to take Angel for a walk. That's about it these days."

***

Jo found herself going back to visit Olivia and the puppies often as their friendship grew. The two would sit talking, endlessly, over afternoon tea and lamingtons. Discussing the books they were reading, art, events in the news, and their day-to-day adventures kept them amused for hours on end. The pups attempted to climb over one another and entertained the two friends.

"Olivia, I adore your house. It has so much warmth within its walls and is always so inviting."

"This home belonged to my parents and their parents before them. There's been many a family celebration within these walls. Lots of children have laughed and played happily in this house. I believe their joy still flows through the rooms."

Jo looked into Olivia's eyes and could almost see the memories running through them. A small pang of jealousy raced through her, but it was brief.

"You're lucky to have had that, and I think you're right; that joy is exactly what I feel when I'm here."

"I was incredibly fortunate. I grew up in a family of wealth. We never wanted for anything. I was privileged to be able to experience a lot of things that others didn't. Though what made me even luckier was to be a member of a family so filled with love. One in which I was always supported and knew I was valued."

"Yes." Jo lowered her eyes from Olivia's view, concealing what might be told through them. "That's something not everyone's lucky enough to receive."

***

Jo lay on the floor, playing with the puppies. Olivia poured her a glass of homemade lemonade. On a side plate, she added two homemade chocolate chip biscuits for their afternoon tea, a ritual that was becoming important to Jo.

"Thanks, Olivia. Sharing afternoon tea with you is the highlight of my day. Talking with you and hearing all the funny tales from your adventures is special to me."

A gentle curve formed in the corners of Olivia's mouth, as she raised her glass from the table. "I look forward to our chats so much. It's wonderful to have someone to share my thoughts with but especially my memories." She took a small sip from her glass before gently placing it back on the oak table that had been in her family for over a hundred years.

Olivia was looking at her hands, twisting one of her constantly present hankies pulled from her sleeve. "The pups are ready to leave their mum now. I think I've got a lady who'd like to take two of them."

Jo's heart sunk. She loved all the puppies but more so her two, special troublemakers. There was something about the tiny, mischievous ones that Jo couldn't seem to resist.

Without looking up from her drink, Jo braved the question, "Which ones does she want?" Unable to look Olivia in the eyes, Jo felt her heart begin to ache.

"She's interested in the two quieter ones. She'd like to show them. The other two are no good for that purpose because of their different coloured eyes."

As Olivia's words sunk in, Jo became aware she'd been holding her breath. She slowly exhaled and looked over to Olivia. "I knew they'd all have to go at some stage, but I pushed it to the back of my mind." Jo shook her head as her gaze fell to the subjects of their conversation. "It's amazing how these naughty, little poop machines can grab hold of your heart strings so tightly, isn't it? I should never have let myself bond with them so much."

Olivia reached across the table, her fingers lightly patting Jo's much larger hand, the affection evident in her touch. "You're who you are, and with that comes a big and giving heart full of love. That's one of the many things that led me to care for you, so don't ever beat yourself up for who you are." Olivia gripped Jo's hand firmly. "It's also the reason why I want you to have your two rascals."

Jo often found compliments unnerving, and today was no different. Although she found the words awkward to hear, they warmed her heart. As she let the sentiment settle, Jo became more aware of the words that had followed. "What? You want me to have the ratbags?"

Olivia nodded.

Jo shook her head. "I couldn't do that. Other people would love to have them, and I know you could get good money for them. They're purebreds, after all. I can't afford to pay you what you could get for them from other people. Besides, I'd never be allowed them at my little, one-room flat. Even if I was, it's way too unhealthy for them."

"Jo, my darling girl, I don't care about the money. I want to know that Angel's babies are going to a good home where they'll be loved. With you, I know that's what they'll get. I see how much you love them and how much they love you. That's all I care about. I know you don't have a lot of money. I'll happily pay for them to be neutered. I can also buy food in bulk and store it in my chest freezer so it keeps the cost down for us both." Olivia made eye contact with Jo and continued in a quieter voice. "I don't just want you to have the pups, Jo. I'd like to offer you the little place I have out the back. The three of you would have plenty of room, and I'd still be able to see these two all the time. Of course, that's if you want them. You might not want to be responsible for two little dogs."

Jo couldn't believe what she was hearing. Trying her hardest to blink back tears, Jo looked down at the tired little balls of fur conked out at her feet. She was overwhelmed by Olivia's kindness and struggled to speak. As much as it was something she wanted to be able to say yes to, she knew she couldn't. "Olivia, I can't believe what you're offering me. No one's ever been so kind to me, but I can't accept. It's all way too much."

Olivia's smile was tender. "Jo, I've grown to love your company. You're a bright, thoughtful, funny young woman who's been given a raw deal in life, so far. Having you stay in the cottage would mean so much to me. I have no other family and, as you know, I get lonely here on my own. As much as I wouldn't need you to be with me all the time, simply knowing you're out there would be a great comfort."

Before Jo could speak, Olivia raised a hand between the two of them, bringing Jo's words to a halt. "I figured you'd see it as too much, so I gave that some thought as well." Olivia lowered her hand, knowing she had Jo's attention. "What if we call it payment? In exchange, you help me out around here. The gardens are becoming too much for me on my own, yet I don't want to hand it all over to strangers. I still love being able to get out there when I can."

Jo jumped up and raced around to Olivia's side of the table. She threw her arms around slight shoulders, holding on tightly as she gave Olivia a big hug. When she let go, Jo ran to the puppies, picking up her two rascals. "You guys are going to be mine. That's right." A shaky breath came before a kiss to each of their tiny, black noses. "You get to come with me, and we can be together every day. You'll get to see your mummy all the time, as well." In true puppy style, they responded by licking Jo's nose and nibbling on her nostrils till she pulled away laughing.

"You've just made me a very happy lady, Jo." Olivia rose to stand beside her. "There's one more thing you could do to make me that little bit happier."

Grooves appeared on Jo's forehead. "What's that Olivia? I'll do anything I can for you."

"Let me take you to collect your things and give your notice now. Then we can come back and get you settled in."

Unsure she could trust her voice to work for her, Jo replied with the slightest nods. After moving her bike around the back, she gave Olivia the address, and they drove to the old, dilapidated building. They found a car park directly outside. A few tenants sat on a collection of torn armchairs, old beer crates, and plastic chairs picked from someone else's rubbish. They drank their beers straight from the bottle, as their children ran wild in the car park. These were the surroundings Jo had been calling home for the past year. She dipped her head low, as Olivia turned the engine off.

"If you wait here, I can run in and grab my things. It won't take long."

Olivia seemed to understand and didn't push Jo. "How about I wait beside the car and open the boot for you when you come back then?"

Jo did her best to offer up a smile. "I'd feel better if you waited in the car until you see me coming." Looking around the neighbourhood, Jo avoided looking at Olivia. "It's not one of the nicest streets. Most of the people are nice enough, but some can be unsavoury. I'd feel better knowing you're in the car, please."

"I'll make a deal. You go and get your possessions, and I'll wait in the car until I see you, but then I get to open the boot."

"Agreed." Jo headed into her one-room flat. She filled two large, plastic rubbish sacks with all that she owned, then made her way back to Olivia to store her bits and pieces in the boot. Olivia again waited in the safety of her vehicle, while Jo went to the owner's flat to give the required two weeks' notice.

Knocking on the door, Jo remembered what Olivia had said, "I don't want you spending another night there if you don't have to. I'll sleep so much better tonight if I know you're safe out the back in your new cottage." Jo knew she would sleep better tonight, as well.

The landlady opened the door, wearing her usual scowl, and Jo was brought quickly back to the here and now.

"Hi, sorry to bother you." Jo received a grunt for her efforts. "I'm just here to give my notice. I've already collected my belongings. I'll make sure the next two weeks' rent is in your account on time, but as I won't be back, you can rent the room out as soon as you find someone new."

The woman simply turned and pushed the door shut with Jo's letter in her hand. Feeling a sense of relief she hadn't expected, Jo almost skipped back to the car.

"Did everything go okay?" Olivia asked.

"Yeah, I told her I won't be there again as of now, but payment will be made as usual. For that I was lucky enough to be grunted at a couple of times and have the door shut in my face." Jo laughed as she finished.

Olivia patted Jo's hand and started the car. "I'm extremely relieved knowing you don't have to come back here again." Looking over her shoulder, she pulled away from the curb. "Now to the next job of the day."

Having no clue what Olivia had up her sleeve, Jo asked cautiously, "What would that be?"

"We need to stop on the way home so you can collect some goodies for your new charges." Before Jo had a chance to argue, Olivia hurried on, "You need to pick out anything you want for them, toys, bedding, clothes, and food. Anything you think they'll need or enjoy."

Both women enjoyed themselves in the pet shop, picking out the essentials along with a collection of squeaky and chew toys, as well as cute little jumpers for the colder days. Olivia insisted on paying for everything, including brushes and flea treatment.

Yet again, Jo was surprised when Olivia turned into the car park of the local supermarket.

Olivia confidently guided the car into one of the narrow parking spaces. "Again, no arguing! We're going in, and I'll be buying anything you need to set up a kitchen. It's important to me that you're able to feed yourself and not be worried about where you'll get the money to stock a pantry."

"Olivia, this is all way too much."

Since they'd first met, the two had spent many hours talking. In that time, Jo had shared some of her childhood with Olivia. Often, when people found out about her upbringing, Jo would be treated with pity. But Olivia had never made her feel inferior.

"Jo, I know how hard it's been for you. I'm just so happy that I can do something to not only bring you some joy but also make your life a little easier and safer. I always fretted about you being in that place on your own, especially at night."

"I don't know what to say, Olivia. Words seem so insignificant compared to what you've given me, but that's all I have to offer at this stage." Moving closer, Jo hugged her. "Thank you, Olivia."

They wandered toward the supermarket doors. "I'll pay you back just as soon as I can."

"Okay, I'll give in on this one." Olivia laughed lightly. "I think I may have met my match. You're as stubborn as I am." She touched Jo's arm gently. "Jo, I'm just so grateful that I'll go to sleep tonight knowing you're no longer in that environment. I'll know you're safe and that means the world to me."

***

Jo settled in straight away. She loved being at Olivia's and made sure to take time out, every day, to enjoy the yard and all it offered. Ruby and Oscar had a safe place to explore and have adventures, while Jo had somewhere to relax. She loved sitting under the big kauri tree, lying back and closing her eyes. The needle-like leaves rustling above her felt like a blanket, soothing and comforting. Sometimes, when she had things on her mind, Jo found herself counting the branches, multiplying and dividing them. The old habit settled her.

Jo had once sought comfort and safety under her rickety old bed. Now, for the first time in her life, she had somewhere truly safe to be. Somewhere she was wanted and somewhere she wanted to be.

Chapter Three

THE LUNCH RUSH WAS beginning to slow. Most customers were heading back to offices or off to meetings, settling into their afternoons. Replacing bar runners with fresh ones, Hope wiped down the soothing wood. *I know, it's good that we're busy, but Aunt Em, working double shifts is starting to take its toll on me.*

One of the draw cards for the café was the two very different spaces it offered. The customers could sit at the more formal tables and chairs to order their meal, or sink into comfy couches or upholstered chairs with overstuffed rolled arms to enjoy their coffee and muffin.

During the winter months, a fireplace provided a warm and cosy atmosphere, allowing people to shelter from the elements for a while. Throughout the summer, the bifold windows were opened wide, offering the feeling of being outside.

The menu provided selections to suit everyone. All the foods were designed to serve up quickly; providing a tasty, fulfilling meal at a fair price within a lunch break. Over time, the café had managed to acquire several customers who were now regulars. Staff knew most by name, enjoying conversations with them about their days, plans for weekends, and everyday chitchat.

Hope didn't work the lunch shifts often. Doing so now, covering Jane's hours, she was surprised to see the relationships that had developed. She was proud of her staff and the environment they'd created. What's more, Hope enjoyed being a part of the comradery.

She was just wiping down the last of the tables when Andy called to her. "Hope, I need to go downstairs to change over one of the kegs so we don't run out tonight. Will you be okay here on your own for a little while? It may take me a few minutes."

"Sure Andy, it's getting quiet now. I'll be fine. I appreciate you doing it for me".

"No worries. I know you won't get a lot of down time until we find someone to take over the lunch shifts, so I'll do whatever I can to make things easier for you".

Hope grabbed a pen and pad to sort out the stock they'd need for the first rush.

12 Coronas
6 Steinlagers
5 Lion Reds

She lifted her head and noticed someone seated at the other end. At first glance, Hope thought it was a teenage boy. But as she got closer, the shape of the body revealed a female. Her beanie covered head was bent down over a book, and she appeared to be alone.

"Hi, is there anything I can get you?"

The eyes that looked up from the book captured Hope the second they met her own. They were the most stunning green Hope had ever seen. "I'd love a Coke and a BLT sandwich, please." The order was followed up with a friendly smile.

Hope's mouth suddenly felt dryer than the Sahara, and she forced down a swallow. "Sure, would you like the Coke now or with your food?"

"Could I have it now please?"

"I'll be right back with it." Hope popped her head into the kitchen and passed on the order before filling a glass with ice, followed by the bubbling, black liquid. Returning to the end of the bar, Hope placed the glass in front of the intriguing stranger.

"There you go. Your sandwich shouldn't be too long."

Glancing up from the book, the eyes smiled as their owner replied, "Thank you," then promptly returned to the book.

Hope walked back to the fridge to finish restocking. As she counted the bottles and cans, she did her best to concentrate on the task at hand. It wasn't easy. Every time she turned back to the paper to write down numbers she found herself looking down the bar. With every sneaky peak, the girl still had her head down and appeared to be reading contentedly.

Hope finished the stock list as Andy came up next to her. "Wow, have you only just got that finished? You should've called me. Sorry Hope, I didn't think it would be too busy. I should have waited another half hour."

"Nah, it wasn't busy, I was just distracted. There was only one customer." She nodded toward the end of the bar.

Andy followed Hope's gaze and laughed when he looked back to his boss. "And what, exactly, was so distracting?"

"At first, I thought it was a teenage guy, but when I got closer I realised he is a she. And she has the most amazing green eyes I've ever seen."

Just then, the BLT was ready. Hope almost ran to get there ahead of Andy, swiftly scooping up the plate before heading back to the end of the bar again. "Here you go, one BLT sandwich. Is there anything else I can get you? Salt, pepper, or another drink?"

Green eyes looked up from the book she was intently reading. The owner returned Hope's smile. "I'd love a glass of water please."

Andy came up behind Hope. "Here you go, Jo, your regular ice water."

The girl Hope now knew was Jo seemed to relax at the sight of a familiar face. "Thanks Andy, just as efficient as ever, I see."

"You know me; I can't resist a pretty face. How are those babies of yours?"

"They're great, just as adorable as ever and full of mischief." Her face lit up as she spoke. "They offer me so much entertainment every day."

"I agree with you, they're definitely adorable."

"Hope, let me introduce to you one of our most treasured customers." Andy faced Hope, as he extended his hand toward the girl with the mesmerising eyes. "This is not only one of our valued customers, Jo here is more like family." He turned back to Jo. "Jo, this is Hope, the café's owner and the best boss in the world." Andy wrapped his arm around Hope's shoulder. "She isn't used to the lunch rush or its most important customers yet. Hope usually works nights but is helping out till we get someone to fill Jane's position."

Jo laughed. "I'm hardly an important customer with my regular Coke, a BLT sandwich, and ice water." Looking to Hope, she said, "Hi, nice to meet you." Jo's eyes flicked back and forth between Hope and Andy. "Have you heard from Jane? How's she doing?"

"She's really well. The little guy's putting on weight, and she's getting used to the midnight feeds." Andy pulled a face. "I don't know how she does it. Once I'm in bed there's no getting me up again till I've had a good seven hours sleep. However, Jane seems to be in her element. I don't think I've ever seen her so happy, or tired." He laughed.

"I'm so happy for her. Please, send my love to the two of them next time you talk to her."

"Better still, why don't you come with me the next time I go to visit? I know she'd love to see you."

"That'd be great, just let me know when. It would be fantastic to see them both."

"Excellent, now eat your lunch and enjoy the book while we get back to clearing tables." Andy pulled a face as he moved away, giving Jo a laugh.

With Andy gone, Hope found herself unusually stuck for words. The best she could come up with being, "I hope you enjoy your lunch."

"I'm sure I will, these are the best BLT sandwiches ever."

"I think so too, but it's great to hear others think so as well." *Why am I so nervous?* She caught sight of Andy out of the corner of her eye. "I'd better go help Andy clear tables and set up for the evening shift. I'll never live it down if he does more work than me." As she walked away, she found herself giving Jo a little wave and feeling excited when Jo returned the gesture.

As they'd finished cleaning, Andy came over to Hope. "Why don't you try and grab a couple of hour's peace and quiet before it's time for the evening crowd to start rolling in?"

"Thanks Andy, that sounds like a good plan. Give me a call if you need anything. I'll just nip home to shower and change my clothes."

"Everything will be fine. I've got it covered; just do what you need."

"When you're settled here, how about coming over before you head home? We can have a quick drink while we look over the applicants for the job."

"Sure, I guess the sooner we find a replacement, the sooner you can have some time back."

Hope grinned. "That sounds good to me."

Hope left out the back door of the café, wandering through the back gate and into her garden. Being so close was handy, it meant she could keep her finger on the pulse, yet still get time to herself and a chance to wind down without having to worry about travel time.

The garden wasn't very big, but it was enough to keep her happy. She walked the path through a grassy pocket to a patio of square pavers. She passed the small, round table and chairs and the free-standing hammock that she loved to lounge in on nice days. Hope unlocked double French doors, opening them wide to allow fresh air to filter through her lounge to the rest of the cosy home.

She made a beeline for the stereo. Rather than the pop music they played in the café, the sound that came from the speakers was an easy-listening, upbeat jazz piece. Hope enjoyed music from a variety of genres, but today jazz called to her.

As the first beats made their way to her ears, Hope wandered to the kitchen to turn the jug on to make a pot of tea. She wouldn't usually have more than one cup but always brewed enough for two. Aunt Em was no longer there to enjoy the second cup, but Hope wasn't ready to change the habit yet.

While the tea brewed, she collected a bread and butter plate from the cupboard and placed a couple of biscuits on it. The plate would wait on the table in the corner of the kitchen, under windows that allowed anyone sitting there to bathe in the afternoon sun. She retrieved her favourite cup and placed it beside the plate of biscuits.

Hope poured the boiling water into the teapot and covered the tea bags with the lid before carrying the pot to the table. At her seat, Hope patiently allowed the leaves to steep before pouring a cup. Her favourite part came next. Aunt Em had taught a very small Hope to dunk her biscuits into the tea before eating them.

Afternoon tea had always been a favourite time of Hope's. Sometimes, the kitchen would be filled with the sounds of their constant chatter. Other times, they would sit in peaceful silence, simply happy to be in one another's company. She'd dunked and eaten all the biscuits and emptied the cup before she looked over the applications for Jane's replacement. Hope heard a familiar knocking at the gate. Glancing out the window, she saw Andy on his way up the path.

"I'm in the kitchen, come on through." Within seconds, Andy took a seat at the table opposite her.

Hope pushed the pile of paperwork in front of Andy. As he began looking over the applications, Hope headed to the fridge, returning with a chilled bottle of Riesling and two glasses. She filled the glasses, placing Andy's in front of him, before taking her seat.

That first sip was held patiently in her mouth, covering her tongue and awakening every taste bud. As the golden liquid slowly warmed, she let it slip down her throat.

"Mmm, that's good."

Andy raised his glass. "To finding someone good."

Gently, they tipped their glasses together before savouring more of the sweet liquid. "You're right," Andy agreed. "This is divine." Both sat simply enjoying their wine for a little, before Andy got back to the papers in front of him. "Are there any in particular you're interested in?"

"I'd be happy with any of these people, but I'm not the one who'll be working closely with them. You are. That's why you're the one who's going to pick."

"Are you serious?"

"Definitely. Like I said, you're the direct supervisor, and you're the person they'll be working with. I need you to be happy with the choice, so I figure the best person to make the decision is you. What's more, I know I can count on you. You're more than just another staff member, Andy. Without you, I'd never have gotten the café where it is today. You've become my right-hand man and my best friend all in one."

Andy leaned over the table taking Hope's hand. "You're my best friend too, Hope. I'm so grateful to have you in my life. You're both a strength and comfort for me." He gave her hand a gentle squeeze. "You're my family." Taking an exaggerated sigh, Andy said, "So, that said, I need your help. I'm scared, Hope."

Hope sat a little straighter, "What of?"

"Getting hurt again."

Hope squeezed Andy's hand tightly in hers. "Talk to me, we can work this out."

"Well, you know my luck with guys. I always manage to find the ones that seem so good to start with, I go and fall in love and open up to them and then find out they're lying, cheating bastards."

Hope nodded. "Yep, that about sums it up, but you can't just give up, mate. There have to be some good ones out there, I mean you're a good catch, so that proves not all are wankers, doesn't it?"

Andy laughed, "Well, that's true, I guess."

"I'm thinking this is about Paul?"

Andy nodded.

"So, how long have you been seeing him for now, a month or so?"

"Just on six weeks."

"Wow, that long," Hope teased.

Andy shrugged his hand out from Hope's and gave her the single finger salute with both hands and they both laughed.

"What's the problem?" Hope asked, her tone serious again.

"I really like him, and so far, he's been really cool. He's fun to be with, but we can have more serious conversations as well. He likes to go out dancing, but is just as happy to stay in and read or watch a movie.

Family seems to be important to him, just like it is to me, and he's out in every aspect of his life."

"And you're just waiting for the real Paul to make an appearance," Hope stated.

"Yep." Andy lifted his chin to the ceiling and took a deep breath. "If I expose more of myself and let him in any more, then I open myself up to hurt again."

"And if you don't, you risk never knowing."

"I've tried, remember. Didn't work out so well for me."

"No, it didn't. But that wasn't your fault. You trusted, like you should, you were respectful, open and honest. All of this is how you should be. You did nothing wrong. Mate, you can do one of two things. Give up on the idea of love and settle for a life of quickies in the clubs, or take a deep breath, believe in happy-ever-afters, and take the chance. This time around, you've taken things slower and Paul isn't just about the clubs and the scene like the others have been. From what you've said over the weeks, he seems far happier away from all of that. Family is important to him, and he has invited you into his world, that's way more than any of the others offered."

"See, this is why I can count on you. You'll always tell it to me like it is. Thanks, Hope. I needed that. Paul may just be the one, but I'll never know if I don't try, and I do want to at least know."

They were no closer to choosing someone to join Andy on the day shift but, knowing Hope needed to get back soon, Andy got ready to leave. "Jo and I will make arrangements to see Jane and her baby. Why don't you come with us? Jane would love it. We could make an afternoon of it, take some nibbles, and have a good catch up."

"Sounds great. Would Jo mind if I tagged along?"

"Not at all, Jo's awesome."

"In that case, I'd love to."

"Excellent." Andy's face lit up. "I'll ring Jane tonight and sort out a day. I can let you know tomorrow."

After Andy left, Hope went to the bathroom to shower and get ready to make her way back to the café. She let the hot water gently massage her shoulders and was shocked to find Jo's image come to her. Most surprising was that the image wasn't of the green eyes that had captivated her but of the smile Jo had thrown at her more than once that afternoon. Shaking it off, Hope finished getting ready for the evening shift ahead.

Chapter Four

FRIDAY'S LUNCH WAS BUSY, yet Hope was disappointed. Every time she checked, Jo's stool was empty. She'd barely spoken to Jo over the previous two days. Jo had seemed intent on her book, while Hope had been busy clearing the tables.

Once the customers dwindled, Hope went home to shower. Meandering through her gate, she bent over to smell the rosebud readying itself to open. Hope smiled as she remembered the day she and Aunt Em had planted the roses years ago. So many fun-filled afternoons of her childhood had been spent in this garden.

She returned to the café feeling much fresher and saw Jo sitting in her usual spot.

"Hi, we missed you today."

Jo turned toward the voice and smiled, as Hope arrived beside her. "Not as much as I missed your BLT sandwiches, I bet. I went straight home from uni to spend some time with Ruby and Oscar since I'm going to be out again now."

Andy appeared from the kitchen. "Ok lovely ladies, are we all set?"

When both nodded, saying yes in unison, Andy wedged himself between them. Wrapping his arms around them both, he led the group to the door.

Outside, Hope pointed down the street. "I managed to get a car park just down there, about fifteen metres."

"Is it warm enough to have the top down?" Hope inquired as they approached her red and white, convertible Mini.

Looking down at the little car they stood next to, Jo nodded eagerly. "It's definitely warm enough."

Andy saw Jo's excitement and agreed with her. "I think going topless is a good idea."

Everyone laughed, and Hope went around to the driver's side and got in. Jo was about to climb in as well, but Andy stopped her.

"No, you don't; I'll take the back seat. You can have the front."

"Honestly Andy, I'm more than happy to be in the back."

"Not on your life." Before Jo had a chance to respond, Andy was in the back doing up his seat belt.

As soon as Jo was in, Hope turned the ignition before pushing a button above the rearview mirror, putting the windows down. She pressed another button, and the roof began sliding back until it was neatly tucked in behind Andy.

Hope easily guided the Mini in between two cars, coming to rest alongside the curb.

"Are we here already?" Jo asked.

"Sure are," Hope replied, as she slid the car into park.

"I was having so much fun, that went way too quickly," Jo said.

Hope grinned. "If you guys want to jump out first, I'll put the roof up. It'll make getting out from the back easier, Andy."

Standing on the footpath, Jo and Andy waited side by side, watching the roof come up.

"That's so cute." Jo beamed. "I love it."

Watching Jo's excitement, Andy said, "You look like a kid on Christmas morning."

"What are you two laughing at?"

"Jo, she's just like a kid on Christmas morning with your car."

"Do you like it?" Hope asked, directing her gaze to Jo.

"Like it? I love it. I've never been in anything so cute in my life. That was so much fun."

"I'm glad I could make you happy."

Before they reached the top step, the door flew open, and Jane rushed out. She wrapped her arms around all three visitors together, pulling them in close.

"Hi guys. I'm glad you could make it. I've been so excited all day."

They followed Jane into her house and through to the lounge.

"Oh," Andy sighed, as he flopped down into one of two oversized, rolled-arm chairs. "I love the windows in here. It's so bright and enticing."

"Thanks. It wasn't always like this. Something happened while I was pregnant, and I went from having a very sleek and clinical house to wanting a soft, comforting home. The chrome and leather I loved so much when I bought it seemed cold. I wanted something warm and inviting to feed Ben in."

"You've definitely got that," Jo reassured her.

Hope nodded. "I agree with Jo; this is so welcoming."

"Thanks guys. Now sit, get comfy."

Hope took the other armchair, while Jo settled at the far end of the couch running her fingers over the soft, red upholstery, a grey, black, and white cushion nestled behind her.

"What can I get you all to drink? I can offer tea, coffee, juice, beer, or wine."

"You know I won't turn down a wine." Andy laughed.

Jane chuckled. "I'd be disappointed if you did. What about you Hope, what do you feel like?"

"I could go for a beer, please."

"Sure thing. What do you think you might like Jo? I've got Coke if you want."

Jo could feel her cheeks reddening. "I might step out of my comfort zone and go for a beer, too, if that's okay?"

"Of course it is, good on you. I'll be right back with the drinks. Andy, why don't you find some music you like and put it on."

Andy jumped up and started flipping through the CD's. Rhiannon, Bob Marley, Ed Sheeran, and Fleetwood Mac. He couldn't help but laugh at the range of music he was finding.

"Any preferences?"

"I'm good with anything," Jo said.

"As long as you don't put on any of that crappy dance music you love, I'll be fine," Hope teased.

Andy poked his tongue out at her. "At least I'm not old before my time."

"Rather be old before my time, with a sense of style, than subjected to that rubbish."

Jane was just entering the room with everyone's drinks, when a cry from down the hallway brought the teasing to a standstill.

"That would be for me," Jane groaned. "He has impeccable timing, just when I was ready to settle into the couch."

Jo took the tray from her.

"Thanks Jo. I'll be back in just a minute."

While Jane made her way toward the crying, Jo placed the tray on the side table. Collecting a glass of wine and a beer, she took them to Hope and Andy.

Grateful for his wine, Andy gushed, "Thanks Jo, I'm really going to enjoy this. It's been a long week."

"Sure has," Hope agreed. "You've earned every last drop of that. I can't thank you enough for everything you've done over the last few weeks, Andy."

"You know I'm always happy to help you out with anything you need. You're not just my boss, you're family as well."

Hope reached out to take the beer. Her fingers brushed against Jo's, and she stammered her thanks.

Those green eyes were right there. So bright and full of what Hope sensed was innocence. Jo threw in another of those smiles she was so good at. They were the sort that could light up an entire room. The type you knew were genuine. They were something Hope rarely saw anymore.

Jo had just settled on the couch, when Jane arrived back carrying the tiniest bundle you could ever imagine wrapped in a blue blanket. In her other hand, Jane held a jug of hot water. In the jug sat a small baby's bottle.

Jo quickly removed the tray the drinks had been on, making a space for Jane to place the jug.

"Thanks." Jane smiled at Jo. "As soon as I've given this little guy his bottle, I'll be able to enjoy my first wine in I can't remember how long. Actually, I can remember." With a chuckle, Jane looked down at her baby. "It would've been the night you were made, my little man."

"Why don't you let me feed Ben his bottle? You can take a break and have your wine," Jo suggested.

"Are you sure; don't you want your beer?"

"It'll still be there when we're finished, won't it, Ben?"

Hope watched, as Jo reached out and very comfortably took the month-old baby from his mother's arms then gathered up two cloth nappies from a stack Jane had in the room. Collecting the jug and bottle, Jo placed them at her end of the couch and made herself comfortable.

Jo settled the baby in the crook of her arm, placed one of the nappies over her shoulder, and reached for the bottle. Shaking a few tiny drops to the inside of her wrist, she checked the temperature. "Just right, little man," she said, looking down at the bundle in her arms.

Jane, watching Jo with her son, relaxed back into the sofa.

Andy pointed to Jane's glass. "Enjoy darling, it looks like Jo here knows what she's doing."

"She definitely does, I'm impressed," Jane said.

"When did you start giving him a bottle?" Andy inquired.

"Two days ago. I wasn't sure about it to start with, because I loved the special connection I felt when I nursed him. But he just wasn't settling for any length of time, and I wasn't sure if he was getting enough from me. I think I was right, seeing as since I began using the formula, he's increased the amount he takes in each bottle by double, and he's started sleeping four hours at a time."

Reaching for her glass, Hope said, "That must be so much nicer for both of you."

"It sure is. At the end of the day, as long as Ben's happy, that's what matters."

"Definitely and, as a bonus, you can have a break while Jo gives Ben his bottle. So, sit back, relax, and enjoy that wine." Andy raised his glass in the air.

Taking a sip from her glass, Jane let out a quiet, low, "Mmm."

"Oh my God, that must be good. That could've been mistaken for someone having an orgasm," Andy teased.

"At the moment, the wine is pleasure enough." Jane laughed back.

"And how would you know what a woman sounds like when she orgasms?" Hope turned on Andy.

"Only what I've heard coming from your office."

Jane snorted. "Ahh the office, where she makes so many dreams come true."

"Come being the appropriate word." Andy burst out laughing.

"I think you two are exaggerating a little. I'm not that bad." As Jane and Andy howled, Hope could feel herself blushing.

"No, of course you're not. By all accounts you're actually quite good." Jane hooted.

"Shut up you two!" Hope didn't know what else to say. She felt uncomfortable with Jo hearing what Andy and Jane were saying.

Now on a roll, they continued their banter and regaling stories of Hope's love life. More specifically, her sex life. Hope stole a sly look at Jo, who hadn't said a word. She breathed a sigh of relief. Jo appeared comfortable feeding Ben his bottle, oblivious to the conversation going on around her. At least, she was hoping that was the case. Just when Hope was convinced Jo wasn't listening to a word of it, Jo lifted her head, looked her directly in the eyes, and smirked.

"So, you're the one. The main attraction who has all the dykes for miles around racing to *Jem's* hoping for some romance with the lady Casanova."

Hope didn't know whether she was more embarrassed by being caught staring at Jo, or by what Jo said. As she felt herself go a deeper shade of red, Hope turned to the other two who, by now, were laughing so hard she thought they might wet themselves.

"What stories about me have the two of you filled Jo's head with?" She turned back to Jo. "Don't believe anything these two may have said. They like to believe I'm something I'm not."

"These two haven't said a word. Your customers are the ones responsible for entertaining me with tales of your escapades." More laughter erupted from the giggling duo. "You'd be surprised how many of the lunchtime patrons are there to gain the attention of the owner."

"Seriously, I doubt that," Hope said, shaking her head.

"I sit in the same place almost every lunchtime, quietly reading and enjoying my BLT. You'd be amazed by some of the things I hear," Jo casually replied, not even looking up from the baby in her arms.

Andy calmed himself long enough to say, "Your reputation precedes you, my dear."

Jo joined in the laughter, but when she made eye contact with Hope something in her eyes softened. Turning her attention to Jane, Jo gently steered the conversation away from Hope.

"Jane, Ben's gorgeous. He's going to look a lot like his mummy."

"Thanks Jo, I think he's just about perfect, but all parents must believe that about their kids."

Hope, deciding to be brave, got up from her seat and walked over to crouch in front of Jo. She saw what Jo was saying, Ben really did look like Jane. The same shaped face, nose, and chin. She'd never really paid much attention to babies before. The truth was, she'd never really known anyone with children before. Hope found herself amazed by how this little being was a miniature version of his mum. Looking up to meet Jo's eyes, she said, "You're right, he's the spitting image of Jane, isn't he?"

"He sure is." Jo smiled down at the infant in her arms. "Do you want a hold? Here, I'm hogging him."

"God no, I wouldn't know what to do. I'd probably break him." Hope stood quickly and took a step back.

Jo laughed. "No, you won't. Sit down. I'll lay him in your arms."

Hope sat next to Jo. She was nervous, but put that down to the fact that she was about to hold a baby for the first time in her life. "Are you comfy?" Jo asked. Hope nodded. "I'll lay Ben in your arms then all you have to do is wrap your arms around him. He'll feel safe and secure then." Reaching out with the bundle of blue, Jo placed Ben gently in Hope's arms. Once Hope had him safely against her chest, Jo sat back. "There, you're doing it."

Hope didn't say anything as she looked down at the baby, surprised by how nice it felt. He was small and cute. She realised how much they needed to be loved and nurtured. Just when she thought this might not be too bad, he wriggled and let out a scream.

Hope's eyes shot up to Jo's. "I've hurt him. Take him!"

Jo laughed softly, quietly and calmly reassuring Hope, "No, you haven't. He's got wind from his milk. I'm going to show you what to do."

"No, you should do it."

"Hope, you're all right," Jo said calmly, as she removed the nappy from her shoulder and laid it over Hope's. "Slide this hand under his bum," she said, guiding Hope's right hand. "That's it, now put your left hand under his head." Jo's hands, as light as feathers on Hope's, guided hers to where they needed to be. "Now gently lift him up so his head rests on your shoulder and hold his body along yours." When Hope had the baby settled against her, Jo continued, "Keep your right hand under his nappy, then use the other to pat and rub his back."

Doing as she was instructed, Hope was soon rewarded with a loud burp. The second it was out, she looked at Jo, rewarded this time with a big smile and a pat on the knee. "Wow, that was a good burp little man," Jo encouraged. "See, Hope, you can do this."

Hope relaxed a little until Ben started to wriggle. She turned to Jo. "Your turn again. Do you think he might want a little more milk?"

"You're a quick learner. I'd say that's exactly what he wants."

Jo calmly placed her hands around Ben and took him back into her embrace. In doing so, her hand brushed across the surface of Hope's breast. Jo didn't appear to notice. Hope, on the other hand, was very much aware of the contact. Rather, her breast was. Her body responded very quickly to the brief touch, sending tingles everywhere, including her slightly erect nipple. *What's wrong with me? First her fingers, and now this.*

Returning to her seat, Hope reached for her beer. *Andy needs to hurry up and make a decision on a new staff member. Working double shifts is obviously taking its toll on me. I'm just fatigued. As soon as I can get some decent sleep, I'll be my old self again.*

Jo finished feeding Ben his milk, winded him, and took him off to change his nappy. She returned to the lounge alone. "Jane, he's all tucked up in his bed and fast asleep."

"Wow, Jo, you're amazing! Thanks. I can't tell you how nice it is to have the chance to sit back and enjoy some adult conversation and laughter, knowing he's in such competent hands. How'd you learn to do that?"

Jo raised both shoulders. "I grew up in foster homes. When you get older there's usually little ones there as well. A lot of the time, if I didn't look after the babies and smaller kids, no one would."

"Sounds like you must have been in some places that weren't very nice," Hope said from across the room.

"Some were better than others," Jo said, before taking a sip of her beer.

Hope observed a slight change in Jo's eyes. A sadness appeared to very briefly sweep over her, and Hope felt she needed to offer a distraction.

"I'm starting to get hungry, what are we going to have for dinner?"

"There's a really good Chinese place just around the corner. We could each pick something different then share all the dishes," Jane suggested.

With everyone in agreement and foods decided on, Hope went to the kitchen to place the order. She returned with drink refills for everyone. Jane protested the wine, saying if she had another she'd be drunk. Everyone laughed.

"You don't have to drive anywhere, and you're not breast feeding anymore. It's okay to enjoy a little time for yourself," Andy encouraged.

Agreeing, Jane accepted the glass from Hope. Jo's cold beer was also greeted with more protests.

"Thanks, but I don't usually drink at all. One's more than enough for me."

Before Hope had a chance to open her mouth, Andy piped up. "Oh no, you don't. If the new mother can agree to push the limits a little, then you can too, Jo. Come on, you're with friends and all we're doing is having a few laughs and some great conversation. You'll be fine."

"Yeah, come on Jo, join us in another drink. I love having you all here," Jane said.

"And I'm driving and will get you home safe and sound."

"I bet that's not the first time you've used that line," Jane taunted Hope, much to Andy's amusement.

The two started giggling again, and Jo was laughing as well. Hope felt herself blush for the third time.

"Oh, you lot are creeps. Here Jo, have your beer," she said, as she placed the cold bottle in Jo's hand.

"Sorry, I'm not laughing at you, really. These two are so full of mischief and then when you blush, it's kind of cute." Jo took a long, slow mouthful then jumped out of her seat and walked past Hope to the toilet, leaving Hope standing there, not at all sure she'd heard everything correctly.

By the time Jo returned, Hope had gathered her composure. The rest of the evening was filled with lots of laughter and amusing and interesting conversation, as everyone got to know each other a little more.

When they were leaving, Hope and Andy each gave Jane a huge hug goodbye. Hope looked over Jane's shoulder, watching Jo to the side. Following Hope's gaze, Jane wrapped her arms around the newest addition to their group. "Don't think you're missing out."

Coming up from behind, Andy engulfed Jane and Jo. "I'm in on this hug too. Come on Hope, group hug." Without letting go, he reached out and pulled Hope into the embrace. Soon, all four were laughing.

When the group hug came to an end, Hope took them home. She dropped Andy off first, seeing as he was the closest to Jane's.

Andy clambered from the car. "This has been such a fun night. Thank you both for coming." He gave Hope a smirk. "It's been very interesting as well. I'll see *you* tomorrow and we'll make a decision on a new staff member." Andy helped Jo out of the back and into the front of the car. "It's been fun spending time with you away from the bar. You have to come with us next time we go see Jane, okay?"

"That'd be cool. I've had a great time."

Closing the door, he headed into his place as they started off down the road.

"Where do I go to drop you off, Jo?" Hope asked.

"Just at the bar is all good. I can walk from there, it's not far."

"Not likely! If it's not far then it isn't going to be any big sacrifice for me. Now, where am I heading?"

"Turn down the street opposite the bar and go all the way to the end...thanks."

"Don't thank me, it's my pleasure. It was a great night, wasn't it?"

"Yeah, it's the most fun I've had in a long time. Definitely the most I've laughed in one evening." Jo smiled at Hope. "I don't really go out much."

"That's a shame, you're great company," Hope replied, surprising herself. As they turned into Jo's street, Hope felt the heat rise from her chest again, grateful for the darkness surrounding them. "How far down am I heading?"

"Right to the end, it's a no-exit. You can just park on the road in front of the gates there."

As Hope pulled the car up to the curb, Jo turned to her. "Thanks for taking me and then dropping me home. I've had a fun time."

"You're welcome. I've had a good time too. It's been nice to have a little time off and get to relax a bit." Hope looked around. "Are you ok getting into the house? Would you like me to walk you up the drive?"

"Nah, I'm fine, I'm used to it. Thanks though. See you next week for lunch." Jo got out of the car and closed the door. She headed off, opening the gate and effortlessly shutting it behind herself.

Chapter Five

ANDY ARRIVED AT HOPE'S office with a large black coffee for Hope and a cappuccino for himself. "No complaints. You know that coffee machine and I don't see eye to eye most days, and today was no different."

Hope laughed as she took the cup from him. "I'll enjoy every drop, knowing you sacrificed life and limb for me and my need for morning caffeine." Hope allowed Andy the time to sit and relax before bombarding him. "So, did you get to look over the applicants? Did you make a decision at all?"

Andy looked at Hope from over the top of his cup as he took another sip, swallowing slowly before answering. "Yep, I got a chance to look at them." Placing his cup on the old rimu desk filling the gap between them, Andy reached into his backpack and produced a folder. "This is the one I'd like to go with."

Hope opened the plain, brown folder. Her lips curved into a smile before she chuckled quietly.

"What? Have I made a big mistake? Is this someone you wouldn't have gone with? I can look over the pile again and pick someone else," Andy rattled off nervously.

"No, the only reason I laughed is because this is the same one I was leaning toward. She must be the right one if we both think she'll be a good fit."

"Thank God for that, I thought I'd stuffed up when you'd gone out on a limb and given me some responsibility." Andy sighed, relaxing back into his seat again.

"Andy, you're my right-hand man, I trust you. You're just as capable of doing the right thing for this place as I am. Stop stressing." Hope was shaking her head while at the same time offering her friend a smile. "Call her with the good news. You'll make her day, I bet."

Panic filled Andy's now wide eyes, "Me? You want me to call her?"

A full, pit-of-your-stomach laugh tumbled free of Hope, bursting through the coffee-aroma-filled air of the office. "You can sort out a start date with her and let me know how you get on. I'm just nipping up the road to get a few bits and pieces. Do you need anything while I'm out?"

"No, I'm all good. I'll give her a call now."

He picked up the phone as Hope wandered to the door, heading out the back to her car. She noticed something on the back seat. She leaned over, grabbing onto a jacket that she pulled to the front. *Jo must have forgotten it was there when I dropped her off last night.*

The scent of Jo greeted Hope, and her mind filled with thoughts of the previous evening. She turned the key in the ignition and a surge of energy made its way from the tip of her fingers all the way through her hand, just as it had when Jo's fingertips had touched hers. Hope's nipples responded to the memory as they had to Jo's touch last night. The physical responses were as much of a shock today as they had been the first time.

Andy and Jane's teasing over her ability to attract women had been pretty accurate. Hope had been involved in a few liaisons with women from the bar. Okay, if Hope were to be honest, there'd been more than a few. But none had evoked responses even remotely close to the ones she'd felt last night. And Jo's actions had been nothing but innocent touches.

"Must be from the lack of down time," Hope mumbled, shaking her head. "Yep, that's it, tiredness. That's all it is."

The supermarket was relatively quiet, and Hope was happy to be making her way back home with everything she needed within forty minutes. With her groceries stored away, Hope was keen to learn how Andy had gotten on. She found him behind the bar, tidying up glasses.

"Hey, I'm back. You got a few minutes to spare?"

"Sure do, I've just finished up here"

Andy followed Hope as she made a beeline for the couch in the office. It was a great place to kick back and relax for five minutes when needed. Andy settled comfortably beside her. Looking up, he noticed her properly for the first time since her return.

"Shit, Hope, you look awful. Are you okay?"

"You sure know how to sweet talk a woman, don't you?" She laughed. "I'm fine, just a bit tired. After I dropped you and Jo off last night I popped back in here. They were run off their feet, so I ended up jumping behind the bar and helping out."

"What time did you get out of here?"

"I helped out till about three, when the place started to clear, then I came in here and tidied up some paperwork. I left around five, I think."

"Okay that does it!" Andy rose to his feet. "I'm working tonight, and you're not allowed to set foot in here until tomorrow afternoon. You need to get some rest; you're going to burn out otherwise."

About to argue, Hope stopped herself. "Thanks Andy, I do have to admit I think I need some rest." Hope shook her head. "I've been responding to things strangely the past twenty-four hours. I'm figuring it's fatigue, but everything will settle down once we get the new girl up and running." Andy was standing in front of her, still wearing a stern look on his face. Hope smiled at his attempt at being bossy. "How'd you get on with that call by the way?"

In an instant, the frown was replaced with an excited grin. "Fantastic! She was so grateful and very eager to get started. She'll be in first thing Monday morning, so give it another week, two at the most, and you can have your days back."

"Wow, Monday, that's brilliant. I thought we might have to wait for a week or two while she worked out notice where she is. That gives me hope; I think I can make it now." They both laughed.

"But you're still having the night off." Andy pointed his finger at Hope in yet another attempt at being authoritative. Although, his face relaxed quickly, as another thought seemed to race through his mind. "How'd you get on with dropping Jo off?

"Fine, she said to drop her off here and she'd walk, but there was no way I was going to do that. I dropped her at her gate. She left her jacket in my car. I just found it when I went up the road. I'll bring it in and leave it here, so we can give it to her next time she comes in."

Andy sat looking at Hope with a smirk on his face.

"What are you looking at me like that for?"

"No reason, just finding the conversation interesting." He continued to smile.

"What's so interesting? You said that last night as well, when I dropped you off."

Settling back beside Hope, Andy looked at her eagerly. "What do you think of Jo?"

"She's nice, why?" Faint frown lines appeared on her forehead.

"No." Andy shook his head. "I mean what do you *really* think of her, and don't try to evade the question."

"I think...she's intriguing. Why?"

"Just curious. Tell me more."

Hope looked at Andy, wondering why he was so keen to find out what she thought. She knew him well enough not to bother trying to escape his prying. She took a deep breath and sighed as she released the air from her lungs. "I don't know, really. She comes in nearly every day and orders the same things, reads her book, and barely says a word. You and Jane have been serving her for longer than I have. Over that time, the three of you have obviously built up some sort of a friendship, which leads me to believe she must have, at some stage, opened up and started talking to you guys."

Andy nodded, "Yeah, it took a while, but she slowly started joining in, bit by bit. So, is there anything else?"

"Hmm." Hope mulled over her thoughts for a second or two. "Last night at Jane's, she was quiet most of the time, yet still joining in. She tends to listen a lot, only adding something when she feels it necessary. Sometimes she's serious, sometimes humorous." Hope spoke slowly, her thoughts forming as she went along. "Then there's how she was with Ben. She was so natural. She even managed to get me to feel comfortable holding a baby."

She felt her cheeks begin to burn. *What's with that?* She usually never blushed. *See, fatigue.*

Unfortunately, the blush hadn't slipped by Andy. "Okay, so what's with this?" Wiggling his finger in front of her face, he pointed at her now crimson cheeks. "I noticed you blushed a couple of times last night, too, and that's not like you. Are you okay?" Andy's voice began to fade before he frowned slightly. "Or is this the 'responding to things' you mentioned earlier?"

Damn him. Why does he have to know me so well? Hope knew he wouldn't leave it alone, but she was going to do her best at any rate.

"It's nothing, really."

Andy simply sat there smiling. "Hope, you know as well as I do that you're going to have to do better than that. The sooner you tell me what's going on, the sooner you get to go home for some much-needed rest."

"You're not going to give up, are you?" Hope sighed.

"You know I'm not, so start talking," he demanded.

"Okay, but it's nothing, really. Like I said before, it's just fatigue." Fully aware her best move was to just tell Andy, Hope carried on. "So yesterday, at Jane's, when Jo gave us our drinks, Jo's finger very briefly, and only slightly, touched mine."

"Yeah, and?"

"There was like a little electrical current running between our fingers, but we hardly even touched. It was so weird."

"Okay, was that it?" Andy looked almost bored with Hope's tale.

Hope thought about telling him that was all there was to it, but knew he'd see through her. *I may as well just carry on.*

"No, there's more." Hope sighed. "When Jo was taking Ben from me, her hand grazed over my breast, and I reacted strangely..."

"What did you do?"

"I didn't do anything. Jo carried on with the baby and didn't seem to notice what had happened." Hope stopped again as she gathered her thoughts.

Andy sat quietly waiting.

"What confused me was that my body responded to such a simple and innocent graze. Or at least started to."

Rubbing gentle circles over his temples, Andy groaned. "Hope, would you just tell me what the fuck is going on?"

"Jesus, Andy, in case you haven't noticed, this is hard for me to say!"

Andy leapt to his feet. "Christ, Hope, get over it. The things I've shared with you are enough to curl hair half the time. There's nothing you could say that will make me feel uncomfortable."

"I'm not worried about you feeling uncomfortable!"

Andy sat back beside his friend, patting her knee.

Hope groaned as she rolled her eyes. "My nipple decided it liked the touch, then a tingle spread through my body." She took a deep breath. "Then a little later, when you were teasing me about my pickup lines, I turned to discover Jo laughing at me, as well. She apologised, explaining she couldn't help herself. Apparently the two of you were so humorous." Hope shook her head. "She casually drops in that her laughter was also because when I blush I'm cute. She then got up and walked straight past me to the toilet. I was left stunned, not really knowing if she'd said it or not." Hope raised her hands and let them flop in her lap. "I mean, what would she have meant by it?"

Andy smirked. "I don't think it takes a brain surgeon to figure that one out, sweetie. It means she thought you were cute when you blushed."

Hope slapped Andy's shoulder. "Yes, smarty pants, but she's so quiet. She comes out with something like that and casually walks away. When she comes back, she carries on like it had never happened."

"Maybe the lack of sleep is just causing you to overanalyse." Andy shrugged. "Usually, you'd just act and not really think a lot about things. You're normally more of an in-the-moment kind, so perhaps it's just because you're really in need of a couple of days to yourself."

"Yeah, that's what I was thinking."

"It's settled then. You're heading home to relax for a while. See if you can have a nap and wind down. Take some time to do something just for you, and then get a good night's sleep. I've got everything here covered, and if there happens to be an emergency, I know where to find you." Andy pulled Hope to her feet, leading her to the door.

Hope wrapped her arms around his neck and hugged him tightly. "Thanks Andy, I really appreciate all you do for me. You're an angel."

"I know, I know." He laughed in her ear gently. "Now, I'll see you after you're feeling better."

Once inside her own place, she went around opening windows and doors, allowing fresh air to flow through the house, before flicking the switch to boil the jug. While the water heated, she changed the CDs in her stereo. With a fresh pot of tea, she sat on the couch and enjoyed the brew. Eventually, Hope sunk down on the couch and dozed off as the music gently surrounded her.

The evening light was beginning to lose a battle against the encroaching darkness as Hope woke. She looked at her watch, surprised to see it was seven thirty. She'd slept almost four hours and felt so much better for it. Slowly stretching, she got up and wandered through the house, closing the windows and deciding as she did so that she was quite hungry.

Hope loved to cook. It was something she'd done with Aunt Em all the time. They'd share their days with each other and enjoy discussing what they had planned for the following day. She stared hard into her empty fridge, hoping something might spontaneously appear. She sighed, swept the door shut, and wandered away. *I know, Aunt Em, my cupboards and fridge are a disgrace, but being in the kitchen alone is no fun. I'm sure you must be turning in your grave knowing the only time I really eat is when I'm at Jem's.* She decided to go for a drive, hoping something would excite her taste buds if she made her way down the restaurant-filled street the café was on. Grabbing a jacket, she shut up the patio doors and made her way to the car.

Jo's jacket lay on the seat. She had meant to drop it over to Andy. Backing out the driveway, a whole conversation played itself out in her mind.

Just go and drop it off to her now. I mean, you're out and about anyway.

What if she isn't there or she has company?

Well, you aren't planning on staying, you're just going to drop the jacket in and go grab some dinner.

Okay then, I'll just run the jacket in. If Jo is there, great, if not I'll take it into work tomorrow.

Hope pulled up outside the gate where she'd dropped Jo the previous night. Grabbing the jacket, she got out of her car and headed for the smaller side gate she'd seen Jo enter. Following a wide drive, Hope could see the broad wooden steps leading to the main home's entrance.

Before she could start down the path, she was met with a mix of puppy yips and warning barks. Two puppies raced around the corner. Hope bent down and slowly put her hand out. Both pups ran to her, jumping and licking her hand.

"Hi, you two. You're gorgeous." Little nibbles followed, and she wrestled the great defenders with her fingertips.

"Hope! Hi, how are you? I wondered what had them excited around here." From behind her new-found friends, Jo's voice startled Hope.

"Hi Jo." Hope stood. "I found your jacket in my car and thought I'd drop it in while I was out. I hope you don't mind."

"Of course not. Sorry I left it behind. You shouldn't have gone to the trouble, but thanks for bringing it round."

"It's no hassle." Hope handed the jacket over then turned her attention back to the little ones at her feet. "Who are these guys?"

"The smaller pup is Ruby. And this chubby one is Oscar."

"They're so cute."

"They are, but they can be a handful at times." The smile that filled Jo's eyes as she looked at her charges overruled her attempts at a grumble. "Do you want a drink, or are you due somewhere?"

"I'm not actually going out as such. I was going to go for a drive while I decided what to do for dinner. I'd love a drink."

"Cool, come on." Jo turned and headed off down the driveway. As they reached the end of the house, another cobblestoned pathway led to a long, wide garden scattered with fruit trees. Along the far fence line, Hope could see a vegetable garden filled with an abundance of thriving plants to be picked and eaten fresh. Blending in nicely with the fruit and vegetables were boxed hedges neatly trimmed and framing the paths, and a multitude of colourful flowers bringing the garden to life.

Positioned perfectly in the centre of all this beauty, a very old kauri tree dwarfed all else around it. Over time, the limbs had twisted and grown over and around one another, strengthening the tree both structurally and visually, drawing one in and eliciting the desire to know the tales this giant could tell.

To one side of the kauri sat two Adirondack chairs with a small wooden table nestled between them. On the opposite side was a swing seat, painted neatly in white, suspended on thick ropes from one of the overhead branches. The full foliage, Hope imagined, would provide an abundance of natural shade when summer fully settled in.

Hope followed Jo past the tree and became aware of a small cottage at the far end of the garden. It appeared to be even older than the main house. The cottage was painted in the same grey and white shades as the main dwelling.

Jo held the door for Hope. "Come in. It's small but it's cosy."

"It's so cute."

"I think so too."

They walked through the small entranceway, and Hope found herself standing in Jo's kitchen. Jo called the dogs in and closed the door behind them.

"Like I said, it's small. You won't get lost." Jo nodded toward the other end of the room. "At the end of the kitchen is the laundry and toilet combined, then through there..." She pointed to the only other door. "...is the lounge."

"I really love it."

"Thanks. I do as well. It's safe and comforting." Jo took the few steps needed to reach the bench. "What do you want to drink?"

"What do you have to offer?"

"Tea, coffee, orange juice, and iced tea. Sorry, no wine or beer."

"An iced tea would be perfect."

Jo got out two glasses, putting ice in both. Reaching into the fridge, she pulled out a large jug and filled their glasses with the slightly sweetened, thirst quenching tea. After returning the jug to the fridge, Jo handed Hope a glass. "Follow me." Jo wandered through the door leading to the lounge.

"Jane's place is really welcoming, I wanted to try and get as close to that as I could with what I've got, so I spent the morning moving the couch to sit under the windows with the TV opposite." Jo shrugged.

"Obviously, I don't have the space or furniture to work with that she does, but I'm happy with this."

Hope took the room in, nodding to the far end. "I love the barn style door."

Jo smiled. "On warm nights, I can open the top half and leave it that way all night. But the thing I love the most is when the sun comes through the coloured glass in the top. Warm reds and yellows spread around the room."

As they sat on the couch, Jo pointed to the loft. "That's my room up there. Like I said, it's small but cosy."

Hope smiled as her eyes wandered the room again. "Do your parents live in the main house?"

"No. That's Olivia's home. She's an older lady I met at the park who's become a very good friend. I don't have a clue where my parents are."

"I'm sorry, it's none of my business."

"It's okay, I'm happy to explain. Like I mentioned last night, I grew up in foster homes. I was taken off my parents when I was ten. After that, I spent years moving from one home to the next."

"Wow, so why did you keep getting moved around?"

"People would rather have babies. They only take on older kids if they have a baby brother or sister. That put me in an age group that most people didn't want. The older you get, the harder it is to be placed until you're around twelve."

"Why's that?"

"By twelve, you're old enough to look after the younger ones and do a lot of the jobs around the house. Unfortunately, a lot of the foster parents that were available when I was younger were only in it for the extra money they could get out of it."

Hope's surprise was evident in the wide eyes she turned on Jo. "So, what were you expected to do at that age?"

"When I was almost twelve, I was placed in a home that had two other kids already. The older brother was two, and the baby was about six months when I first got there. When the kids woke up in the morning, I had to get up with them, give the baby his bottle, and feed the two-year-old his breakfast. It was up to me to make sure they were dressed as well as change their nappies. Then I'd have to get myself ready for school and make my own lunch."

"Oh my God, Jo, you were just a kid!"

Jo shrugged, curling her top lip slightly. "Yeah, well, that meant nothing to them. I had to make sure I kept the boys quiet. If they woke the lady up before eight thirty, when it was time for me to leave for school, I'd be punished."

"Jo, I won't pretend to know much about kids, but even I know that little ones make noise."

Jo chuckled. "They sure do and keeping them quiet was really hard work, especially when there wasn't much food. A lot of the time, I'd go without so they'd have a little more. After school, I had to get all the vegetables ready for dinner, look after the other two—changing them when needed—as well as making sure they were bathed daily. Not that the lady cared about any of our hygiene, it just meant we were out of her hair for that much longer."

"Did she even look after them when you were at school? Did she feed them all day?"

"I don't know. I think some days she was better with them than others. It all depended on how hungover she was. Food was always second to booze in that house. They barely ate most of the time, but he liked a big dinner every night. He'd get home and expect his dinner ready to be dished up right away. As soon as he finished, I had to have a cold beer ready to set on the table in front of him."

Hope leapt to her feet in outrage. "How were they allowed to have you all in their home when they treated you like this? They were as abusive in their own way as what you had probably been taken from!"

"That was a picnic compared to what I came from." Suddenly realising what she had let slip, Jo tried to cover it over. "The problem was, no one ever really checked back then. They do now, things have changed a lot in the last ten years."

"So, what would it be like when they started drinking? Would things get worse?"

Jo lifted her drink to her lips and took a sip. "We'd have to eat dinner in our bedroom. The three of us had one room to share. When they'd only had a couple of drinks, I'd do the dishes and put the others to bed. If I was quiet while I did the dishes and made sure they had their beers, they basically ignored me. As soon as the little ones were asleep, I'd finally sit and do my homework. I wouldn't ask for help, because I'd get punished for interrupting their time."

"Oh my God, Jo, that's horrible."

Jo shrugged lightheartedly. "That wasn't the worst of the homes. That was pretty average. The worst part was that you'd start to care about the other kids, then you'd be taken away again. I'm not even sure why I got moved half the time."

She felt Hope's hand on her forearm. "Jo, you said that place was a picnic compared to your parents' home. Why was it you were put in care in the first place?"

Jo looked up toward the loft, her mind working to sort words into clear sentences.

"You don't have to answer, I'd understand. We only just met, really."

"I'm okay to talk about it." Jo took another sip of her tea. Condensation dripped to her shirt. She cleared her throat before placing the glass back on the wet coaster. Jo's voice was soft when she spoke. "I was taken off my parents because they were drug addicts. They never had any money. It all went on their next fix. When they were high, they had no idea where I was, or what I was doing. When they came down, it was all about finding the next high. They'd be on edge, and I'd be too much for them and they'd hurt me. Then it got to the point where even though I'd keep out of their way, I was the reason everything was bad in their lives, as far as they were concerned."

Jo looked over to Hope, took a deep breath and let it out slowly. She returned her gaze to the floor in front of her. "When I was taken from them, the social workers took me to the hospital. I was malnourished and had a broken bone in my forearm. X-rays showed that I'd had other bones broken before, but they hadn't been seen by any doctors, and they'd healed on their own. Luckily, they weren't major. They were fractures more than real breaks so they all managed to heal without causing me permanent problems. Also, I had some burns on my chest, upper arms, and back. The doctors think my parents may have used heated knives on me. I do know some were from cigarettes, but there were others that were different. I also had cuts all over my stomach up to my chest."

Jo looked up at Hope again to discover tears in her eyes. She immediately covered Hope's hand with her own. "I'm sorry, that was too much. I shouldn't have told you so much."

Hope reached out, making a hand sandwich with hers covering Jo's. "Please, don't ever apologise for telling me. Thank you for sharing that. Jo, I'm the one who's sorry. I'm so sorry you had to go through that."

"It's okay, my mind has blocked some of the worst memories. I remember a lot of what happened but not the worst of what they did. I remember more clearly from the day that I was taken to the hospital."

"If all of this is too much, please just tell me, Jo, but I'm curious, how was it you ended up at the hospital?"

"I'm okay. To be honest, in a way I can tell this because I do it almost on auto pilot, like it happened to someone else. Another coping mechanism I'd say. As well as that, except for Olivia, the lovely lady who owns this place, I haven't really told anyone else. It's something you do your best to keep to yourself so others won't treat you differently."

"Jo, I feel honoured that you feel comfortable enough with me to share your story." Hope gave Jo's hand a squeeze.

The responding laugh was short and sharp. "I have to say, I'm surprised I'm telling you, but it doesn't feel awkward or wrong, so that's a good thing."

"Yes, it is. So, if you still feel all right about it, I'd like to hear how it is you ended up in the hospital."

"Well, my parents had been really good at making sure any marks were in places that others wouldn't see. Most of the time it was my father, but my mother was nearly always there, watching, encouraging. Sometimes she'd join in, either to help restrain me or to do damage herself. They were careful to make sure bruises were in places that clothing would cover and that I never missed a day of school, so no one would check up on me or ask me if I was ok. This night, they must have been super strung out, because they did more harm to me than they usually would in one go.

The next day, when I woke, they were still passed out. I got myself ready and went to school as I always did. Getting dressed and walking to school that day was so painful. I still remember that. Every inch of my body was in pain. I did my best to cover the wounds with toilet paper so my shirt wasn't touching them, but the wounds started to weep and bleed while I was at school. Without my realising it, the blood had made its way through my shirt. My teacher noticed and called me over. I went to her and she slowly lifted my top. As soon as she saw the toilet paper I'd wrapped around myself, she lowered my top and took me to the nurse's room."

They were quiet for a moment. Hope gave an encouraging squeeze with her hand.

Jo took another sip from her drink. "Once we were in the room with the nurse, my teacher let me know she was going to take my shirt off so she could see what was going on. I tried really hard to convince her that I was fine, but she wouldn't be persuaded. After she lifted my shirt and unwrapped the paper, she gasped in a way I'd never heard before. I wasn't sure what it meant. I looked up and saw tears in my teacher's eyes. She asked me, 'What happened? Who did this?' but I didn't speak a word. I was scared I'd be in even more trouble when my parents found out. I just wanted to put my shirt on and go back to class.

"It didn't take long for me to understand that I wouldn't be going back to class but, instead, to the hospital. My principal was called in, and she took pictures of me. I had weepy, infected cuts and burns, as well as so many bruises that most of my back and stomach was literally one entire bruise. I had lumps and cuts along my spine, the back of my neck, and on my head, hidden by my hair. After the pictures were taken and the cuts washed up, my teacher took me to the hospital herself. That was the first time I ever knew what it was like to be hugged, comforted.

"While I was at the hospital, the lady from social welfare showed up. I saw my parents at the court room the day they were sentenced for the abuse they had inflicted on me. They simply glared at me. My father made the action of slitting his finger across his throat and pointing to me, while no one else was looking. That was the last time I saw either of them."

Night settled around the silent women, and the cicadas' sounds filled the air before Hope realised she still had her hand on top of Jo's. Her thumb rhythmically stroked back and forth on Jo's hand, still comfortably rested on Hope's arm. The simple touch created the same intense currents as the night before.

Jo moved, breaking their contact as she stood. "I'm not great in the kitchen, but could I tempt you with an omelet?"

"I don't want to put you out. I've already interrupted your evening."

"Hardly, I had nothing planned. I was thinking of making an omelet for myself, anyway, and was just going to watch a little TV and read a book. Stay. It's no trouble."

"If you're sure, then I'd love to," Hope replied with genuine joy. The idea of staying in Jo's company was very appealing. Hope followed Jo through to the kitchen. "What would you like me to do? I'm not too bad in a kitchen, so you may as well put me to use."

"Oh no, don't tell me that, you'll really know how bad I am if that's the case. Thank God I decided to make something I'm not too shabby at." Both laughed easily before Jo suggested, "You can top up our glasses if you like and just sit at the table while I cook."

"Well, I'm happy to top up our glasses, but I'm not going to just sit and watch, so let me know what would be helpful."

Jo wasn't going to win this one. "In that case, I thought we could have spring onions, courgettes, capsicums, ham, and cheese in our omelets. Are you all good with that?"

"Yum!" Hope delivered full glasses of tea to the kitchen bench. "How about I do the vegetables, while you do the cheese and ham?"

"I'm all good with that."

Jo got out all the ingredients, a couple of chopping boards, and two sharp knives. The two worked comfortably, side by side, to prepare their simple meal.

"Mmm, capsicum sends little explosions of flavour over my taste buds every time I bite into one." Hope popped another forkful of omelet and salad in her mouth. "I've been working so many extra hours the last few weeks that I've only been grabbing a toasted sandwich or nachos from the kitchen at work." Hope placed her knife and fork on the side of her plate. "Don't get me wrong. The food is good, and I could get something more from the full menu, but I've been eating on the run. It's just so good to be able to sit and enjoy every mouthful."

"I'm glad you like it, but I'd say that's thanks to your help. Like I said, I'm not great in the kitchen. I can come up with something nice, but I don't do flash and fancy."

"I like playing in the kitchen. I've been known to manage flash and fancy, occasionally." Hope's face broke into a full smile. "I like experimenting but haven't done that in quite a while."

"Well, anytime you want someone to sample one of your experiments, just call out. I'm prepared to sacrifice myself like that."

Both laughed as they went back to the food in front of them. Before long, they'd eaten, washed up, and were back in the lounge with a coffee each. The two chatted freely, with no awkwardness. The brief moments of silence were comfortable, relaxed.

"So, how did you come about owning a café-come-bar?"

Staring into her tilted cup, Hope ran her finger slowly around the rim. "My Aunt Em bought the place when I was just little. I lived with my aunt and grew up in the house directly behind the café. A few years back, I felt the need to travel, to explore the world. Aunt Em was so supportive, encouraging me to see as much as I could."

"You're very lucky, Hope. You have someone who loves you enough to encourage you to leave, to follow your dreams. That's special."

"You're right, I am. Aunt Em always loved me unconditionally." Swirling the remainder of her coffee around the base of the hefty piece of pottery, Hope spoke softly, "I was in Switzerland a little more than a year ago. I received a call from her best friend, Mr. Riley. He was also her lawyer, and he called to let me know Aunt Em was in the hospital, that she'd had a heart attack." Lowering the mug to the table, Hope extended her arms, pushing it away from her. Bringing her hands back to the edge of the table, Hope ran the pad of her right thumb over the nail of her left, making slow small circles. "I did everything I could to get back here as quickly as possible. It meant a lot of swapping planes and very little sleep, but it was worth it. I managed to get back in time to see and talk with Aunt Em." Closing her eyes, Hope took a deep breath. When she spoke again her words were barely a whisper. "We spent the night cuddled together on her hospital bed. When I woke in the morning, she had passed."

Moving her hands under the table, Hope wiped her clammy palms over her pants before planting a forced smile on her face. She cleared her throat, and her voice grew stronger. "After that, I spent plenty of time wondering what to do. I spent hour after hour just thinking, so many things running through my head. Suddenly, it was clear to me." Hope raised her eyes to Jo. Exhilaration now filled her expression and her voice. "I want to be here, keeping Aunt Em's love alive. Gutting the interior was the hardest part of the past year. To see Aunt Em's prize become nothing more than a shell almost crippled me. The café brought Aunt Em joy. The regulars, people Aunt Em had been feeding for decades, weren't simply customers, they were friends. I grew up with these people, in this place. The café is just as much home to me as our little place out back." Draining the last of the coffee from the uniquely crafted vessel, Hope set it on the table. "I went about looking at the best way to do that and came up with a clever idea. The café could remain open during the day. But I'd see how things would go if I were to try transitioning to a cross between a pub and a club in the evenings."

Jo reached over, gently running her hand over Hope's forearm. "I'm so sorry about your aunt. The way you speak of her and light up at the mention of her tells me how special your bond was."

"She was an amazing woman, and I owe everything to her. She took me in and raised me. She was my world, and I miss her every day." There was weighty sadness in Hope's words.

"How was it that you were raised by your aunt?"

"My parents were young...my father was Aunt Em's brother. My mother's parents disowned her when they found out she was pregnant. It didn't fit with their high society friends, especially seeing as my father, in their eyes, was a commoner. They told my mother she was never really wanted and had always been a disappointment. That getting pregnant was such typical behaviour from her. To do something so selfish to them."

"Seriously?"

"Apparently so. Seeing as it was Aunt Em that told me this, and she never lied to me, I have no reason to believe it would have been any different."

"So, where did your mother and father end up, if you were raised by your aunt?"

Hope laughed, the sound lightly floating through the air. "That's right, I was getting to that, wasn't I?"

Hope could feel Jo's hand still resting on her arm, its warmth spreading through to her core. Not wanting Jo to remove it, Hope looked Jo in the eyes hoping to keep her focus there. "My grandparents were older than most parents when they had Aunt Em, and then a lot older when they had my dad. Aunt Em was fifteen when he was born. Both my grandparents passed away, and Aunt Em raised my dad. She was in her early twenties when they died within a couple of years of each other.

"When my mum was almost eight months pregnant with me, a drunk driver ran into my parents. My father was killed instantly. My mother was alive long enough for the emergency crew to get her to the hospital. Doctors delivered me by caesarean section, but she passed away on the operating table as they were stitching her up."

"Wow! Your aunt sounds like she was an amazing woman."

Hope guided her fingers over Jo's, her touch featherlike. "She was. I was lucky, unlike you. What you went through is unthinkable." Hope shook her head, bringing herself back to the present. "It disgusts me to think that people who were meant to love, care, and protect you, were the ones to hurt you. No child should ever have to go through that!"

Head hanging low, Jo barely made her whisper heard. "You're right, what was done to me should never happen to any child."

Seeing the little girl Jo must have been, the sadness and fear tore at Hope's heart. Not wanting to see it any longer, she decided to try and lighten the moment. "So, tell me, when am I likely to see you in the bar at night?"

Jo's face lightened, as she began to smile. "That will not be happening."

"Why? It's a nice place. Good music..."

"Oh, I know, but it's not for me."

"So, you've been before then?" When Jo nodded, Hope was intrigued. "When was this? Tell me all about it."

"That's a story for another time, I think."

Chapter Six

HER TALL, BLACK STOOL was vacant. Jo wove her way through the crowded room, the other customers and their chattering nothing more than a dim buzz around her. Securing her sneaker on the silver rail, Jo pushed herself up onto the stool and swivelled around, scouring the room until she located Hope. Eyes locked and both smiled. In the week since Hope had joined Jo for dinner, this had become their daily ritual. By the time Jo turned back to the counter and settled herself on her usual seat, Hope was reaching over with Jo's Coke.

"Your sandwich won't be long."

As Hope spoke, Jo took a few big gulps from her glass. "Ahh. Thanks for the Coke; it's just what I needed. And thanks for placing my lunch order."

"You make it easy by having the same thing every day," Hope teased.

"Is that your way of calling me boring?" Jo was playing along.

"You? Boring? Trust me, Jo, if there's one thing I do not consider you, it's boring."

Opening her mouth to reply, Jo was interrupted by Andy. Before she had a chance to get the words out, he called to Hope from the other end of the counter.

"I'll be right back. I'll just go and see what Andy's hollering at me for this time. I tell you, he's worse than a wife."

Jo laughed. She loved the way Hope and Andy teased each other.

Jane's replacement, a lithe woman with Chinese heritage, served Jo her usual BLT. Throwing Jo a wide grin and extending her hand with more confidence than Jo could dream of, the new hire didn't hesitate to introduce herself. "I'm Tara. I've seen you here every day since I started, but this is the first chance I've had to say hi."

Jo shook Tara's hand and introduced herself and the two shared some friendly chitchat until Tara's next order came up. Heading off toward the waiting plates, Tara turned back to Jo. "I'll see you around," she promised, throwing a wink Jo's way.

Alone again, Jo sat with her mouth open, staring after Tara and wondering what had just happened. No one had ever winked at her before, let alone a sexy woman. Blinking, Jo pulled herself together before drool dribbled down her chin.

Biting into her sandwich, her thoughts returned to Hope and Andy, smiling at the way they played with each other. As she swallowed her bite of sandwich, Jo gave herself a mental shake. *Wait, Hope and I banter like that. When did that happen?*

Jo considered her interactions with Hope and realised the relaxed joking between the two of them had developed naturally over the past week. Since the evening, Hope had called in at Jo's, they'd found it easy to talk. The teasing was simply an extension they'd slipped into. A warmth had settled between them, and she imagined it was like what a small child might feel, snuggled into a cuddly blanket. Comforted. Hope had a way of helping Jo to relax, and Jo liked the way it felt. Lost in her thoughts, Jo was startled when Andy suddenly appeared at her side.

"I've sent Hope on a wild goose chase so I could talk to you quickly."

"Oh, okay. What's up?" She was both surprised and intrigued by Andy's behaviour.

"It's Hope's birthday next Friday, and this will be the first without her aunt. I know Hope enough to realise she won't say a word to any of us about it being her birthday. Jane and I thought we'd keep up the pretence that it's just another day and say nothing, but come in that night for dinner. Jane's going to get her sister to babysit, and I'll arrange cover for Hope so she can have dinner with us. We want you to come too."

"That's a wonderful idea, Andy, and I'd love to be a part of it all, but I really don't do well with the night crowds."

Sad, puppy dog eyes begged her. "Please, Jo, I get that it's not really your thing, but it's for a special occasion. You and Hope have developed a great friendship, and I know it would make it more special for her if you could be there too."

Jo felt torn. She wanted to be there to celebrate with Hope, Andy, and Jane, but the idea of coming back to the café at night, when it was a club, made her nervous.

"I promise you we can make it earlier on, so by the time it starts to get crowded you can be back home."

Andy did a quick look around, checking to make sure Hope was still occupied. Jo figured if they could eat earlier, then she would be able to handle the smaller crowd.

"Okay, I'm in. It'll be nice to help Hope celebrate. Especially seeing as it'll be a tough day for her."

Jumping up and down, Andy let out a quiet squeal. "Yay! Thanks Jo." Sobering, Andy added, "Remember, none of us know it's her birthday. It's just another day."

Jo nodded. "Got it." She spoke a little louder. "Yeah, please Andy, another Coke would be great."

Understanding this was Jo's way of letting him know Hope was back, he went along with the hint. "It is hot out there today, isn't it?" Offering Jo a wink as he took her glass, Andy made a hasty retreat, leaving her smiling.

"What's he up to now?" Hope wondered.

"Nothing, what makes you think he's up to something?" Jo asked, an innocent look plastered over her face.

"This is Andy we're talking about. When is he not up to something?"

Jo giggled. "You do have a point." Andy was generally full of funny tales or teasing people about one thing or another. Although as much as he liked to joke, he was never nasty and was always happy to be teased in return.

"I swear, he is so onto it most of the time, but some days I really wonder if he's slept at all. Today is one of those days. Earlier on, I went into the office, and he was on the phone to Jane but couldn't remember why he'd called her. Now, when he just called me away, he needed me to count the wine supplies in the cellar to make sure he had the numbers correct. When I mentioned to him that he does this successfully all the time, he insisted I double-check today as he was sure he had made a mistake. He hadn't."

Without thinking, Jo rested her hand on Hope's. "He's just having one of those days, I guess. We all have them from time to time. However, he does seem in a particularly good mood, full of smiles. Maybe he's in love."

Hope slapped the palm of her hand to the side of her head, laughing as she rolled her eyes. "Of course. That would be right. He does like to fall in love and does so easily and often. This time around, fingers crossed, he has the real thing. He's been seeing this one for a while now and all seems well so far."

Arriving back with a fresh Coke for Jo, Andy asked, "So what's the gossip?"

Jo removed her hand from Hope's to take the glass, as Hope answered. "We were just wondering if your dizzy blonde moments today have anything to do with being in love."

Feigning shock, Andy flung his hands up to his chest. "Me having dizzy blonde moments? Never!" All three laughed before Andy admitted, "However, I may indeed be in love."

"Andy, you being in love is no big news. You fall in and out of love more often than I change my underwear," Hope mocked him.

"Well, now I am the one who's shocked. I never thought you wore underwear," Andy threw back.

As the two continued back and forth like a stand-up act, Jo laughed so much her sides ached.

Chapter Seven

""ARE YOU SURE IT'S not too much trouble having these two?" Jo patted Oscar as she spoke to Olivia.

"I promise they're no problem to have. Look, Ruby's already tiring herself trying to get Angel to play. Once you go, Oscar will get in on the act. As soon as they realise Angel isn't going to come to the party, they'll chase each other like fools for a while then settle in one of the beds."

"I just don't want you to feel you have to watch them. I could stay home. I mean, it's not like Hope knows I'm planning on going anyway, and I'm sure the others would understand."

Olivia looked at Jo for a minute, and then spoke in the gentle tone that warmed Jo whenever she heard it. "Jo, darling, I understand this really isn't the type of place you feel at ease visiting, and I'm sure the others will understand if you decide not to go. Like you say, Hope isn't aware of anything, so you wouldn't be disappointing her in any way."

Jo took a deep breath before exhaling a large sigh. "I know, but I did tell Andy and Jane I'd go and it is for a really good reason. I didn't go in for lunch today, because I planned on being out tonight. So, if I don't go now then I'll have missed seeing Hope on her birthday."

"The two of you seem to be getting close. I've noticed you talking about Hope a lot more since your outing to Jane's."

"Yeah, we get along really well. Ever since Jane's, we've spent time together most days. It actually felt weird not seeing her today." This was the first time Jo had thought about it, and the awareness left her with deep lines across her forehead.

"Do you think the two of you might become more than friends?"

Her head lifted sharply, and she stared at Olivia. The frown was replaced with eyes as round as saucers. "Me and Hope?"

Olivia chuckled almost silently. "Yes, you and Hope."

"No, that's not likely." Jo shook her head emphatically.

Tilting her head slightly, Olivia frowned. "Why ever not? The two of you seem to enjoy one another's company, and you're both single. Aren't you?"

Jo could feel the redness covering her cheeks, unsure of how to word things, not wanting to say anything inappropriate to Olivia. "Yes, we're both single. I think Hope's happy to remain that way too. From what I gather, Hope attracts a lot of attention when she works nights and has enjoyed the company of quite a few women." Fixing her eyes on the floor just in front of her, Jo was frank, "I don't want to be one of those women. It's not who I am."

Olivia held Jo's hand, gently stroking the back. "Good, you deserve more than that."

Jo gathered herself up and lifted her head, smiling at Olivia. "Thank you."

"I know you've been on your own for a long time, but you're not alone anymore. You have someone who believes in you and cares about you now."

"I may not always say it, but it does feel good. Thank you for all you've given me, Olivia. Somewhere to live, and the puppies are huge gifts. But you've given me family, something I never thought I'd have, and there is nothing that compares to that."

"Well, you've given me family in return, so I guess we are both very lucky women."

Jo nodded, a wide grin lighting her face. "Olivia, please don't think badly of Hope based on her reputation with women. When we're together, I never see any sign of that Hope. When she's with me, Hope's very kind and gentle. She's understanding and interested in me as well as interesting to be with."

"Sweetheart, I've lived long enough to know better than to judge a book by its cover. I take people as I find them. From what I've seen of Hope when she's with you, she makes you happy and I see her smiling a lot too. I think it's a wonderful thing and, as long as she is good to you, then I have no issues with anything else." Olivia clasped her hands together. "So, the million-dollar question: Are you going tonight or not?"

How on earth does Olivia manage to take a serious conversation and make me feel so at ease, then simply move on? Jo laughed. "I guess I'm going. Time to be a big girl."

Olivia hugged Jo to her, "That's the way," then gave her a gentle push. "Off you go then. You don't want to be late."

Jo shook her head, chuckling at she made her way to the door. "Thanks, Olivia."

"You're welcome, my dear." Olivia gave Jo's hand a squeeze. "Remember, people do change."

Chapter Eight

JO MET ANDY AND Jane outside, and all three walked in together. Approaching the bar, Jo couldn't see Hope initially. As they got closer, she recognised the top of Hope's head as she crouched in front of one of the fridges with pen and paper in hand.

Jo was happy to head for her stool, relieved to see it still vacant. Andy had a different idea. He grabbed her hand, pulling her behind him as he led the way. Walking slowly behind the bar, he stopped close to Hope, Jo and Jane right behind him.

Hope stood, moving toward the end of the bar but not lifting her eyes from the paper in her hands until she'd almost walked into Andy. With a start, she lifted her head. Her eyes grew wide as they moved from Andy, to Jane, and then to Jo.

"Oh my God, what are you three doing here?"

"We've come to have dinner with you," Andy declared, bouncing up and down on the spot.

"I have to stay behind the bar. It's Friday night. It's going to start to get busy soon." The look on Hope's face told everyone that she wasn't happy about the situation.

Andy wrapped his arm around her shoulder, beaming. "Lucky I thought of that. Your cover will be here any minute now. In the meantime, I'll look after things here while you go sit with these two stunning women." Andy extended his arm, floating it through the air before Jo and Jane. Both smiled in return. Andy shuffled them all out from behind the bar. Hope went along with it and made her way around to stand beside Jo.

"I expected you to put up more of a fight than that, but it turns out you're easy after all," he teased in true Andy style.

"Funny, it's not my name and number I have to keep scrubbing off the walls in the men's toilet," Hope threw back.

Andy erupted in laughter. "Get your sexy asses over to the dining area. Sandy has a table ready for us."

The three wandered off, doing as they were told and laughing as Sandy showed them to the table. They'd only just sat when Andy joined them.

"That was fast. Who's covering?" Hope asked.

"Tara."

Pausing with the napkin suspended over her lap, Hope cocked her head to the side. "Tara. The Tara that just started this week?"

"Yep, that's the one. Don't panic, she's worked busy clubs before and so far, has shown amazing common sense. I thought we should try her at the bar in case we need her to cover some time. She was more than happy to help tonight, and I figured at least this way we're here, if needed. What's more, we wanted to celebrate your birthday with you." Leaning over, Andy placed a kiss on Hope's cheek. "Happy birthday, sweetie."

Hope's mouth dropped open. She looked from one friend to the next, her eyes beginning to glisten. "I can't believe you guys have done this." She looked around the table again. "How did you guys know?"

Jane leaned over to take Hope's hand. "A little birdie told us."

"Tweet. Tweet." Andy flapped his elbows. He lowered his head as he made his confession. "I might've snooped a little to find out when your birthday was. All three women laughed. They ordered their meals and Andy ordered a bottle of wine. With glasses topped up, he raised his to toast Hope. As they ate, Jane updated them all on Ben's latest accomplishments. It was evident that being a mum suited Jane a lot. She beamed every time she mentioned her new son.

After their plates were cleared, Andy pushed his chair back from the table. "I just need to go toilet. I'll be back soon."

"Great to know, thanks for keeping us all in the loop," Hope said, looking smugly at Andy.

"I'd hate to think you were worrying or anything." Andy gave Hope a gentle push as he stood. "What about you, Jane? Do you need to go as well?

"Oh, ah, yeah, now that you mention it, I do."

Hope watched the two wander off toward the toilets together. "Those guys are just weird sometimes."

Jo shrugged. "Yeah, but they're funny as well."

"That's true." Hope leaned in and nudged Jo slowly. "I missed you at lunch today."

"I couldn't trust myself not to blurt out happy birthday, so figured it was safer to stay away today." Jo blushed as she reached into her pocket and pulled out a small, square package neatly wrapped in red paper. "Happy birthday, Hope."

Hope sat looking at the gift, her mouth open.

"I didn't know if I should get you a gift or not, sorry, I shouldn't have done this." Jo knew she was rambling but couldn't stop herself. As Jo moved to withdraw the small box, Hope reached out challenging, "Don't be sorry. My reaction made you think you'd done something wrong but you haven't. I'm so sorry for that." Hope reached her hand out to touch Jo's. "Please, look at me." Jo raised her gaze from the table. "I thought that ignoring my birthday this year would make Aunt Em not being here easier, but it didn't. I've missed her so much all day that it's hurt. I've felt so alone and lonely today, and that's my own doing. I spent all morning waiting for lunchtime, so I could see you, knowing that would cheer me up. When you didn't come in, I was in a real funk all afternoon. Having you three turn up and surprise me was just what I needed." Hope lowered her voice. "When you showed me the gift, I was doing all I could to not cry, and that left you feeling as though you'd made a mistake. Jo, I'm sorry."

Relieved she hadn't overstepped any boundaries, Jo's mood lifted quickly. "Let's try this again." She presented the gift again. "Happy birthday, Hope."

Hope accepted her present and opened it. Inside the wrapping was a small, woven, flax pouch. Hope opened the top and dipped her fingers into the kete, pulling out a black leather cord. Bound to the end of the cord was a pendant made of greenstone. The cool, emerald-coloured stone was sprinkled with black specks and carved into a spiral.

"It's beautiful." Hope ran her fingertip gently over the necklace.

"To the Maori, the spiral shape represents the unfurling frond of the silver fern. The koru symbolises new life, growth, strength, and peace. I thought this fit you well."

Tears balanced unsteadily on the edge of Hope's eyelids, ready to tumble at any moment. "I love it. Could you please place it around my neck?"

Jo stood, and Hope passed her the necklace. As Jo eased the looped cord over Hope's head, she shared the stone's history. "The father of one of the guys in my creative enterprises class is a carver. He has a permit to gather a certain amount of greenstone every year so he can make pieces of jewellery. Before he works with the stone, he has it blessed. It's then customary to have the finished piece blessed before it's given as a gift, so I made sure to do that."

"Wow, I never knew any of that."

Jo returned to her seat. "It was so much fun learning all of this. Tama was so good, taking time to talk and share with me. He's a quiet guy, so getting time with him was great. I got to know him more as well as his culture."

Hope ran her fingers over the stone that now rested around her neck, snug against her skin. "I still can't believe you did this for me." Reaching over, Hope wrapped her spare hand around Jo's, squeezing gently. "Thank you."

"Happy birth...day, to...you. Happy birth...day, to...you." Andy and Jane returned, placing a candle-topped chocolate cake in front of Hope. Jo joined in, although she did so at a much quieter volume than her companions. The singing ended, and Andy clapped his hands together excitedly. "Blow out the candles and make a wish."

Hope took a deep breath before releasing it all with gusto, making sure to get all the candles blown out. With pieces cut and on everyone's plate, Hope dug into her slice. "Mmm...this is the best chocolate cake I've ever had. Where did you get it?"

Andy pointed his finger in Jane's direction. "The creator of this delight is sitting right there."

"Jane, did you bake this yourself?" Hope asked before devouring a second forkful.

Bobbing her head, Jane confirmed.

"You could do this as a business! How did you learn to bake like this, and why did we not know about it till now?"

Jane laughed. "I had never baked a thing in my life until I was pregnant and then, for some strange reason, I had this desire to bake all sorts of things. When I first started, there were many disasters; I can tell you."

Jo had been busy eating her own slice. "I can promise you, you've managed to perfect baking. Hope's right, this is amazing. People would pay good money for cakes this delicious."

Andy served himself seconds. "I think I should try another piece, just to be sure."

Chapter Nine

"JO, I KNOW YOU didn't enjoy your last trip here at night. If you need to head off I'll understand," Hope said. After dinner, Andy and Jane managed to convince Jo to join them at the bar. Jo, figuring it was a special occasion, decided she'd stay a while longer. She was enjoying the company of her new friends.

The table Hope chose was in the back, off to the side of the bar. She pointed it out to the group, but looked right at Jo, seeming to ask her if it would be ok. The table was near Jo's stool, far from the crowds and dancing. Jo barely nodded and found herself pulled forward as Hope took her hand, keeping Jo close behind her. Hope's hand felt safe wrapped around Jo's, and unsettling at the same time. All too soon, they reached the table, and Hope pulled out a chair.

Jo took the seat Hope held out for her. Once they were all around the table, Jo could view the bar and the dance area with ease. She found Hope already watching her. When their eyes met, Hope mouthed, okay? Jo nodded and smiled, and Hope appeared to relax. Andy arrived carrying a tray with another wine for himself and Jane, and a beer each for Jo and Hope.

"Jo, I know you don't drink often, but you seemed to enjoy the beer the other day at Jane's, so I grabbed you one. If you don't want it, I can get you a Coke or water."

"Thanks, Andy. Seeing as it's a celebration, this will be great." Jo reached for the ice-cold Lion Red.

"Oh fabulous, darling." Andy raised both hands in the air before clapping excitedly. He almost squealed. "Yay." The women just laughed.

Halfway through their third wines, Andy and Jane disappeared to the dance floor. Jo had put her foot down about dancing. She was nowhere near ready for that. When she'd declined the offer to join Andy and Jane, Hope graciously stayed with her at the table.

The dance music got louder, and Hope moved her chair up against Jo's before leaning over to speak near her ear. "Thanks for staying a while."

Jo leaned in too. "You only have one birthday a year, and I wasn't ready to stop celebrating this one with you." She felt Hope's hand reach for hers under the table, entwining their fingers, and met Hope's grin with a shy smile.

The two sat hand in hand for some time, leaning into one another on and off to comment about a song, a cute couple, an unusual haircut, or other such simple things that caught their eye.

Zoe made her way over to Hope with a query. Hope leaned over to Jo. "I just have to go and sort something out, but I'll be right back."

Jo nodded, and Hope squeezed her hand gently before making her way to the bar. Jo watched as Hope spoke with Zoe again before disappearing to the back. She soon reappeared, talking to Tara and Zoe, who smiled as they proceeded to push Hope back toward the table. Jo watched her return and felt her heartbeat quicken.

About halfway, Hope was intercepted by an attractive woman with long, blonde hair, bright-red lipstick, and way too much eye makeup. The woman draped herself over Hope like a cat stretching itself out on a blanket in the sun. Jo watched as the woman ran her hand up and down Hope's back. Her hands went lower, cupping Hope's butt, and Jo noticed Hope look toward her. Embarrassed at having been caught watching the performance, Jo looked away quickly.

Minutes later, when Hope still hadn't returned, Jo looked to where she'd last seen her with the blonde. Not finding Hope there, Jo looked around the room until her eyes locked on Hope once again. The blonde was no longer attached to Hope, and Jo felt a sense of relief wash over her. Hope was on her way back in Jo's direction, this time with a Coke in one hand, a fresh beer in the other.

Jo's smile was quickly wiped away when a tall, attractive woman stepped in front of Hope, the latest to hinder her return. She kissed Hope long and hard. Hope's hands remained at her sides, holding the drinks in place, while the woman continued to kiss her.

A weight settled in the pit of Jo's stomach as she rose to her feet; she made her way to the front and burst through the door. The cool air of evening washed over her as she quickened her pace. Jo hurried down the path, crossing the road quickly. At her own street, she broke into a run, only slowing as she neared the gate.

***

Hope was convinced ignoring her birthday would work. *Was I ever wrong. Seriously, what was I thinking? That if I ignored the day, if no one said happy birthday, then Aunt Em not being here wouldn't hurt so much? Ha, what a fool. From the second I woke up, I've been more than aware of what the day is, and even more aware that it will never be shared with Aunt Em again. It's time to face the truth, I'm on my own from here on in.*

As she double-checked the premix stocks, Hope kept repeating the same mantra over and over. "Just get through the night. Just get through the night."

Hope was heading to the cellar. If she collected the contents of her list now, there'd be enough in the fridges to get them through the Friday night crowd. Her eyes still on the paper in her hands, her mind a million miles away, Hope stopped suddenly when she almost walked right over the top of someone. Looking up to apologise, Hope was stunned to find Andy in front of her. Jane and Jo were behind him.

She couldn't believe how happy seeing Jo made her. Hope had missed Jo when she hadn't come in at lunch, her mood spiraling down even further after that. Seeing Jo standing behind Jane lightened Hope's mood, instantly.

Laughing with her friends over dinner was exactly what Hope needed. She noticed Jo blushing as she reached into her pocket and pulled out a small, square package neatly wrapped in red paper. "Happy birthday, Hope."

Oh no, I'm going to cry. I can't cry. Come on, open the box. As her fingers reached toward the bottom of the package, Hope felt something cool. Pinching the object carefully between finger and thumb, she removed the unexpected gift.

She discovered a beautifully crafted pounamu pendant, and tears threatened once more. Thankfully, Jo began explaining the meaning behind the koru, allowing Hope a distraction. She listened intently, as she ran her fingertip tenderly over the stone, tracing its shape.

"I love it. Could you please place it around my neck?"

Jo took the necklace. Moving behind her, Jo placed the gift delicately around Hope's neck. As it settled in place, Hope felt the coolness of the stone slip away, leaving in its place a radiating warmth.

Hope couldn't believe how appropriate the necklace and its meaning were. That Jo had chosen a gift that represented new beginnings was so fitting to the day and Hope's mood. It felt like Jo could read her mind.

The meaning of the koru was one thing, but that it had been made by someone who holds his heritage and beliefs close, allowing them and his past to be a part of his present, was the shakeup Hope needed. Aunt Em may be gone, but her love and all she had taught Hope would be with her always.

Andy and Jane appeared with the most delicious chocolate cake Hope had ever had, spoiling her even more. Thanks to her friends, what had started as a miserable day wound up filled with laughter. Now, sitting with Jo while Andy and Jane danced, Hope found she was smiling, and it wasn't an effort.

Leaning in closer to Jo in order to be heard was nice. Reaching out and holding Jo's hand was even nicer. When Jo didn't pull away, instead giving Hope a smile, Hope entwined their fingers. It felt soothing and exciting all in one. Nice. Hope thought hard but couldn't for the life of her remember the last time she'd held someone's hand like this, if ever.

"Sorry to have to interrupt your night off, Hope, but we are getting low on raspberry vodka," Zoe cut off Hope's reflections.

"Shit, that's my fault. I'll be right there."

Zoe wandered back to the now-busy bar to rescue Tara from the thirsty patrons, and Hope leaned in to Jo again. "I'm really sorry, I just have to go and get the drinks I was in the middle of restocking when I nearly ran Andy over. I forgot all about them in my excitement."

"It's okay, I'm happy here doing some people watching."

The smile Jo sent Hope left her a little worried about standing. She wasn't sure her knees would handle the extra weight now. With an extra squeeze of Jo's hand, Hope took a deep breath and stood, relieved when she didn't fall back down.

She double-checked with Zoe and Tara in case there was anything else they needed from the cellar. They couldn't think of anything Hope didn't already have on the list she'd made earlier, so she went to collect the beverages.

Hope arrived back upstairs and was shocked to see how much busier the bar had gotten in the five minutes she was in the cellar. It was going to be a crazy night; she could tell. The Auckland weather had changed this week. The sun had been out every day, chasing away the rain that had made itself so at home for months now. People's spirits were lifted, their desire for fun obvious.

Hope made sure both Zoe and Tara knew she was back and would be crouched down restocking the fridge, placing the drinks in. The last thing she wanted was for one of them to fall over the top of her. With the drinks in and the box discarded, Hope approached the women again. "It's getting pretty busy. I'll just thank the others for an amazing night and then be right back to help."

The two employees looked at each other, then, without a word, placed their hands on her shoulders, pushing her toward the end of the bar. "We've got everything here covered so just go and have a good time. If we need you we'll come get you, we promise," Tara said.

Hope raised her hands in surrender. "Okay, okay, I'm going."

Feeling a mix of guilt and relief, Hope began making her way through the predominately female crowd. She knew Tara and Zoe would be run off their feet for a little while, but was happy to be able to spend some more time with Jo. Just thinking about getting back to her brought a smile to Hope's lips.

Just as she reached the outer edge of the crowd at the bar, Hope's trek back to Jo was brought to a standstill. From out of nowhere, a blonde materialised before her. Hope had seen the woman in the bar at times but had never spoken with her.

"I heard through the grapevine that it's your birthday," the woman slurred before draping herself over Hope.

The woman grabbed her ass and Hope looked to Jo, hoping she wasn't watching. Looking directly into Jo's eyes for the briefest of seconds before Jo averted her eyes, Hope hissed, "Damn it." Without a word to the woman, Hope shrugged away from her hold and made her way back to the bar. She needed to gather her thoughts, and getting herself another beer and Jo a Coke would buy her the time she needed.

All she wanted to do was get back to Jo and feel her hand around Jo's again, to sit close and feel Jo's breath on her cheek as she leaned in to share something she'd seen. Jo's warmth beside her was gentle, welcoming, comforting. *Shit, what do I know? Jo saw everything. Do I carry on like nothing happened? Do I apologise? Think Hope, think.* She was halfway back to Jo with the drinks and still didn't know what she was meant to do when she got there.

Her body came up hard against a human blockade in front of her. She looked up, but saw nothing. Hope's mouth was taken over by soft, plump lips. The kiss was aggressive and demanding. It was also one-sided. Hope remained still, her hands at her sides, holding the drinks she carried firmly in place before stepping back, breaking free from the unwanted kiss.

Finally, able to see the person so keen to make herself available to her, Hope recognised the woman. She hadn't seen her in a few months. The last time she had, the woman was replacing clothing as Hope made her way out of her office and back to the bar.

"Sorry, I couldn't help myself. I heard it's your birthday and thought maybe I could offer you a surprise gift."

Unable to recall a name, Hope did her best to be polite yet clear. "Sorry babe, I don't mean to be rude, but I'm celebrating with friends tonight and need to get these drinks back to them."

As Hope moved away, she heard the reply, "Sure, maybe another time."

Praying Jo hadn't seen that as well, Hope carried on back to the table as quickly as she could. Finally reaching the table, Hope discovered it empty. She stood on a chair to search the room and managed to glimpse Jo as she bustled through the front door.

"Fuck!"

Chapter Ten

OSCAR AND RUBY RAN energetically after one another, while Angel rested at Olivia's feet, raising her head occasionally to see what the two rascals were up to.

Popping the last of a beetroot chutney and brie topped cracker into her mouth, Olivia sighed. "It's so nice to finally have the sunshine again. Winter was long this year."

"Yeah, it was. Long and wet." Jo rolled her eyes.

A comfortable silence settled between them. Jo loved that she could sit with Olivia without feeling she had to talk constantly. She'd never really had that with anyone else. The truth was, she'd never had any of what Olivia gave her before. Olivia offered a home, safety, security, friendship, love—family.

In the beginning, Jo had been reserved, not wanting to open herself up to disappointment and hurt, but Olivia had been patient. Slowly, Jo lowered her defenses and began trusting Olivia. It had been a risk but one that paid off.

Olivia gently and slowly pulled Jo from her thoughts. "Jo dear, is there anything you'd like to talk about?"

"No, I'm fine."

Nodding, Olivia watched Jo as she spoke. "I'm sure you think you are, but this is the fifth day in a row we've eaten lunch together. Now, don't get me wrong, I love your company, but I can't help but wonder what's caused this sudden change in your daily routine."

Jo thought about what to say, or more to the point, what she was feeling.

"If you'd rather not talk, then I need you to know I'm not going to be angry. It's also really important that you know I'm always here for you."

Jo looked at Olivia, not bothering to try and hide the tears that threatened to spill. "I know Olivia. Thank you. Honestly, I'm not sure what I'm thinking."

"Would you like to try and figure it out, with a little help?"

Normally, Jo wrapped the walls tightly around herself. That had been her only choice in the past, her only method of coping. Close yourself off and shut down. She'd learned that at such an early age. But was that the only way to deal with things? She didn't think so, and with Olivia on her side Jo thought maybe she'd be able to find a new way, a better way. Jo nodded. Olivia stood and came to her. Bending down, Olivia kissed the top of Jo's head.

"Let me take our plates inside and get us fresh juice, then we can talk."

Jo rested her head against the back of the chair, her face turned up to the sun. She watched the kauri's branches above her. They were strong, yet so supple, swaying from side to side in the early summer breeze, their many leaves sheltering her. They rustled together to create a rhythmic tempo Jo found comforting.

Olivia returned with their glasses full. The pups, after running around full speed for fifteen minutes, were happy to settle beside Jo's chair, asleep in seconds.

Jo took a deep breath and held it in before slowly exhaling. "The thing is...I'm not really sure what's wrong or why."

"But you can agree that there is something wrong?"

Jo nodded.

"Do you mind if I point out a few things I've noticed then?"

Again, Jo nodded, not fully comfortable yet in sharing her thoughts and feelings. If she were honest with herself, this was the first time she'd ever allowed herself to take notice of her feelings. In the past, her walls would have locked everything out, and in. This whole feeling and trying to understand it was bloody scary.

Olivia held Jo's hand in hers, tenderly. "If I were to take a guess, I'd say whatever is going on for you has something to do with your outing last week."

"You'd be right." Jo fidgeted with the buttons on her shirt with her free hand.

"There we go," Olivia enthused, her voice full of light. "We have somewhere to start." Olivia squeezed Jo's hand. "Why don't you tell me all about the night so we can try and work out what's worrying you so much."

Jo did as Olivia asked, telling her all about how surprised Hope had been, the fun and laughter they'd all shared over dinner, the present she'd given Hope, and how much Hope seemed to like it. She told about the change of tables, how they'd enjoyed watching the people, Andy and Jane dancing up a storm together, and Hope holding her hand. Finally, she told Olivia about witnessing the two women who threw themselves at Hope.

Olivia sat quietly, taking in all Jo shared. When Jo finished, Olivia remained silent for what seemed to Jo to be hours. The silence was almost too much for Jo to bear.

"I have two questions that I'm going to toss at you together. Firstly, when these women threw themselves at Hope, what did she do? Second, when she returned to you, how did she behave toward you? What did she say or do?"

Lowering her head muffled Jo's voice. "I didn't wait to find out."

"So, you saw this then got up and came home before Hope managed to get back to you?"

"Yes."

Again, Olivia sat silently while Jo continued to stare at her lap. With a gentle pat of Jo's hand, Olivia asked, "What did you feel when Hope held your hand?"

Jo raised her head cautiously. "It felt nice."

"That's great, Jo. Did it feel anything else?"

Jo thought for a little then smiled. "It felt comforting and exciting all in one."

Olivia squeezed Jo's hand. "Excellent, that's what I was after. Now, for a slightly harder one. What did you feel when you saw the women all over Hope?"

Heat rose from Jo's neck, and she looked away again.

"Don't look away, darling. You can share anything with me and know it's safe. I won't judge you or laugh at you, ever."

Jo returned her gaze to Olivia and swallowed hard. "I felt sick to my stomach in an instant. I had to get out, get some air. I stood up and raced to the door, and as soon as I was outside I had to get away. Get home."

"And seeing as I've been blessed with your company every day so far for lunch, I'm guessing you haven't seen or spoken to Hope since."

Jo shook her head. "No."

"Why would that be?"

"When I got home, I spent all that night thinking. I couldn't get it out of my head. I thought about her holding my hand and what that meant. It must have meant something different to me than her. Why did I feel the way I did when those women were touching and kissing her? She isn't my girlfriend, so I had no right to feel anything. Then I thought about the two of us and our lives. Why on earth did I ever think, even for a second, that we could be more than friends? We come from different worlds. I knew all about Hope's reputation long before I even met her."

"Well, that's an awful lot of thinking. So after all of that, what answers did you come up with?"

Jo took a few sips of her drink and swiped her mouth. "I decided I'd been foolish to think maybe there was something developing between us. She was just being friendly. Hope would never be interested in someone like me, not when she has so many women interested in her that she could choose from."

"Jo, my darling, I need you to look at me before I say anything more, because I really need you to hear this." Olivia waited while Jo gradually raised her sight to look Olivia directly in the eye. "You are far from foolish. You are an intelligent young woman, and what's more, you're very attractive. Even more important than either of those, you are a beautiful person in your soul. Anyone, and I mean anyone, my dear, would be very lucky if they were to receive your affections. Hope included."

Jo blushed deeply, unaccustomed to such praise. Not knowing how to deal with Olivia's words, she again became silent.

"Jo, you still haven't answered something for me."

Happy with the change in direction, Jo sat up straighter in her seat. "What's that?"

"Well, you told me about the women freely throwing themselves at Hope, but you never told me how she reacted to them. Did she receive their contact well? Did she respond to them? Was she happy about this attention, do you think?"

Realising she'd never thought of any of this, Jo took her time. When she looked back at the events, and remembered Hope's reaction, she was a little surprised at what she recalled.

"I have to be honest here."

"What would that be then?"

"Well, until you asked me these questions, just now, I hadn't thought about Hope's reaction at all."

"Jo, that's understandable. You were in the middle of coping with the way this was making you feel. But now, a few days later, and with someone else's help, maybe you can make some sense of this all. So, tell me, what did you come up with?"

"Thinking about it now, I don't recall seeing Hope respond in any way at all. Her hands remained at her sides, and she made her escape as soon as she could. I think maybe she was trying to get away without being hurtful."

"Well, that says a lot, my dear."

"Hmm, I guess it does. But the reality is, I think this was all a good thing. I mean, Hope has made it clear to plenty of others that she isn't interested in anything serious, and I wouldn't be interested in anything casual, so it's best that we keep moving on with our lives."

"Does it mean that you couldn't still be friends? From what I gathered before all this, the two of you seemed to get along well and enjoy each other's company. You seemed to laugh easily together and that is something to be treasured. Maybe all you will ever be is good friends, but perhaps something more will grow of it in time. You never know. People grow and change."

Jo laughed for the first time in days and it felt so good. "I'll think about what you've said. I do enjoy being around Hope and we do laugh a lot together. I've missed that. But I need to make sure I can be around her, knowing it will only ever be as friends and not let myself want or wish for more. That would only lead to heartache, I think."

Olivia moved over to Jo and hugged her close. "You're wise beyond your years in so many ways."

Feeling safe, Jo returned the hug. "Thank you."

Chapter Eleven

AS SHE WALKED ALONG the corridor to her office, Hope banged her hand down hard on a pile of boxes stacked outside the storage closet. "I guess if I want these away I may as well do it myself." Hope placed the last of the paper towels on the shelf. Standing upright to move out of the closet, she thumped her head on the shelf above. "Shit on it," she spat, as she slammed the door before storming into her office.

Seconds later, there was a light rapping at her door. Uninvited, Andy slowly opened the door and tentatively popped his head around the side. "Can I come in?"

"Sure, not that I really believe I have a choice in the matter," Hope grumbled.

Andy sat on the couch and watched Hope pick up and dump piles of paperwork from one side of her desk to the other and then back again. When he didn't speak, she threw him a glare before snapping again, "Did you need something, or am I simply your afternoon entertainment?"

The second the words were out of her mouth, Hope regretted them. She wasn't usually a bitch to anyone, but to talk to Andy like that was unforgivable. "Crap! I'm sorry, Andy, that was really unfair and rude."

Hope moved from behind her desk and joined her friend on the couch. She rested her head in her hands. Andy leaned over, wrapping his arm around Hope's shoulder.

"Ever since your birthday, you've had your knickers in a twist over something. And every day, after a certain customer doesn't show up for lunch, your mood deepens. You can be as grumpy as you want, but neither of us are leaving this office until you talk to me."

Hope threw herself back on the couch, staring at the ceiling. "I don't know what the hell's going on."

"Then start at the beginning and let's figure it out."

"That's just it." Hope threw her hands in the air. "I don't know where the beginning is so I have no idea where to start."

Andy gave Hope a hug. "Hey, it's all right, we'll sort it together." When Hope gave him a look that said not likely, Andy simply laughed. "Can we both agree that this has been brewing since your birthday?"

Hope nodded her head and sighed.

"Right then, we've got a starting point." Andy clapped his hands together. "Everything seemed to be good while we had dinner."

Hope nodded again.

"When Jane and I came back with the cake, I noticed you were wearing this lovely greenstone carving." Andy leaned over, gently lifting the carving on his finger. "Dessert was filled with laughter, then we went through to the other side and everyone was still in good spirits."

"Yep, that was all good. The shit happened after we moved to the other side."

"Okay, so maybe you do have an idea," Andy said, eyebrows raised.

"I guess, maybe," Hope muttered. When she looked at Andy and his eyebrows were still up, she punched his arm. "Would you stop with the look?"

"Well, would you stop with the bull and just tell me what happened?"

"Oh, all right then, we were having a great time, getting along together really well. While you and Jane were dancing, Jo and I moved closer to each other so we could hear better. I reached out and held her hand, and she didn't pull away. Zoe needed my help for a minute. On my way back to Jo, some woman decided to drape herself all over me while wishing me a happy birthday. When she grabbed my arse, I backed away very carefully. I was praying Jo hadn't seen it but when I looked over at her, she was watching."

"Oh no, she wasn't very happy about it, I'm guessing."

Hope laughed a sharp sound that had no sign of humour in it. "Well, she may have been okay about that but it got worse."

"Christ, what else happened?"

"I didn't know how to handle Jo seeing that woman all over me, so I headed back to the bar to get us fresh drinks. I figured it'd give me time to think and something to take back and maybe break the ice with."

"Seems like a decent idea to me."

"I was almost back to her, but before I knew what was happening, someone else was in front of me, planting her lips on mine."

Andy covered his face. "Oh God. What did you do?"

"Nothing, I kept my hands at my sides and moved away as soon as I could."

"What did Jo do?"

"She took off. By the time I got to the table Jo was gone. I stood on one of the seats just in time to see her race out the front door."

"Did you go after her?"

"No, I didn't have a clue what I'd say to her. That's when I went and helped behind the bar. I didn't last there long though. I was in such a foul mood, I figured it was better to go home where I downed a bottle of wine and fell asleep on the couch."

"And since then she hasn't been in at all?"

"Nope. Every day I hang around at lunch even though Tara's got everything covered. I hope she might show up. Then when she doesn't I get shitty."

"What are you going to do about it?"

"Nothing."

"What do you mean nothing?" Andy asked, the pitch of his voice an octave or two higher than normal.

"Just that, nothing."

"Why are you doing nothing?"

"Jesus, Andy, how long have you known me?"

"About a year."

"And in that time, have you ever known me to show any signs of being the settling down type?"

Andy paced the floor in front of Hope. "No, but then again I've never seen you concerned with what another woman might think. I've also never seen you look at anyone the way I see you look at Jo, or smile so easily in anyone else's company."

Hope's head lifted quickly, her eyes darting to Andy. "What do you mean, 'The way I *look* at Jo?'"

"Do you really want to know the answer to that?"

"Yes!" Hope stood, moving in front of Andy. "You can't come out with something like that then want to back out."

"Okay, but promise not to hit me," Andy teased.

"I'll hit you if you don't hurry up and tell me." Hope glared.

"You look at Jo the way a puppy does its owner, like she's the best thing since sliced bread."

Hope shoved Andy lightly. "Bullshit, I do not."

"Ah...yes...you do."

"Well it doesn't matter anyway. I mean, we're two very different people. She's so quiet and shy, and I'm not. I love the night life and all the people, and to Jo that's like a form of torture. We're from different worlds. What's more, I'm not the settling down type."

"That the story you've been telling yourself all week, is it?"

Flopping back onto the couch, Hope sighed. "It's not a story, it's the cold, hard facts."

Sitting next to Hope, Andy put his arm across her shoulders and pulled her in close. "Bestie, I think if you let this go, you'll regret it. Even if all you can ever be is friends, the two of you are good for each other from what I can see." He got up and walked to the door. "On that note, I'm going to leave you to do some thinking." Andy walked out and shut the door behind him. A moment later, he opened it again. "Oh, and by the way, I love you."

Hope smiled. "I love you, too. Thank you."

Andy blew a kiss before disappearing for real.

.

Chapter Twelve

JO'S WEEK WAS NOTHING more than a blur. She'd attended classes and had been out to take pictures for the end-of-year exhibition she needed to show for her final grade, but she could recall little. Now, as she sat in the garden, the dogs playing at her feet, Jo looked down at the book in her hands. She was halfway through, but if anyone were to ask what had happened so far, she really couldn't give a great deal of detail. Beyond the basics, they were simply lost words.

"Damn it," Jo muttered, as she dropped the book to the ground beside her.

With no book to hinder her, Ruby climbed into Jo's lap. Running her fingers gently over the silky hair covering Ruby's ears, Jo spoke gently to her companions. "What should Mummy do, guys? I really miss Hope and seeing everyone at lunchtime, but I don't know what to do. I can't just start turning up again like nothing happened, and I don't know what to say to Hope. I have to do something though. At this rate, I'm an accident waiting to happen. I can't stop wondering how she is, what she's up to."

Ruby, seeming to sense Jo's sadness, clambered up her chest, licking Jo on the tip of her nose. Jo laughed. "Thanks Ruby, I love you too, my baby girl." Collecting up her glass and book, Jo headed back inside. "Come on guys, I need to at least try and get some work done on my exhibition."

***

Andy's words ran through Hope's mind as she folded the crisp, freshly washed sheets. Jo was good for her, and she was sure she was good for Jo as well. They laughed easily together, and with Jo she felt an ease she'd never felt with anyone else. Not even Ang and PJ, and they'd all flatted together.

Another week had passed by with no contact from Jo. Instead of moving right along, maybe distracting herself with the attention of other women, Hope had to admit she missed Jo. Last night, at the bar, Hope had become increasingly agitated with every woman that blatantly flirted with her. In the past, the attention would have made Hope feel wanted. She would have taken someone up on the offers they were throwing her way and moved on.

She flopped onto the bed. "Why the hell was I getting so pissed off last night?" Ten minutes of staring at the ceiling produced no answers, and her thoughts were still on Jo. She jumped to her feet. "Enough's enough!"

As Hope approached the little house, all the bravado she'd had in the car disappeared. With every step she took, her pulse seemed to increase. Her tummy felt like there were little people in there playing the drums, and her heart was thumping so hard she was sure it would burst through her chest at any second.

She was within a couple of metres of the front door, able to see Jo seated at the kitchen table. She came to a sudden stop. *You can turn around and she'll never even know you were here.* Dipping her head, Hope sighed before moving hastily to the door. She had to knock quickly, or she'd end up listening to the fear in her head.

Jo's jaw dropped when she saw Hope standing there. Slowly, Jo placed her pen on the table and stood. Hope watched her approach the door as she might an animal she didn't know, curious, yet cautious. She opened the door, her eyes never leaving Hope's. The two stood watching one another.

"Hi," said Hope.

The corners of Jo's mouth twitched a little before she smiled. "Hi."

"I'm sorry to just turn up, again, but I couldn't take it any longer. I just had to bite the bullet and come over."

Jo moved to the side. "You'd better come in then." Jo moved back to her seat at the table, and Hope followed Jo's lead and sat opposite her.

"Jo, I'm sorry."

"No, Hope, you have nothing to be sorry for. I was the one who took off without a word, and I'm the one who hasn't been able to face you since. It's me who owes you an apology."

"I understand why you left."

"I had no right to behave the way I did. When I came to my senses, I was too embarrassed to see you. With every day that passed and I didn't come in, it just got harder and harder."

Hope could see Jo's hands shaking and wanted to be able to calm them, to hold them in hers, but knew that was too much for now. Instead, she'd have to use words, something she usually tried to avoid. "I miss you." Jo looked up and Hope saw eyes filled with tears that were trying very hard to break free.

"I've missed you too."

As relief washed over her, Hope smiled for the first time in what seemed like forever. "Shall we try again?"

Jo nodded. "Yes please."

Hope stayed, enjoying a drink with Jo and filling her in on how Andy and Jane were. They laughed effortlessly again and, when it was time for Hope to leave, she reminded Jo of a promise.

"As I recall, I still owe you a meal, and you still owe me a story about your first visit to the bar. How about I get Andy to cover for me tomorrow night? I'll cook you a fancy dinner and experiment on you. In return, you can tell me your story."

Laughing at Hope's persistence, Jo agreed, "Sure, how can I refuse an offer like that? You're determined to hear my story, aren't you?"

"You'd better believe it."

"In that case, tomorrow night will be great. What would you like me to bring?"

"Nothing, I'll have everything covered." Hope rubbed her hands together. "Oh, my mind is ticking away already. It's feels like forever since I cooked up a storm."

As she was leaving, Jo gave Hope her mobile number, just in case Hope decided she needed something picked up at the last minute. Hope also gave Jo her number. "Just in case you want to chicken out."

Chapter Thirteen

HOPE WOKE AFTER FINALLY getting a full night's sleep. Her mind wandered to Jo. She smiled as she remembered the way they'd worked alongside each other in the kitchen. It felt nice to be in the kitchen with someone again.

Getting to know Jo was fun. She was unlike most of the people Hope got to meet through the bar. Those were far more superficial conversations, most of which bored Hope. Jo, on the other hand, didn't bore her at all. In fact, Hope found herself more and more intrigued by Jo with every encounter they shared.

Jo had been so open with her about her childhood. Hope was a little surprised. Most days, Jo came for lunch at the café and barely said a word. She was never rude, just shy and reserved. But when it was just the two of them, Jo was happy to answer any questions Hope put to her. Added to that, Jo was fun to be around.

Hope was still surprised at her own actions as well. Other than Andy and Jane, she hadn't invited anyone else to her place since she'd been home. She wasn't sure what brought about the invitation. Yes, she was interested to know what Jo had against the bar—or bars in general.

Whatever the reason, Hope was in too good a mood to spend time trying to analyse it. A shower left her feeling ready to face the day, and she made her way out to the garden with a freshly brewed pot of tea. She savoured the heat of the mid-morning sun on her skin and felt alive for the first time in a long while.

Hope ran through some ideas as to what she'd cook that night. She'd come up with two options, and she suddenly wondered if Jo had any allergies or foods she just really didn't like to eat. As much as Jo offered to be a guinea pig, Hope still wanted it to be something she'd enjoy.

Hope tried to send Jo a text only to discover herself typing and deleting time and time again. *Why is this so difficult?* She shook her head and started on yet another attempt.

Hi just wondering if there's anything you don't or can't eat? Hope.

Hope stared at the screen for a while, trying to decide if that would be all right. Laughing at herself, she couldn't believe she was over thinking something so simple. She pushed the send button before she changed her mind again. "There. All done."

She started pulling weeds from the rose bed, but the little "voodoo" tweet beckoned from her phone. Hope grabbed at the phone and smiled when she saw Jo's name on the display. She swiped her thumb across the screen.

Hey there. Nope I can and do eat anything! Should I be worried?

Hope read the message and couldn't help but laugh. This woman, who was usually so quiet and withdrawn, had so many hidden sides to her. Hope decided to play along.

You'll just have to wait and see!

Hope popped her phone back on the table and was still smiling when she heard the tweets again. She picked up the little screen and slid her thumb, all in one motion.

I can't wait.

Hope shook her head and decided to concentrate on the meal she should be planning. She chose a recipe she'd seen a little while ago and wanted to try. To cook it for one had seemed pointless to her. Tonight would be the perfect excuse to give it a go.

Excited now about her plans, Hope abandoned her weeding, wanting to head out straight away to get everything she'd need for the meal. She quickly wrote her list and grabbed the keys to the Mini.

***

Jo woke to a stunning morning, the skies a crystal blue with not a cloud to be seen anywhere. She and Olivia wandered with the dogs to the park. The pair spread a blanket and sat. The puppies amused them as they enjoyed a light picnic for morning tea. Tangling themselves amongst their leads as they clumsily flopped on one another and chased their tails, they made Jo and Olivia laugh, but Jo's distraction with her phone caught Olivia's attention. "Is everything all right, my dear?"

Closing over her phone, Jo apologised, "Yes, sorry, that was very rude of me."

"Jo, you may be a number of things, but rude is definitely not one of them. I don't mind you answering your messages whatsoever." Olivia passed Jo a shortbread biscuit. "It's just not like you to be on your phone. In fact, I think this is the first time I've seen you use it, to be honest." She snapped the latches on the plastic container. "Actually, I'm more curious than anything."

"Why is that?"

"Well, as much as I may not have known you a lifetime, I feel I know you pretty well. I have to say, the way you smiled when you read those messages is something I haven't seen from you before. So, I'm curious just what, or who, it is that has brought about this joy."

"That was Hope. She's invited me for dinner at her place tonight so she can experiment on me. She enjoys cooking, but since her aunt passed away, hasn't felt much desire to cook for just herself." Jo knew she was babbling, and could feel the warmth rising from her chest. She hoped Olivia wouldn't notice.

Olivia was smiling at Jo. "That was nice of her. I gather this means the two of you have made up?"

Jo nodded, looking from her feet to the children playing. "She came by last night, and we talked." Feeling the heat fade from her skin, Jo returned her gaze to Olivia.

Olivia wrapped an arm around Jo's shoulder. The two sat on their blanket for a little longer before Jo checked her watch.

"Do you mind if we head home now, Olivia? I want to make sure I have time to feed and settle Oscar and Ruby before I head out."

Olivia agreed and together they packed away the blanket, flask, and biscuits, along with a collection of puppy toys, before making their way home

Chapter Fourteen

JO SHOWERED, WHILE OSCAR and Ruby were outside eating. The warm water was relaxing, and as she emerged from the bathroom Jo felt energised. She scaled the ladder to her loft in a flash and opened her wardrobe, wondering what she should wear. She wanted to be comfortable. Jo opted for her favourite jeans and t-shirt with a lightweight jacket, in case it got colder once the sun went down.

Looking in the mirror, she wondered what to do with her hair. She usually wore a cap or a beanie. They were the best ways to keep her unruly mop under control. She'd always disliked her hair. When she was younger she'd been teased about it by other kids. All her foster parents had hated that no matter what anyone did, it always looked messy. That is, those that bothered to try and do anything with it.

Her hair was brown with naturally lighter streaks running throughout, and it was curly. But not just regular curly. Oh no, that would have been too simple. What Jo had was unruly. She would have loved to pull her beanie down over the ringlets that refused to be tamed, but she knew that wasn't suitable. If Hope was putting in the effort to cook for her, the least Jo could do was to try and sort her hair.

Reaching for the latest product that claimed to control the most challenging tangles, Jo rubbed some between her palms before running her hands through her hair. She used her fingers to comb it into place then stepped to look at her reflection in the mirror. There. She was a little surprised that it didn't look half bad. *I bet it doesn't last half an hour.*

She played with the pups a while. If they were tired out, they wouldn't get too upset when she left. When it was almost time to head off, Jo took Oscar and Ruby inside to their enclosure. She made sure they had water, toys, and a chewy bone each. Satisfied they'd be fine while she was out, Jo turned the TV on to the music channel. She liked to do this so they wouldn't feel alone. Making one last stop at the bathroom to check on her hair, Jo was astounded to find it still looking the same as before.

As she wandered up the road, Jo couldn't help but notice there was a spring in her step. Smiling to herself, she decided she liked the feeling. Hope had said she'd come and pick her up, but Jo would have none of that. Arthur Street was directly behind the café, an easy five-minute stroll. Reaching the top of Tole, Jo was almost directly opposite the café. Now that she was on Ponsonby Road, she was joined by others out for the evening. Most were wandering along the busy street in search of somewhere appealing to eat.

Jo crossed at the pedestrian walkway. Within seconds, she was on the footpath that would lead her to Hope's. Checking the house number one last time, Jo folded the paper and put it in her back pocket. With a deep breath, she turned into the driveway.

***

Hope sat in her kitchen and took a long, slow sip from her cup, feeling herself relax the instant the dark liquid slipped down her throat. Knowing she had time, Hope savoured every sip. A lot of what Hope planned to make could be prepared ahead of time. That way, when Jo arrived, she could join Hope in the kitchen to keep her company as she finished things off.

Hope stood and reached into a slow stretch before walking to the fridge and removing the bits and pieces she required. Before beginning, Hope made sure she had something light playing through the speakers. Her Benny Tipene CD was perfect. She always enjoyed singing as she cooked.

It didn't take long to get organised and have everything ready to throw together when Jo arrived. She washed and dried the dishes and wiped down the counter, then returned to the stereo. Selecting six new CDs, Hope filled the music cartridge and pressed play, adjusting the volume so the music could be heard nicely from the kitchen.

Although she'd showered that morning, Hope went to the bathroom and quickly rinsed off before getting dressed, humming as she entered the bedroom.

Hope didn't have any particular style of dress she preferred. Sometimes she liked to wear skirts and dresses, while other times she was far more comfortable in pants. For the bar, cargo pants were the most practical so, for some time, that had been standard wear. Looking into her wardrobe now, her eyes were drawn to her favourite skirt. Without hesitation, Hope removed it from the hanger and slipped it up over her hips.

The hem of the white, cotton skirt fell just above her knees, beneath a black silhouette of Albert Einstein. The second she'd seen the skirt in the shop window, she'd loved it. She still didn't know why. She chose a short-sleeved, black blouse to go with the skirt.

Studying her collection of shoes, Hope caught sight of her knee-high, black 'Doc' Martens she'd bought in London. As much as she loved them, she didn't get many opportunities to enjoy wearing them. Sliding her feet into the boots, Hope was grateful she'd bought the zip version instead of the lace-ups. The softened leather pulled tightly around her calves as she stood straight. Taking a step back to look in the mirror, Hope was happy with the choices she'd made.

She slowed in front of her dresser, taking notice of the collection of perfumes sitting on top. She didn't often bother with scents, but maybe tonight it would be nice. She told herself it was because she was wearing a skirt for the first time in she couldn't remember how long. Hope, having applied only a little Chanel so it wouldn't be overwhelming, was on her way back to the kitchen when she heard the knock at the front door.

Chapter Fifteen

HOPE BARELY RECOGNISED JO. Having only ever seen her in a hat of one kind or another, she'd never really given much thought to what Jo's hair might look like. Jo's eyes had always drawn Hope's attention, so much so that she hadn't taken time to appreciate Jo's other features.

As Hope looked at Jo now, she was very aware of so much more. Jo had the most amazing curls. Tightly wound, they looked as though they may go ping at any moment. Hope was intrigued by the hues. If she didn't know better, Hope would have thought Jo's hair had been exposed to the sun day after day. There were so many shades, all blending together, that it would be difficult to say what colour Jo's hair actually was.

The naturally bronzed tone of her olive complexion complemented her eyes perfectly. Those eyes. They were the green of ocean waves as they curl toward the shore.

Hope, still mesmerised by this vision of Jo, received a smile that drew her back to the moment. "Hi, how are you? Please, come in." Hope stood to the side welcoming Jo into her home.

"I'm good. How are you doing? Did you have a good day?"

Hope closed the front door before leading the way to the kitchen. "I'm great; I had a fantastic day. It was so nice to get to sit in the sun for a while. I thought maybe while I cook you might like to join me in the kitchen. That way we can talk at the same time."

"Sounds like a great idea. I'm more than happy to help out too."

"Thanks, but tonight is my chance to experiment. Remember? Your job is to be my tester. So, why don't you take a seat, and I'll get started. Would you like a glass of wine?"

"That would be lovely, but only if you're going to be joining me."

Hope laughed lightly. "Oh, I think you can twist my arm."

From the small cupboard above the fridge, Hope took out a bottle of Oyster Bay Merlot. Not only was the Hawkes Bay wine one of her favourites, but the flavours would perfectly complement the dish she had planned.

Effortlessly removing the cork, Hope poured two glasses. She offered one to Jo, then extended her own glass. "Here's to new friends."

"Yes, to new friends," Jo nodded, lightly touching their glasses.

Taking a sip, Jo raised her eyebrows. "That's really nice. It glides down so smoothly."

"Glad you like it; it's one of my favourites, and it just happens to go perfectly with our dinner."

"So, what is it you're cooking?"

"No, can't tell you. You'll just have to wait until it's dished up to find out," Hope teased.

"What, not even a clue? I bet you're one of those evil people who love to taunt others with gifts wrapped and under the tree for weeks before Christmas."

"Oh, you know me so well already." Hope laughed, heading to the oven.

Hope enjoyed baiting Jo's curiosity as she worked around the kitchen. In no time at all, she was dishing out their dinner. "That smells divine," Jo said, making Hope laugh as she stretched her neck to get a glimpse of the secret menu.

"Hopefully it tastes divine, as well."

Hope set a plate in front of Jo and a second where she would sit. Turning back to the counter, she gathered the Merlot and, once seated, refilled their glasses.

Hope noticed Jo was staring at her plate. "Is everything okay? Is there something on there you don't like?"

"No! This looks amazing. How did you do that? You haven't even been in the kitchen for an hour and you dish up something that looks like it should be on the cover of a cooking magazine."

"I did most of the prep work earlier so it wouldn't take too long now. This is an easy recipe to make. We just have to pray it tastes as good as you think it looks."

"If the smells coming from my plate are anything to go by, you may end up with me at your table every night."

Laughing along with Jo, Hope said, "That'd be all right with me. At least then I'd have a reason to cook."

"You may regret saying that," Jo warned. "Do I get to know what this is called now?"

"Veal marsala, with creamy mashed potato, caramelised carrots, and broccoli."

"Wow, you did all this yourself?"

Laughing at the look of surprise on Jo's face, Hope nodded. "Yes, but wait till you try it. This may just be one huge disappointment." Hope's eyes filled with mischief. "Seeing as your role tonight was to be my guinea pig, you should take the first bite."

Jo eagerly picked up her fork. She took up a bit of meat and potato and eased the fork into her mouth. She closed her eyes and held the morsel in her mouth for a moment. "Yum, this is so gooood!"

Unaware she'd been holding her breath in anticipation, Hope exhaled slowly. "Whew! You never know, when it's the first time you've tried something, just how it will turn out."

"I can guarantee you, this is amazing."

Hope took a bite and had to agree. "Oh yeah, this is one of my more successful experiments."

"Have you had many failures?"

"More than I'd like to count. Poor Aunt Em was always so polite about them, never wanting to hurt my feelings. She'd smile and tell me everything was lovely." Hope shook her head. "Then I'd take a mouthful and need to run to the sink to get rid of it."

An hour later, Jo took their plates to the bench top and filled the sink with hot, soapy water.

"What do you think you're doing?" Hope questioned from behind Jo.

"I'm just going to wash the dishes."

"Not likely, you're my guest!" Hope attempted to reach around Jo to get hold of the dishcloth.

Jo wriggled between Hope and the sink, holding tightly to the cloth. "I'm also a guest who loved every mouthful you prepared for me, so as way of thanks, I will be doing the dishes."

Seeing that she had come up against someone as strong willed as herself, Hope gave up on that battle, grabbing a dish towel from the cupboard instead. Picking up a glass to dry, Hope was again put in her place. Jo turned, placing firm hands on Hope's shoulders, and directed the cook back to the seat she'd just vacated.

"You'll stay right there while I sort these out," Jo insisted before topping up Hope's glass. "Sit back and relax for a minute."

Not used to being told what to do, Hope was a little taken aback. She was stunned to discover yet another side to Jo. This aspect of Jo's personality was surprisingly assertive. Deciding she liked this trait in Jo, Hope sat back and sipped her wine.

Chapter Sixteen

"SHALL WE MOVE INTO the lounge? The couch is a lot more comfortable than these chairs," Hope suggested, as Jo finished the last of the dishes.

"I'll bring the wine."

"Is the music okay? If you don't like it, I've got a wide range you could look through."

"This is great. I'm enjoying the mix that's playing." Feeling comfortable in Hope's company, Jo relaxed enough to be playful. "It was fun when you sang along while you were cooking."

Immediately blushing, Hope covered her face. "Oh no, I can't believe I did that."

Jo automatically rested a hand on Hope's thigh. "You've got nothing to be embarrassed about. You've got an amazing voice, Hope." She gently squeezed Hope's thigh and felt a small tingle in the pit of her stomach when Hope's hand covered her own. "Like I said, I enjoyed it. You were so at ease. Singing seemed to be something that went hand in hand with cooking for you."

"I love to sing when I'm cooking. It was something Aunt Em always did when she was in the kitchen. It's one of the many gifts she gave me." A small smile softened the sadness that crossed over Hope's eyes.

Sadness was something Jo had seen in many people over the years. It was an emotion she had become almost immune to, so it surprised her when she discovered she didn't like to see it in Hope. Maybe a change of topic would help.

"I like it when we get to hang out together like this, away from *Jem's*. It's been cool getting to know you more. I mean, there's no way I would have heard you sing at *Jem's*. It was a bit of a surprise, but a good one. I'm enjoying getting to know you. Spending time with you away from the café is allowing me to see new sides to your personality. Your singing is one that both surprised and delighted me."

"Well, I'm not the only one with hidden surprises around here, missy."

Jo frowned. "Who, me?"

Hope gave a hearty laugh. "Yes! You go from this person who sits in the café eating the same lunch most days, barely speaking, and keeping your nose buried in a book, to someone who has a hidden sense of humour I find I really enjoy. Someone who seems wise beyond her years, and as much as you may have a gentle, quiet side, there's an assertiveness carefully resting below the surface. You, little Miss Innocent, are full of surprises."

The tingle Jo felt earlier returned at the thought of Hope having noticed so much about her.

"And to top that off, you turn up tonight with no hat for the first time since I met you. When I opened the door I nearly didn't recognise you. If it wasn't for those eyes, I'm not sure I would have."

Jo dipped her head, lowering her eyes to the floor. "Yeah, sorry. I usually wear a hat, because my hair's so unruly and difficult to deal with. It's much easier to just keep it covered."

With a light touch of fingertips beneath Jo's chin, Hope raised her face until they were looking one another in the eyes. "I think it's a shame to keep it covered. Your hair is gorgeous. It complements the most alluring eyes I've ever seen." Hope smiled smugly.

A crimson-cheeked Jo responded quickly, "What about you?"

"What about me? What have I done?"

"I was pretty shocked when the front door opened and there you were dressed like that." Jo swept her hand in front of Hope before pointing a finger. "And in those boots!" The words were out of her mouth before Jo had a chance to think, and she wished there was a hole somewhere she could crawl into.

"So, do you like this look, or do you prefer the cargo pants and shirts you generally see me in?"

Wanting to play a little, Jo crinkled her nose. "Well, the cargo pants and shirts are pretty hard to beat." Her cheeks were well and truly on fire before the words were even out. "But this look is amazing."

Jo stared, as Hope came closer and lowered her mouth to Jo's lips, touching softly, tentatively.

As much as they'd been playing with one another, flirting a little even, Jo was surprised by the kiss. An even greater shock was her body's response to Hope. The wine was still warm on Hope's breath, and Jo tasted its sweetness as she leaned in, her tongue skimming over Hope's lips. The instant Jo's tongue slid over Hope's, the kiss filled with a hunger Jo hadn't expected. One she hadn't known before. Melting into the taste of Hope, Jo was barely aware of Hope's arm sliding around her back, pulling her in closer. Her own hand, that so far had remained on Hope's thigh, made its way to the back of Hope's head. Pulling Hope in, bringing their mouths down harder on one another, Jo fed the hunger.

With a new-found confidence, Jo allowed her fingers to run through Hope's hair before guiding them to the top button of Hope's blouse. At the same time, Jo felt Hope's hand brush up under her t-shirt. Smooth fingers ran over Jo's back as she awkwardly attempted to undo Hope's top button. Hope assisted Jo, moving down her shirt one button at a time until all were freed.

Bringing a shaking hand inside the blouse, Jo's fingers skimmed over the lacy material shielding Hope's breasts from her touch. Filled with an overwhelming desire, Jo gently squeezed and kneaded the soft flesh below her palm. The moan from Hope's throat was low and deep. Her arousal, evidenced by the nipples that hardened under Jo's touch, intensified the fire blazing within Jo.

Need fueled determination, and she slipped her fingers beneath the edge of the material shielding Hope's tender flesh. Lifting the silky cup, Jo exposed Hope's breasts to the air. She took her ravenous lips from Hope's mouth to one nipple and then the other, sucking tenderly as she felt them harden even more against her tongue. Hope arched her back, which forced yet more of her flesh into Jo's mouth.

Jo rose to her knees and straddled Hope's thighs. Wetness developing between her own legs signalling her desire. She slid Hope's blouse from her shoulders before releasing the hooks of her bra then lowered her mouth to kiss the freshly exposed skin of Hope's collarbone.

She was kissing her way to Hope's neck. Suddenly, Jo stopped and drew back. Hope's fingers were at the hem of her shirt, pulling the material up. Jo's mind cleared quickly. Her hands moved at lightning pace, and she grasped Hope's fingers.

"I'm so sorry, Jo. That wasn't what I asked you here for. I should never have taken things in that direction. I understand if you want to leave, but would really like it if we could still attempt a friendship."

Without hesitation, Jo responded with total honesty, "No. Hope. I don't want to leave, and you have nothing to be sorry for. I responded to your kiss. I surprised myself by taking things one step further." With a little laugh, Jo admitted, "Okay, maybe a little more than one step." To her relief, Hope laughed too.

"What was it I did to upset you?"

"Hope, you didn't do anything wrong at all. I panicked at the thought of you seeing me without a top on. No one, other than doctors or nurses, has ever seen my scars. I even managed to get through multiple foster homes without ever showing them to anyone else." Jo sighed as her fantasy crashed with reality. "No one should ever have to see that ugliness."

Cupping Jo's face in her hands, Hope spoke very gently, "Jo, they are an unfortunate reminder to you, every day, of the cruelty shown to you by those who should have nurtured and protected you. You've been through more than anyone should have to endure." Lifting her lips to Jo's face, Hope kissed her cheek softly. "I wish I could change that for you, but I can't, any more than anyone else could. You're a survivor, and those scars are now as much a part of you as your hair, eyes, and nose. Jo, I want to know you better, and I am very attracted to you. I can't explain any of this, but I want to touch you, kiss you, stroke you, and see you. Please, Jo, trust that I'm safe, and that I won't cause you any more pain where your scars are concerned."

Hope didn't feel like a risk; Hope felt right, safe, so Jo simply nodded her choice to trust, and Hope competently cast off her t-shirt before nimbly removing her bra. Jo felt light fingers caressing her skin and soft kisses to her stomach, before Hope's tongue softly trailed from one scar to the next, where Hope would leave yet another kiss.

Sitting atop Hope, Jo looked down into her eyes and could only guess that what she saw on Hope's face was desire. Claiming Hope's mouth again, Jo savoured it passionately before laying a string of kisses along a delicate collarbone. Moving up a creamy neck, Jo nipped and sucked, eliciting a low moan from Hope. Her breath was warm on Hope's ear as she whispered, "Your room," before raising herself to her feet. Without speaking, Hope stood, took Jo's hand in her own, and led them to her bedroom.

Liberated from years of restraint, Jo turned Hope to face her, walking her backwards the few remaining steps, while again claiming the sweet connection of their mouths. Hope's legs came up against the mattress, and Jo eased her to a seat on the edge. Taking Hope's hands in her own, she guided them to the button at the front of her jeans. She focused on Hope, who obliged, slowly lowering the zip. As the tab reached the bottom, Jo stepped back, swiftly removing both jeans and underwear in one movement.

Standing there, exposed and vulnerable, Jo had no idea where her courage had come from. Second guessing herself now simply wasn't an option. Covering the distance between them, Jo placed her hands on silky shoulders and gently laid Hope back on the bed. Jo moved back, first lifting one boot-clad foot and slowly undoing the zip before removing the soft, black leather, and then doing the same with the other.

Jo edged her hands to the waist of the trendy skirt. Hope raised her hips slightly, allowing Jo to slide the material down over her hips, past long slender legs to the floor. She did the same with the thin, lacy underwear, revealing smoothly shaven skin.

Releasing a stuttering breath, taking in the beautiful sight of Hope sliding herself slowly up the bed, Jo followed, knees either side of hourglass hips. Excited when Hope raised her hips, pressing their bodies together, Jo was encouraged to hungrily reclaim soft lips. Without separating their mouths, Jo lowered them both to the duvet; her knee spreading thighs, she settled herself in the welcome warmth.

She found Hope's ear with her lips and gently sucked the lobe into her mouth, simultaneously rocking her hips back and forth, allowing her thigh to gently glide over the juices beginning to escape. Hope gasped. Jo felt fingernails digging into the flesh just above her ass.

Jo pressed herself against the thigh between her legs, and heat erupted deep within, increasing the flow of warm wetness. Jo's desire spread across Hope's leg, as they increased the intensity of their movement. Raising her body just enough to bring her mouth over Hope's breast, Jo drew in the taut bud. She flicked her tongue over the sensitive nipple while maintaining the steady rhythm her hips had developed.

Moving her mouth now to the other erect and needy tip, Jo closed her teeth around the swollen nipple, biting with just enough force to entice pleasure. Nails scraping Jo's back, a low rasping groan, and a tensing body indicated Hope's climax was near.

At the feel of Hope's release, Jo's body followed suit, a violent pleasure erupting from within her. Hearing her name escape Hope's lips, Jo clenched the sheets beneath her hands as the waves of pleasure rolled in.

With the last of the spasms subsiding, Jo slowed her hips, not yet ready to stop entirely. She moved tenderly, slower now, wanting to savour the sensations right up till the last. Unable to endure any more, her clit became too sensitive. Jo lay down alongside Hope, planting gentle kisses on her neck. Hope's fingertips raised goosebumps all over Jo's back.

Jo carefully rolled to the side and lay on her back beside Hope. "Wow!" She continued to stare at the ceiling as she gathered herself together. "I'm so sorry."

Hope raised herself on an elbow, looking down at Jo. "What are you sorry for? That was beyond amazing."

"I don't do things like this," Jo answered honestly. "I have never in my life had a one-night stand, and I've definitely never been so forward."

A frown formed across Hope's forehead. "What makes you think this would be a one-night stand? Is that all you want it to be?"

"Well, I guess I assumed that's all you'd want. I've heard the stories about the elusive bar owner who gains the attention of so many women for an evening, but no more than that."

Hope flopped back against the bed. "Oohh, oww. That hurt, but I guess I deserved it in a way."

"I'm sorry Hope. I didn't mean to hurt you. I guess I've just never been in this position before, and I don't really know what to do or say."

***

Hope watched Jo for a few seconds, then gave a little smile. "How would you feel about me pulling the blankets up and the two of us having a talk? I think there are a few things I should probably share with you."

"Okay."

She pulled the duvet over them, a snug refuge from their emotions. Hope lay on her side facing Jo, who was still staring at the ceiling. Hope reached a feather-light finger to Jo's cheek, needing Jo to look at her. Jo obliged, allowing Hope to begin. "I'm not going to lie or try to convince you the rumors you've heard about me are untrue. I don't know what these so-called stories are, and to be honest, I don't want to know. I imagine what you've heard will have some validity to it. But I'd like to tell you some things that you wouldn't know. Things no one else knows."

"I'd like to hear whatever you feel comfortable talking about, Hope."

Hope ran her fingers through her hair. "Yes, the truth is, I have pleasured a number of women that I've met in the bar. However, I'm not sure the numbers are quite as bad as they've been made out to be. The part to all of this, the bit that you couldn't know, is that none of those women ever pleasured me."

"What do you mean by that?"

"What I mean is, I may have taken several women to my office, enjoying their company, and I may have pleased them sexually, but not one of them ever got to touch me. Plenty tried, but I had no desire to be touched by them. I would bring them pleasure and be happy to leave it at that. It gave me a sense of power, I think, and that was thrill enough for me. I wanted nothing more from them. Most of the time, I'd be back behind the bar serving drinks before they were even dressed again."

Jo lowered her gaze to the sheet that lay between them. "Oh, I see."

"Jo, please look at me," Hope pleaded. Dark pupils overshadowed the soft green Hope loved. "I doubt you do, even I don't really get it. What I get even less is why tonight, with you, it was different." Hope took Jo's hand in her own. "It wasn't just a little different, it was totally different."

"What do you mean?"

Releasing Jo's hand, Hope ran her fingertips along Jo's arm. "Not only did I want you to touch and please me, you were by far the more dominant of us tonight. I have never experienced that with anyone else. Not ever!"

An unsteady, nervous laugh slipped from Jo. "Well, it was definitely a first for me, as well, so I guess that makes two of us who have no idea what went on."

"Oh, I know what went on, and I enjoyed it a great deal," Hope teased.

"No, I didn't mean that."

The deep blush flooding Jo's face was very cute, and Hope laughed. "I know what you mean. I was just trying to lighten the moment a little." Hope gently stroked the side of Jo's cheek. "Jo, I don't know what any of this means, but for some reason, with you, things have been different. Right from the first time I saw you, I've been intrigued by you, and I've enjoyed learning more about you. When I'm with you, I feel like we've known each other forever. And when I'm not with you, there's so much about you I want to know."

"Okay...I think that's a good thing."

"What I'm trying to say, very unsuccessfully, is that I don't want this to simply be a one-night stand. I'd like to continue getting to know you, to see where this goes."

She watched as Jo lay silent for a moment. Hope's own fears matched the swirling storm in Jo's eyes.

"Hope, something you need to know about me is that I believe in honesty. I will always be honest with you, and in return, I need the same. So, the truth is, I am very intrigued by you and very drawn to you. That scares the shit out of me. I'm very inexperienced when it comes to relationships, of any sort. I've spent a long time keeping myself safe from hurt by avoiding people. If I'm not careful, I could wind up getting really wounded here."

"Then we have that in common. I've spent a lot of years keeping a safe distance, too. Avoiding heartache. So, I'm thinking I'm probably as scared about all of this as you." Lifting Jo's fingers to her mouth, Hope kissed them delicately. "Jo, I can't guarantee us happy-ever-after, but I can return your honesty and promise you that if we decide to explore whatever it is that's developing between us, you'll also have my loyalty."

Hope gave Jo time to process her words, all the while maintaining eye contact. Jo finally spoke, her voice carrying a tremor, "If I'm going to expect honesty from you, then I need to offer that as well. Hope, I don't have a clue what this is between us, but I know there's something. I've never felt anything like this and it scares the shit out of me, but I don't want to run away from whatever it is. I want us to see where it goes."

Holding Jo's face between shaky hands, Hope kissed her the best she could while smiling.

"So, does this mean I might be able to get another dinner out of you?"

Hope laughed heartily. "If you play your cards right, you may just get tomorrow morning's breakfast out of me." Hope's mouth met Jo's. Exposing their fears gave this kiss a new tenderness, and Hope thought she might melt.

Chapter Seventeen

HER EYES WERE SCRUNCHED up; she opened first one and then the other, aware of the warmth beside her. Rolling to her side, Hope propped herself on her elbow, and looked down at Jo, still asleep. Although Hope wondered how it all happened, sleeping with Jo, being intimate with her, had felt amazing.

They'd made love again after their talk. With more patience and taking turns, they began learning more of what the other enjoyed, finding where each liked to be caressed, sucked, and licked. Both were exhausted by the end of their second round of discovery. Hope had pulled Jo close, and they'd fallen asleep wrapped in one another's arms.

It was the first time in many years Hope had woken next to someone. It warmed her through to watch Jo sleep beside her. Hope took in stunning features, amazed how oblivious Jo was to her own looks.

As her gaze wandered a lazy path down Jo's uncovered torso, she felt an anger building inside. So many scars. The fury behind many still evident in the intensity of their flaming hues. She was shocked by her desire to protect Jo, but very quickly found an easy place to settle the emotion. She shook her head. Just how many more surprise emotions would Jo throw at her?

Hope had surprised herself when she first kissed Jo, but that had been nothing compared with the shock she'd felt, and enjoyed, when Jo took charge. It was all new territory. She tried to figure out why, last night with Jo, she'd allowed things to be different.

Sleep-heavy eyes began to flutter. Jo reached her arms up above her head in a good stretch. The sheet slipped down, further exposing her chest to Hope's view. Hope smiled her appreciation at the sight.

"Morning," Jo said sleepily, noticing Hope watching her.

With a genuine smile that lit her eyes, Hope was full of life. "It's not just morning from where I'm lying; it's a fantastic morning." She brushed her lower lip over Jo's smile. The kiss was gentle, not filled with the hunger and passion of last night. This time, Hope offered reassurance that she still felt the same way. When Jo gently stroked the side of Hope's face as she returned the kiss, Hope felt relief that Jo was offering comfort in return.

"Are you hungry? I could get you that breakfast I mentioned last night." Hope delicately traced Jo's collarbone with just her fingertip.

A sly grin snuck across Jo's face. Hope suspected she was recalling the events of the night before.

"I'm starving, but I need to get home. Oscar and Ruby will be beside themselves."

Hope was disappointed; she wasn't ready to end their time together just yet, especially when she wasn't sure when she'd be able to get more time off over the next week. But, she understood the puppies would need their mum.

"I don't know how you'd feel about it, or what you need to do today, but you could come with me. We could spend some time at my place, if you like."

Hope grinned. "Or, you could take my car to go get the little ones, along with a few bits and pieces they may need, and bring them back here. While you're gone, I could make a start on breakfast."

"Are you sure you'd be okay with them coming here? I mean, they're house trained, and I could bring their enclosure so they shouldn't damage anything, but I know some people aren't too keen on pets in their homes."

"I'm fine with it. We can shut the gate securely, that way the back is safe for them, and they wouldn't need to be enclosed all the time. We could eat and then take them for a walk after, if you like."

Jo pulled Hope in for a kiss that lingered a little, an offering of more to come. "I'd love to do that with you." She placed a kiss on Hope's cheek. "Thank you for understanding."

"How about you go get them, then you can thank me later." Hope wiggled her eyebrows at Jo. "I have a few ideas on how you might be able to do that."

"Oh you do, do you? Sounds to me like I might enjoy getting to thank you."

"I plan on both of us enjoying it a lot."

After double-checking Jo knew how to drive a stick shift, Hope handed over the keys. Once the car headed out the drive, Hope went to the kitchen. It didn't take long to come up with an idea for breakfast.

"Yes, Aunt Em, I know, it's a good thing I finally got some groceries. I'm going to make one of your favourites. It feels good to be doing this again, even if it isn't with you".

By the time Hope heard the car pulling back into the carport, she was well organised. Once Jo had the dogs all settled, she'd need only a few minutes to cook the last bits. Hope greeted Jo as she climbed out the car. Looking at her watch, Hope was surprised to find it had only been twenty minutes since Jo left, yet she was excited to see her again. She placed her hands on Jo's hips leaning in to give her a welcoming kiss. They held each other tight in a warm hug.

As they moved apart, Hope looked into the car to see two very excited puppies looking up at her and wagging their tails. "So, shall we get them in and settled?" Hope smiled through the window at the balls of fluff.

"Yep, that's a good idea. I'm terrified one of them will have an accident in your car," Jo said with a look of concern on her face.

Hope shrugged. "If they do, it can be cleaned."

"I can't believe you're so casual about it."

"Babies do these things. Getting stressed or angry won't make the situation any better; it will only cause them to be scared." She threw Jo an easy smile. "So, how can I help?"

"If we grab a pup each and put them in the bathroom, they could wait there while I set up their enclosure."

Hope helped carry things in then gave Jo a hand to get the sides of the enclosure slotted together. Jo made sure there was water and a little basket of toys set up, while Hope double-checked the gate.

The instant Jo opened the bathroom door, the two little dynamos came rushing out, leaping at her legs. Jo knelt to calm them with hugs and pats. With the puppies quieter, she stood. "Now that you've helped me, what can I do to assist with breakfast?"

"Nothing, I've got it all under control." Hope winked at Jo. "If I remember correctly your job is to thank me."

Jo gave her a long, sensual kiss, pulling back just enough to whisper, "Are you sure you want to wait till we've eaten for me to thank you?"

Looking up at the ceiling, Hope let out a jagged breath. "You're making it very tempting, but I can't help think maybe I'll get better thanks if you have a full stomach," she murmured.

Jo moved her lips to just under Hope's chin and slowly ran her tongue down to the top of her t-shirt, causing Hope to shudder lightly.

Placing her hands on either side of Jo's arms, Hope held her in place as she took a step backwards. "You are constantly surprising me. You know that?"

"Is that a good thing?" Jo's face was all innocence.

Not able to help herself, Hope laughed as she wrapped her arms around Jo's shoulders. "It's a very good thing."

Hope kissed Jo again, maintaining some control over the encounter. As their lips parted, Hope slid her hand down to take Jo's in her own, leading her to the kitchen table, where she offered her a seat.

Coffee. She brought a mug for Jo, placed one on the table for herself, and went back to the stove. She soon served a breakfast of bacon, scrambled eggs, and cinnamon French toast. As they ate, both realised they were much hungrier than they'd thought. They devoured everything on their plates, while Oscar and Ruby played around their feet.

Chapter Eighteen

HOPE REACHED ACROSS THE table, running her finger over the back of Jo's hand. "Is there anything you either want or need to get done today?"

Jo shook her head. "No, Sunday's are usually lazy days for me. Often, all I do is take the two hounds for a walk to the park and take pictures."

"Would you still like to do that? I'm happy to go for a walk with you guys, if you don't mind me joining you."

Jo's eyes shone back at Hope. "Of course, we wouldn't mind if you joined us. Having you with us will be a treat."

They quickly tidied the kitchen, working together with ease in the confined space. As soon as everything was spick and span, Jo readied her charges for their outing. Hope gathered Oscar's lead from Jo, before entwining the fingers of her free hand with Jo's. Not wanting to overstep any boundaries, she watched Jo's reaction. What greeted her was a warm, full smile.

At the park, Jo led them down a path that soon became a dirt track, weaving its way amongst the trees. Above them, Hope saw the three distinctive levels of trees so common amongst the bush in Auckland. The totara, miro, and other conifers, provided the high canopy. Below these, the broadleaved trees created a shady cover, often just overhead. The taraire were loaded with their purple, berry-like fruits, and several kereru were perched amongst the trees. The large wood pigeons filled themselves on the fruits ripening in the warmer spring temperatures. The lowest level was a variety of native tree ferns, shrubs, and ground covers.

As they moseyed along the leaf covered path, Jo pointed out the features ahead. "This track loops around in a semicircle. At the far side, there's a stream with an open space where I usually take Oscar and Ruby's leads off so they can have a good run around. They're getting braver and beginning to investigate the water. It's so cute to watch."

Hope noticed the stream was gentle and clear when they reached the clearing. Jo took first Ruby's and then Oscar's lead off. Guiding them to the water's edge, she gently encouraged them to have a look. Hope watched as Jo patiently allowed them the time they needed to feel safe. Ruby was the first to attempt dipping a tiny paw into the water. She turned tail and ran at the slightest drip of the water on her fur, Oscar following.

Hope laughed heartily. Jo stood and walked to her, sliding her hands around Hope's waist. "I'm trying to get them used to it, but as you see, they're not too convinced."

"No, they don't look it." The two rascals were now sitting side by side, looking up with big, puppy eyes.

"Maybe they'll be keener to give it a go when the weather warms up a little more. At least, I live in hope." Jo's lips brushed lightly over Hope's.

Hope met Jo partway, carefully taking Jo's bottom lip between her teeth. Jo ran her hands down Hope's back, covering Hope's rear, bringing them closer together.

"I think we should keep moving, because I can't be sure I'll behave myself if we keep this up."

Laughter rumbled up from the pit of Hope's belly as she touched the tip of Jo's nose with her finger. "Yep, I think you're right. I don't know if I can be trusted either, and I don't want to lose these guys the first time I come out with you."

Jo bent to reattach Oscar's lead.

"If you pass me the other one, I can get Ruby ready to head off," Hope said.

They emerged from the bush hand in hand, and Jo led the way to a park bench not too far from the playground. "I love to sit here on Sundays, watching the kids play. The best part is seeing the mums and dads play as well." Her eyes continued to survey the people. "The joy in the kids' faces when their parents are having fun with them is something no amount of money can buy. They could be given the most expensive toy in the world and it'd never compare to the feeling of being loved and important."

Resting her arm around Jo's shoulder, Hope leaned over, kissing her cheek. Nothing more was said for a while, both watching the people around them.

"Do you feel anger toward your parents for all they put you through?" Hope asked

"No, not anymore. I used to, a lot, when I was younger. But I grew to see that if I continued holding onto that anger it'd consume me, and they'd still be getting the better of me. I refuse to give them that level of control over me. They no longer get the right to dictate any part of my life in any way. They lost that a long time ago."

"Jo, you've got so much inner strength and courage. I think you're an incredible person to have overcome all you went through."

Jo shook her head. "Thanks Hope, but believe me, I'm far from incredible. I'm just doing the best I can to better my life. I have to, because I can't ever let myself become anything like them."

Hope's hands on Jo's face were affectionate, her tone serious. "Jo, you're nothing like that, and you don't need to ever fear becoming them. You're getting an education, making something of your life." She leaned down to pat Ruby. "Then there are these little guys. The way you love and care for them shows me that you'd never ever be anything like your parents. And I saw how you were with Jane's baby. You're gentle, naturally kind. You'd make an amazing mum one day."

"I don't think I could ever do that. What if, after a while, I changed and became like them? What if there's some inherited gene that would predispose me to becoming violent?"

The fear in Jo's eyes was very real, and Hope knew she was serious. "Jo, I really don't think there's any gene that causes that. I'm sure some people are simply nasty, regardless of how they're raised or what their circumstances have been. Then there are others, like your parents, who possibly became very different people once drugs got hold of them." She softly stroked Jo's cheek. "Jo, I've met a lot of people on my travels, and I see and meet all sorts in the bar. Trust me when I tell you that you're very special. You're gentle, loving, intelligent, and strong. You'll never be anything like your parents."

"Thank you. It means a lot that you see me that way." Jo skimmed her fingers over Hope's thigh. "What about you, Hope? Would you like kids one day?"

Hope raised her eyebrows. "The truth?"

"Yeah, definitely, I'm curious."

"Well, the truth is, I've never thought about kids for myself in any way, shape, or form. Jane's the first friend I've had who has a kid. The thought of me ever having one hasn't even come close to entering my head. I've never been in the position to have to consider it. My lifestyle, up until just over a year ago, was footloose and fancy-free. I didn't stay put in any one place for too long. Not really a suitable life for a child." Hope quieted for a moment, mulling things over. "Although, I guess I have certain ideas about what I believe children should receive."

"Like what?" Jo sat up straight, intrigued by the topic.

"I think a stable environment is important. That's not to say I think there needs to be two parents, or if there are, that they need to stay together. Sometimes, I think it's better for the child if parents separate, rather than just be together for the child, and then have them in a home filled with tension." Hope was watching Jo's reactions. Jo nodded in agreement. "I think positive role models, routines, discipline, and affection all help a child to know they're loved and let them feel safe." As these last words rolled from her tongue, Hope frowned. "Do you think you may have been a different person today had you grown up in a stable environment?"

"Definitely, I feel safer and a lot more comfortable in my own company, or with just one or two others, than I do in large groups. I hardly ever join in discussions, too worried to express an opinion. In my past, if you had a voice you'd be seen. Being seen often resulted in some form of abuse. Also, I'm very guarded. I don't open myself up to others or let them in often." Jo looked intently into Hope's eyes for a moment. "That's why I don't know what came over me last night. I've never felt like that before. And then, to actually act on my feelings is such a foreign concept." Jo laughed nervously. "My turn to be honest. All of this, last night, today…now…it's terrifying."

Hope ran her fingers along Jo's back. "This may sound strange, but I understand better than you probably think I do."

Jo knit her eyebrows together. "How's that?" She reached to take Hope's free hand, giving it a gentle squeeze.

"Like I told you last night, it had been many years since I'd allowed anyone else to touch me. I've been with a lot of women, I guess, but you're the first person to pleasure me since I was eighteen."

"Why's that? What caused you to feel that way? To guard yourself so protectively and then let that guard down for me?"

"It was simple really; I fell in love with the wrong person. I got hurt, and decided I never wanted to feel that pain, ever again. The simple solution was to shut myself off to any form of intimacy." Hope was grateful for the quiet pause and Jo's gentle stroking of her back while she collected her thoughts. "It was the first time I'd been in love, and I made the mistake of thinking she loved me too. I thought we were going to live the happy-ever-after life. She did a good job of letting me think that was the case. When I came out to Aunt Em, she was amazing. She told me there wasn't anything I could do, or be, that would cause her to stop loving me."

"Your Aunt Em sounds like an amazing woman."

"She was. She was a rare breed, that's for sure. I was so lucky."

Hope stared at the sky as though she could see her past on display. "I met Lisa just before my eighteenth birthday. I was at a friend's party, and Lisa was a cousin of that friend. We hit it off from the beginning. Before I knew it, we were inseparable. It was like that for about six months, then slowly, I began to see less and less of her. She'd always have an excuse, she was working late or had to help her mum out, things like that. It got to the stage where I'd only see her a couple of times a week, and she'd turn up late. When she did finally come over, we'd make love then she'd be gone again. As this went on, I felt more and more like I was simply there for her pleasure and that was my role to fill. Then, one night, she was meant to be picking me up to go to a movie. At the last minute, she called to say she couldn't make it. Aunt Em could see how upset I was by being let down, yet again. She told me to get ready; I was going to get to see that movie, no matter what. As we were lining up for our tickets, we noticed this young couple, a boy and girl, a few spaces in front of us in the queue. They were all touchy and cuddly, kissing and giggling, and I was thinking how that should've been Lisa and me. When they had their tickets, they turned around...It *was* Lisa with some boy she'd met at work."

"I'm so sorry." Taking Hope's face, Jo gently kissed her cheek. "That was a cruel thing to do to you."

Hope shrugged. "I swore I'd never let myself hurt like that again. That's why, for all these years, I've been happy to have brief affairs. Some lasted a couple of months, but I'd never let myself be emotionally invested. For that reason, no one ever got to touch me. It was my role to please them. That way, I was in control. And if I was in control then I couldn't be hurt again."

"What made it different last night, with me?"

"I don't know." Hope gave a short laugh. "For some reason, a lot of things have been out of my control since I met you, none of which I understand. I have given up trying to figure out or control what is happening and I'm just going with what feels right."

Hand in hand, they made the journey back to Hope's in comfortable silence. Pondering why she'd opened up to Jo in a way she'd only ever done with her aunt, Hope decided she didn't need to know why. All she needed to do was embrace that she was happier than she'd been in a very long time.

Chapter Nineteen

THE FUR BABIES WERE asleep before Hope latched the door to their enclosure. "I don't know about you, but I need a shower."

Jo nodded. "I could do with one myself. I brought a change of clothes with me, would you mind if I had one when you're finished?"

Hope tilted her head to one side. "Or you could have one with me."

A cute chin jutted out slightly, as Jo seemed to study the ceiling while tapping her index finger against her cheek. "I think that'd be a good idea, that way I don't waste your water."

Laughing, Hope grabbed for Jo's hand and pulled her toward the bathroom. "You're so thoughtful and considerate. They're two of the things I like best about you."

Hope turned the shower on before snatching the hem of Jo's shirt and pulling it up over Jo's lifted arms and unceremoniously flinging the material behind her.

"What else do you like about me?"

"Your eyes are amazing. From the first time I looked into them, I haven't been able to get enough." Hope placed gentle kisses on each of Jo's eyelids before marking a trail of faint kisses down Jo's neck to her shoulder. When Hope felt Jo shiver slightly, she looked at her. "And I love how your hair has a mind of its own."

Jo looked away. "I hate my hair. It's always such a mess; that's why I wear hats all the time."

Hope brought Jo's gaze back to her. "It has the most amazing colours, almost every shade of brown anyone could imagine, with lighter streaks complementing your skin tone and eyes. When I look closer, I can see near-white strips threading through, blending in."

Hope reached behind Jo to unhook the clasps on her bra and free Jo's breasts. The piece of clothing was soon on the floor along with Jo's shirt. Hope covered each enticing mound with her hands. "And I like the way, when I do this..." The thumb and forefinger of each hand gently pinched a nipple each, "you respond to my touch instantly."

Jo's rounded buds hardened beneath the touch. Hope lowered her head, gently blowing on each nipple. She watched as they hardened a little more. Happy with the results, Hope left a trail of kisses as she made her way to Jo's mouth. As their lips met, Hope was taken aback by the hunger in Jo's response.

Still kissing, Jo reached for Hope's shirt, removing it with haste. Hope sensed Jo's urgency and quickly removed the rest of her clothes. Stepping under the warm water, Hope extended her hand. Making short work of discarding the remainder of her own clothing, Jo accepted Hope's hand, following her under the stream. Their mouths met, tongues finding one another with hunger and passion.

With a deep need to please Jo, Hope released Jo's mouth, controlling her own passion. She turned Jo around and stepped behind her lover, easing her body against Jo's back. She explored Jo's body with smooth fingertips gliding from firm shoulders, over a full chest, and along Jo's flat stomach. Hope took her time, allowing her hands to rest briefly on slightly rounded hips.

Hope reached for the soap and quickly lathered her hands before positioning them back on Jo's hips, sliding her hands leisurely back to Jo's breasts. Smoothly working nipples between her fingers, Hope lowered her mouth, allowing herself the pleasure of sucking Jo's neck. The mixture of soft pleasure and slight pain received the response Hope had been looking for. Jo arched her head back, a low groan escaping her throat.

Hope continued to alternate between sucking and lightly biting Jo's neck, her hands making their way down over Jo's stomach and reaching the soft tendrils in the v of Jo's legs. Unhurriedly exploring the area, Hope gently slid her fingers between Jo's folds, eliciting yet another deep groan. Slipping a finger inside, Hope could feel her own desires growing and knew she was as wet as Jo.

Jo's hips began a rhythmic movement against Hope's hand. Hope slowly added another finger, positioning her thumb to glide over Jo's clit. When Jo cried out, Hope knew they'd both be ready to climax soon. Continuing to move her fingers in and out of Jo, Hope moved her free hand down, gliding fingers between her ready lips and over her own swollen bud. With the first touch to herself, she released a moan that was immediately echoed by Jo. Feeling Jo begin to clench around her fingers, Hope let herself go. They climaxed together in a symphony of cries and whimpers.

As their bodies relaxed, Hope removed her fingers from both Jo and herself. Turning Jo to face her, she stared at Jo's lips, bemused and besotted, before claiming that mouth. When the kiss subsided, they held onto one another, regaining their breath.

Lazy fingers stroked Hope's back, and Jo's voice was raspy. "Wow, that was amazing. Thank you."

Hope chuckled lightly in Jo's ear. "I agree. Wow!" Grinning, Hope admitted, "I don't know about you, but after that I think I'm ready to join the puppies in an afternoon nap."

"I think after that we both deserve a little rest," Jo added with a shy giggle.

"It's agreed then."

***

Jo watched the mid-afternoon shadows creep across the bedroom. Needing the toilet, she moved gently, doing her best not to disturb Hope. But as their bodies began to separate, Hope tightened her arm around Jo, one eye opening slowly.

"Hi," Hope mumbled. "Are you okay? Where are you going?" She quickly sat up. "You're not leaving, are you?"

"No, I was just trying to slip out to the toilet without waking you. Sorry, I wasn't very successful."

Exhaling, Hope flopped back on the mattress. "I thought you were going to sneak out before I woke up."

Jo lowered her mouth lightly to Hope's. "No," Jo whispered, just before they kissed. Her breath softly caressed Hope's lips as she moved away. "Not even close. I'll be right back."

Hope watched Jo wrap the discarded towel around herself before wandering to the toilet. *What the hell is up with you? You're the one who sneaks from others beds, not them from yours. Shit, you don't even let others in your bed!*

Hope was all set to analyse what was going on with her, when Jo wandered back into the room. The second she saw Jo, all anxieties seemed to vanish. The only thought present in Hope's mind now was how beautiful Jo was. Slipping back under the covers, Jo sidled up to Hope.

Hope gently stroked Jo's hair. "Feel better?"

"So much better." Jo chuckled.

"You know, I really do love your hair," Hope complimented the woman stretched out naked beside her.

Jo buried her face in Hope's chest and mumbled, "I know it's awful, you don't have to try and make me feel better about it. I've got a beanie in my bag. I can throw it on if my hair's in your way."

Shocked by Jo's words, Hope slightly moved Jo so she could turn and prop herself on her elbow. "No, I think your hair's stunning, amazing. Why would you think I'd want you to cover it up? Have past partners been unkind to you about your hair, Jo?"

"There haven't been any past partners, but I was given a hard time about my hair when I was a kid. I learned the best thing to do was cover it up so people didn't notice it and it didn't annoy anyone."

Hope stared at Jo for a long moment. "What do you mean by 'there haven't been any past partners?'" Hope asked, a little confused.

"Just that."

"So, what you're telling me is you've never been in a real, long-term relationship?"

"You could say that. Or you could say that you're the first woman, first person full stop, that I've been intimate with."

Before Hope had a chance to stop and think, her mouth engaged. "Are you serious?" When Jo looked away, Hope saw the embarrassment and hurt in her eyes. Realising just how harsh her words must have been, Hope turned Jo back to look at her again. "Jo, I'm sorry." As Hope ran her finger over Jo's chin, she smiled softly. "The fact is, I was surprised. My reaction was based out of concern for you."

"What do you mean concern?"

"Jo, if I'd known this was your first experience, I would have been a lot different with you. I would have gone slower, been gentler, and I would have tried to be less hungry in my desire."

"So, you'd have desired me less if you knew I was a virgin?"

"No! That's not what I mean." Getting flustered, Hope laid back beside Jo, rubbing her hands over her face.

"I'm sorry, I should have told you so that you had a chance to back out." Moving toward the side of the bed, Jo's voice was barely audible. "I'll just get the puppies, then I'll leave you be."

Hope lunged for Jo grabbing her hand and pulling her back down. "No, that's not what I want. Jo, hop back in beside me and let me start over. I've done nothing but muck this up from the beginning." She saw Jo hesitate. "Please."

Jo moved back into the bed, and they sat themselves up against the pillows. Hope pulled the covers over them both. Once they were comfortable, she took Jo's hand in her own. "Jo, I don't think there's anything that would've been able to make me desire you less. I've no idea what's going on between us, and I must admit, I'm a little confused by it all. But for whatever reason, it feels right." She tried to reassure Jo with a nervous smile.

"Having feelings for someone is foreign to me, and because of that I don't really know what I'm doing any more than you, I guess. But I do know, if I was going to change anything, it wouldn't be sleeping with you. It would be the way in which we went about that. If I'd known it was your first time, I would've been gentle, patient with you. Instead, I was greedy. Your first time should've been a much nicer experience than the one I provided."

"I'm sorry, I guess you're right, I should have told you."

"Can I ask, why? Why now with me?"

"Honestly, I didn't plan or expect it, but when you kissed me, I just went with what felt right in the moment. Being with you felt very right. I thought you'd guess, I mean, you're experienced. I figured my lack of knowledge would have said it all anyway."

"What?" Hope couldn't believe what she was hearing. "Oh my God, Jo. For someone who is new to all this, you have nothing to worry about. I had no idea it was your first time. Every move you make is like you know exactly what you're doing. Every kiss, every touch, every look, is exquisite!"

"So, I haven't disappointed you?"

Wrapping her arm around Jo's shoulder, pulling her in and kissing the top of her head, Hope wanted to bundle Jo up in her arms, keeping her safe and warm forever. "Far from it, Jo. Whatever you do, don't doubt yourself. You're beautiful, and you know just the right things to do to excite the heck out of me. As I said before, this is all foreign to me as well. I don't know what's changed or what this is between us, but I'm keen to see what's going on if you are?"

Jo looked up. "I don't know what's going on either, but I like it, and I'm keen to find out as well."

Hope kissed Jo tenderly as they sat propped up in bed, Hope's arms around Jo, protectively holding her close as she stroked that beautiful hair. Hope ran her hand soothingly over Jo's shoulder. "What happened when you were a kid, with your hair?"

"It was always so difficult to keep control of. It was hard to brush and maintain, always a problem for the adults I was placed with. They didn't like the extra time it took to get me ready before school or that it took longer to wash and dry than the other kids. Most of the time, when they'd brush it, they'd hurt me, pulling it and slapping my head when I wriggled. As well as that, the kids at school would tease me. So, one day, I just started hiding it. It was easier for everyone."

An anger swirled in the pit of Hope's stomach. Disgusted by the ill treatment Jo had suffered time and time again, Hope marveled at the woman Jo had become. Pulling Jo tighter to her, Hope kissed the top of her head. "I love your hair. Around me, you never have to worry about covering it."

Chapter Twenty

OSCAR AND RUBY WOKE, whining their discomfort, and Jo dressed quickly to take her puppies outside. Hope threw on some clothes before going to the kitchen to switch on the jug. Jo came up from behind and wrapped her arms around Hope's waist, snuggling into her back. She felt Hope relax into her and smiled. "What are you doing?"

"I'm just going to make a pot of tea. Will you have a cup?"

"Mmm. That'd be nice."

The sound of the water boiling in the jug pulled them from their thoughts. Jo let Hope go and wandered over to the table. Hope poured the water, and brought the teapot and cups over to the table. She took the seat opposite Jo and reached down to give the pups a pat.

Jo watched as Hope patted her babies, touched by how caring and understanding she'd been toward them. "Thanks for being so patient with them, Hope, I appreciate it."

"You don't have to thank me for anything. They're cute and they've been no problem at all. I've enjoyed having them around, to be honest." Hope looked at Jo. "I've enjoyed having their mum around too."

"Their mum likes being here with you. What time do you have to be at the bar?"

"I don't need to head over there until about eight tonight. We could have some dinner together before I have to go, if you like."

"That'd be great. Maybe we should cook at my place. That way I can get these guys settled again. After dinner, you can come back here and relax on your own for a little while before you head over."

"That sounds like a good idea. We could head off soon."

"I'll go get our stuff sorted out after we've had our tea. That will give us plenty of time without needing to rush at all."

***

While gathering up her shampoo and deodorant from the bathroom, Jo thought she heard voices. She returned to the lounge to collect Oscar and Ruby's toys and discovered she'd heard correctly. *I wonder who she's talking to.*

Jo didn't want to interrupt and was happy to wait, but the little ones ran to investigate.

"Oh, how precious are you two? Where did you come from? Hope, when did you get these guys?"

Finally, able to answer a question, Hope laughed at Andy. "They're not mine; they belong to Jo. The cute little one here, hiding behind my leg, is Ruby, and that little rascal trying to devour your shoelaces is Oscar."

Jo headed toward the kitchen to collect the ratbags.

"Oh my God they're even cuter in the flesh than in the pictures Jo showed us. How come they're with you? Are you looking after them?"

"No, Jo's here with me as well." Jo noticed Hope didn't hesitate in her answer and it felt good. She walked into the kitchen, offering Andy a grin.

"Hi Andy, how are you?"

Eyebrows raised, Andy looked from one to the other. Hope reached an arm out to circle Jo's waist, pulling her in close enough to plant a kiss on her temple.

"Well, you two are the dark horses, aren't you? So, how long have you been hiding this from me?"

"We haven't been hiding anything from you, or anyone else for that matter. This is a very recent development. It was as much a surprise to the two of us as I'm sure it is to you," Hope said.

"Oh, it may be a surprise to you darling, but it's no surprise to me!"

"Really, and what makes you say that?"

Andy shook his head, smiling at the pair. "Because I've spent the last few weeks watching the two of you. I've seen the way you look at each other. I've watched the way you talk, laugh, and light up when you're together." Thrusting his hands into his pockets, Andy grinned at them like the cat that got the cream. "Like I say, it may have taken the two of you this long to work it out, but I've known since the night we were all at Jane's."

Hope threw a tea towel at her friend and poked her tongue out at him. "Obviously, we're not as astute as you. Now, what's brought you over here anyway?"

"That's right, I almost forgot about that. Just wanted to make sure you were all right for tonight?"

"I'm great for tonight. Thanks to your pep talk, I feel so much better."

Andy let out a sly snicker. "I'd say all the thanks go to Jo for that."

"Hmm, you may be right," Hope agreed. "She definitely makes me feel good."

Jo felt her face getting hotter and hotter, and Hope giggled as she kissed Jo's cheek.

"Well, this is all too sickly sweet for me. If you're sure you're fine, I'm going to head home."

Chapter Twenty-one

HOPE'S WORKLOAD EASED UP. Andy's confidence was well placed; Tara was a blessing. She'd taken to staff, as well as customers, easily and quickly. Hope's new-found freedom was a relief, but not at all for the reason she would have expected. A few weeks ago, Hope had craved some time to herself, a chance to just be. Now, the relief was knowing she'd have more time with Jo.

Since their first weekend together, Hope had been a regular visitor at Jo's. They spent hours learning more and more about each other, surviving on little sleep. Between Hope having to lock up every night, and Jo needing to be in class every morning by nine, their hours together were limited.

In the early hours of the morning, their legs wrapped around each other, Hope ran her fingers over the swell of Jo's breast. "Tell me more about school."

"What would you like to know?" Jo asked.

"Anything, everything. How about, what exactly it is you study? I mean, I know you have lessons every day from nine till one, but I don't know much else and I'm interested."

"I'm doing a Bachelor of Creative Enterprise. In the first year, they spend a lot of time teaching us about creative thinking and professional practice. It's a real hands-on learning style. We get to work alongside professionals, collaborating on projects, allowing us a chance to see a variety of different ways art can be used in the professional world. After the first year, you can move more into a field that interests you. For me, that's photography. It always was, and as much as some of the other things I saw and learned about were interesting, they never came close to how I feel about seeing the world through a lens."

"I love seeing you light up. You do that whenever you talk about taking pictures and when you talk about Oscar and Ruby. Tell me more," Hope snuggled Jo in closer.

"It's a three-year course if you take it full time. When I started, I thought I'd have to do it over six years. I didn't want to take out a loan, I'd rather not be in debt like that. I didn't have enough money to do more than one semester. But then, through the course, I met someone who put me onto this guy. One thing led to another and before I knew it, I had a job. My work is easy and is all done on computer. Dave, the guy I work for, travels around the schools. He does class photos and individual packs the parents can buy. Basically, he takes the pictures, and I use different applications to enhance the shots. When the orders are placed, I bundle them up for him. It's easy work that I can do from home, and it pays my way through school."

"I'm so happy that you get to do what you love, Jo."

Jo moved closer, her tongue teasing the edge of Hope's lower lip. With a jump, she suddenly moved away. "Hey, I just had a cool idea. I've learned a lot from Dave. I could probably get some really nice portraits of Ben for Jane if that's something she's interested in having."

"I'm sure it is. That's a really neat idea. I've been meaning to call her, anyway, so why don't I give her a ring today and see if she's keen?"

"Please, I'd love to be able to do that for her."

***

Jo gradually eased her finger down on the trigger button, whirring her Canon into action again. She couldn't believe how calmly the session was going. Ben was such a contented soul, making Jo's job both easy and enjoyable.

Jane and Hope helped move the furniture around, and they transformed Jane's living room into a makeshift studio. Using the natural light the many windows offered, Jo took picture after picture of Ben. She'd started off with the little bundle lying on his back, but when she discovered how obliging the infant was, she made the most of the opportunity. She placed him on his tummy and side with the aid of a sheepskin, a basket, and a giant teddy bear. Aware she was pushing her luck and knowing she had more than one stunning picture, Jo turned her camera off and set it in her bag.

"You're such a good boy," she cooed, moving to scoop Ben into her arms. Wrapping a blanket around him, she turned to Hope and Jane. "He's such an angel to work with, but I think we could be pushing our luck if we keep going for much longer." Jo snuggled Ben against her, as she turned her eyes to Jane. "If there's anything else you'd like to give a go, I think your little man here will be compliant for a little longer, though."

Jane moved toward Jo and her son. "You've already given me so much. I feel rude asking, but there's one more thing I was wondering if you could do. If you'd rather not, then it's okay to say so."

Jo noticed that Jane seemed nervous, a trait she hadn't seen in her before. So far, whenever they'd been together, Jane had always come across as someone with confidence. This change in demeanor had Jo curious.

"What is it?"

"How would you feel about taking a couple of pictures of Ben and I together?"

Jane's words, as simple as they seemed, only worked to enlarge Jo's curiosity as to why this would have Jane acting a little unsure of herself.

"The thing is...I'd ummm...could you...would you...

"For Christ's sake, Jane, spit it out," Hope said, nudging her friend.

"What I have in mind would mean I'd be either naked, or at least topless. If that would make you feel uncomfortable, I'd understand."

Jo had never photographed anyone naked before and was caught off guard by Jane's request. When she hesitated, Jane went on quickly.

"I'm sorry, Jo, forget I asked. I'm more than grateful for the pictures you've already taken."

Jo shook her head. "Don't be. I was just caught off guard and to be honest, I've never actually taken pictures of people without clothes on before. I knew it could happen at some stage. I guess I always thought when it did the request would come from strangers."

Joining them, Hope smiled broadly. "I have a solution. You should both take your clothes off. That way no one has to feel awkward."

Keeping Ben safe in one arm, Jo reached over to swat Hope on the butt. "Trust you!"

"Hey, I'm only trying to help." Hope grinned, wiggling her eyebrows playfully.

"Yeah, help satisfy your dreams." Jane shoved Hope's shoulder playfully.

"Hey, you can't blame a girl for trying," Hope said, offering up her best look of innocence.

"No, you can't," Jo agreed. "Any more than I want to deny Jane the chance of the pictures she'd really like."

Jo could see how much effort Jane was putting into not smiling as she said, "Are you sure, Jo?" The second Jo's head bobbed up and down, Jane gave up, releasing the grin she'd been suppressing.

"In that case, why don't I head out and get something nice for lunch while you finish up," Hope offered.

"Oh my God, don't tell me the legendary womaniser is being chivalrous?" Jane teased.

"Don't kid yourself. I'm starving. Right now, my stomach wins out that's all."

Hope was playing right along with Jane but the faint blush didn't pass without Jo noticing. Keys in hand and heading for the door, Hope called over her shoulder, "Be back soon."

***

While Jo and Hope put furniture back, Jane fed and changed Ben. With a full tummy, Ben settled in his bed instantly, exhausted after the morning's excitement.

Reaching for another piece of sushi, Jane asked, "How did you get into photography, Jo?"

"I've always been drawn to art in one form or another. As dark as some days might be, art let me see that there's still beauty in the world. If I opened my mind and my eyes, I'd always be able to find something positive. Art helped me get through times that were pretty miserable. My aim is to one day produce something that will offer someone else a glimmer of hope. Photography was the art that called to me the strongest. I can sketch fairly well, and I like to play around with pencils and charcoal. I don't enjoy paint though. I'm not sure why. It never really felt comfortable to me. But looking through a lens to find beauty in a tree's branches, a pet's love and adoration, a thunderstorm, or a smile, that's what feeds me. It makes me want to get up every morning; it excites and inspires me."

Hope squeezed Jo's hand. "You light up when you talk about taking pictures, and that excites me."

Ducking her head, Jo felt her cheeks warm. "Sorry, I guess I can be a little over zealous when it comes to certain things."

"Don't ever apologise or be embarrassed by that," Jane assured. "It's a rare thing these days, and who am I to moan about that anyway. I think I'm turning into one of those mums who can talk about nothing but her child."

"Now it's my turn to tell you to never apologise, not for that. That's how it should be," Jo lightly touched Jane's arm.

"Having Ben was the best decision I've ever made, despite many people telling me I was anything and everything from a fool for wanting a child, to being selfish for bringing one into the world on my own."

"I can tell you, through experience, that having two adults in the house doesn't guarantee a child will be better off. As long as a child is safe and loved, then whether it's by one, two, or a dozen people it doesn't matter. I've spent time in plenty of homes where there were two parents and in place of love there was resentment and instead of feeling safe kids lived in fear."

"No person should have to be subjected to that, let alone a child," Hope stated.

"You're right," Jane agreed. "And I may not be in a position as a single mum to provide my son with everything and anything, but he will always know he's loved and that he's my number one priority."

Hope pushed her glass out in front of her as she stretched her legs out under the table. "There's something I've been wanting to talk to you about actually, Jane, and this seems like the perfect time."

"What's that, Hope?"

"Well, I have a proposition for you, and before you get all excited, it's business not pleasure."

Playing along, Jane lowered her head with a disappointed look on her face. "Wow, you really know how to crush a girl, don't you?"

All three laughed and Jane asked, "What's this all-work, no-play proposition you have for me? You have me curious, despite being crushed."

"Before I start, you need to know if it doesn't fit in with how you envision being a stay-at-home mum, then that's all good."

"Since my birthday, and that amazing cake you made, my mind's been at work. When I was young, Aunt Em offered the customers amazing homemade baking. I was thinking, if you were interested, then maybe we could go back to offering that again. Jane, that cake was delicious. I was thinking maybe you could bake for the café, and I could pay you for the goodies you produce."

Jane looked from Hope to Jo, then back to Hope. "I think that would be awesome, but I don't think my kitchen is big enough to do the job in."

"Well, if you were okay with bringing Ben out, then you could use the kitchen at *Jem's* first thing in the morning, or in the afternoon, after the lunch crowd dies down. I figure it would be a few hours a day. Ben could hang out with me in the office. I'm sure between Andy and I we could keep him safe for that long, and besides, if we needed you, you'd be right there."

"And I could help out as well. My classes are only in the morning, so I'm finished by one every day," Jo said.

"What if we give it a trial run for a week and see how it works for everyone? If Ben isn't too much for you guys, and being there in the afternoon fits in okay, then I think this could be a good thing," Jane offered with a huge grin.

"Really?" Hope sat forward, and when Jane nodded she jumped from her seat, rounding the table and hugging Jane. "I thought I was going to have to work harder than that to convince you. I'm sure we can make this work." Moving back to her seat as Jane and Jo laughed she went on, "I'm not just happy on a business level. This will mean we will all get to spend more time together again, and I like the idea of that."

"Well, don't get too excited, it might not work out, but I'm excited to at least give it a go."

***

As she walked around her bedroom efficiently collecting a change of underwear, t-shirt, and a pair of shorts for the morning, Hope caught sight of herself in the mirror that sat over the drawers she had been using since she was a child.

Hope back-peddled. Standing directly in front of the mirror, she took in her reflection. Something was different, but she wasn't sure what it was. Her hair was due for a trim, but it wasn't overly long or untidy. She'd stepped on the scales just the other day, the numbers that flashed back at her confirming she hadn't lost or gained any substantial amount of weight, so that wasn't it. There was something though. Looking closer, Hope found the difference. It was her eyes. They were vivacious, alive in a way she couldn't remember seeing in a very long time, if ever.

The more Hope looked, the more she became aware that it was more than just her eyes. There seemed to be a light that radiated around her. It began deep within and came shining out through her eyes. Hope couldn't remember ever seeing herself in this way before.

Her thoughts wandered to Jo. This was far from uncommon. Hope was lucky if she could go an hour without thinking of Jo. As her head swam with thoughts of her lover, Hope could see for herself that Andy was right. Everything about her face had changed. Her eyes deepened in colour, and the faint lines around the outside edges were enhanced as she smiled, while her whole face had softened.

Hope shook her head as she tossed the clothes into the bag at the foot of her bed. With the zip closed, she scooped the handles into her palm and headed for the door. She wanted to get to Jo's as soon as she could. The night had been slow, and Hope was very happy that it was only eleven thirty. If she hurried, Jo might still be awake. Remembering at the last minute the bottle of wine on the kitchen bench, Hope grabbed it before locking up and making the short drive to Jo's.

Oscar and Ruby scampered around her feet before she'd quite reached the door. They were obviously happy to see her. Hope set the bag and wine safely on the ground beside her, as she patted the playful babies. "Hi, ratbags. This is a nice welcoming."

The sound of Jo's light laughter reached Hope's ears. She straightened and turned in the direction of the sound. Moonlight illuminated Jo's face in a soft, white glow, while the trees hid the rest of her within their shadows. Jo's features were almost angelic, drawing Hope to the woman that had managed to turn her very controlled world on its axis.

They stopped in front of one another, close enough for Hope to feel Jo's warm breath settle over her like a silk sheet. Jo's hands slipped around her neck, and their bodies slid up against one another. On tiptoes, Jo brushed her lips over Hope's, whispering softly, "Hi there."

"Hi yourself," Hope managed, barely. With her hands settling on Jo's hips, Hope responded to Jo's mouth deliberately moving against her own. Soft words caressed Hope's heart as they floated between Jo's feather-light lips.

"You're so cute with Oscar and Ruby. I love that you accept them. Thank you, sweetheart."

Hearing the term of endearment, Hope was caught off guard by this woman who seemed to be constantly surprising her. Hope made a point to never use pet names that might mislead a woman into believing there was more to what they shared than there really was. She'd also been very quick to correct those women when they'd called her by anything but her real name. *So why now, when Jo calls me sweetheart, do I have no desire to correct her? Instead I want to hear the word float from her lips again* Before Hope had a chance to find the answers, Jo covered her mouth again, this time with more need, the kiss deeper, her tongue circling Hope's slowly before running the length of Hope's lip.

As they slowly parted, Hope smiled. "You don't need to thank me for loving the two cutest puppies alive. But if you ever decide you want to, that there," Hope touched Jo's lips gently with her finger, "is the perfect way."

Hope ran the back of her fingers gently over Jo's cheek before sliding her thumb under the edge of the beanie, scooping it back off her head. Jo's hands immediately tried to control the wayward locks, but Hope gathered Jo's hands in her own, holding them to her chest. "I wish I could capture you right now, the moonlight revealing your natural beauty, like a spotlight on a delicately painted canvas, your curls its natural frame." Placing her hands on either side of Jo's face, Hope held Jo as she would an exquisite piece of china. "You're stunning."

Leaning in, Jo hid her face against Hope's chest. Releasing one hand, but keeping the other firmly in her grasp, Hope moved toward the house. "Let's get inside and settled. I brought wine in the hopes that you may still be awake enough to enjoy a glass with me."

.

Chapter Twenty-two

JO STIRRED, FEELING THE warmth of Hope's body tucked in behind her. Hope's arm lay limply across Jo's waist, bent at the elbow, allowing her hand to rest cupped around Jo's breast. Jo found this to be both protective and possessive in its action. Strangely, she found she liked how both felt, almost like a comforting blanket tucked in around her. The deep, even rhythm of Hope's breathing let Jo know she was still sound asleep.

Her mind wandered back to the previous night. Hope had been gentle and patient with Oscar and Ruby, even when she thought Jo was nowhere to be seen. The way she treated the puppies didn't change as soon as believed she was alone with them, and this meant so much to Jo. Her heart melted a little at the kindness in Hope's tone as she'd spoken with the babies.

She remembered stepping out from the shadow of her special tree and seeing the look in Hope's eyes as the distance between them shortened. She'd looked into those eyes, seeing something there she was unsure of. A look she was unfamiliar with.

Now, here in the safety of Hope's embrace, Jo remembered the image. As she'd closed the gap between them, Hope's eyes had softened in the moonlight. Warm and inviting pools of chocolate. Jo wondered if, perhaps, this was the look of desire. She'd never had anyone desire her before, so maybe, just maybe, that's what it was.

Jo lay still, trying to decipher it all. The hand on her breast gently squeezed before the fingers moved. Taking Jo's nipple between thumb and forefinger, Hope gently pinched, and Jo's body responded immediately. As her nipple hardened, a small moan passed by her lips.

"Mmm, I like the way you wake up."

"And I like waking up to you," Hope whispered in Jo's ear, her breath warm over Jo's cheek.

"I can't think of a better way to begin the day."

Hope's lips were now on Jo's neck, leaving little kisses, and the leg moving forward between her own encouraged Jo to open her thighs. When she cooperated, Hope slid her leg between them, pushing hard against Jo's centre.

She felt Hope's hips against her backside, the bristle of Hope's curls against her skin causing slick juices to coat Hope's thigh. Hope pushed harder, her hips moving slowly back and forth against Jo's bottom. Jo easily synced her body to move in time with Hope's.

Sensations everywhere, Hope set a steady pace with her hips as her fingers continued to move over Jo's breast, her fingertip now flicking the pert bud. The very tip of her nail only just skated over the tip of Jo's sensitive nipple. Torn between the two distinct areas of her body screaming out to her, Jo did her best to keep the cadence their hips had developed. She arched her back, filling Hope's hand with the soft flesh of her breast. Hope moaned between what sounded like tightly clenched teeth. The need to touch Hope was so strong. Jo tried to turn so she could face her lover only to be held firmly in place.

"Not this time. This morning I get to touch, and you get to receive."

As those fingers continued to squeeze Jo's nipple, she felt a warm mouth come down on her neck. There were soft kisses before Hope sucked the now wet skin into her mouth. The pressure of a very wet thigh against Jo's throbbing mound increased, as Hope sucked harder at her neck.

Just as Jo felt her body was ready for release, Hope removed her mouth from Jo's bruised neck and withdrew her thigh. Before Jo had time to complain, Hope had repositioned herself with her hand between Jo's legs and her fingers running along the edge of swollen, wet lips.

Hope mounted Jo's leg, leaving a slick coating of her own desire. Jo's clit was erect and waiting for the fingers that slid in a little deeper. Slow touches over her enlarged bud were torturous, and Hope's fingers hovered over Jo's entrance for a moment before one finger slipped inside.

Jo instinctively lifted her hips from the mattress, thrusting herself up to Hope. Her fingers gripped the sheet on either side of her. When Hope withdrew her finger, Jo lowered herself back to the bed only to, moments later, feel herself filled again as Hope added a second finger. A groan worked its way from the pit of Jo's stomach, as she met Hope's fingers thrust for thrust.

The fingers kept their blissful rhythm inside Jo, as Hope ground herself against Jo's leg. Their bodies moved fluidly in a private dance. Jo felt Hope's breath warm against her skin, when a surge of nerve endings awakened along the length of her spine.

Moving against Hope's hand in a semicircular pattern, Jo was rewarded when Hope groaned, "Oh God." The sound of Hope's voice brought Jo closer to the edge, and when Hope pressed her thumb firmly against Jo's clit, moving it only slightly, Jo could hold on no longer. Her climax washed over her in waves. Still gripping the sheet in tightly clenched fists, her face turned and pressed against the bed, Jo cried out, "Oh my God, Hope, oh fuck." Hope joined her in release.

As their bodies stilled, Hope laced her fingers with those that had moments before been white knuckled as they gripped the bedding. Arms bent and locked hands drawing them close, Jo let herself be pulled along as Hope rolled to her back. Jo lay along the length of her, resting her head on Hope's chest. When Hope kissed the top of Jo's head, she raised her face, bringing her lips to Hope's and kissing her long and slow before returning her cheek to Hope's breast.

They lay with limbs woven together for some time, each lost in their thoughts. Jo began tracing lazy figure eights lightly over Hope's stomach. "Tell me about your time overseas, I've never been anywhere and would love to hear all about your adventures."

"Hmm, where do I begin?"

Hope's fingers began their own lazy trails over Jo's back as she thought. Jo was content to wait quietly within the comfort of Hope's arms. She sensed Hope was filtering through memories as she found a place to start.

"I think," Hope paused briefly, lifting her head to kiss Jo's forehead, "the best place to begin would be back here, in Auckland, before I left. I was aware of my sexuality relatively early on but still tried to convince myself that it was just a passing phase. When I finally could admit to myself that it wasn't going to change, I spoke with Aunt Em. I was so lucky, Jo. I was always able to come to Aunt Em with anything, she was always there, happy to listen, to offer advice if I asked, and to provide support but never judgment."

"Not too many people have that. She sounds like an extraordinary lady."

"Yes, she was." Hope grew still. Jo could almost see the memories rippling through Hope's thoughts.

"That day, after I had my heart broken at the movie theatre, Aunt Em wrapped me up in her arms and pulled me in tight for a little while. She told me, 'Hope, sweetheart, the most important thing is for you to find who you are. Don't be scared of it. Don't try to hide from it. Doing so will only make you unhappy. When you find who you are and accept that, then you'll be able to find love. Then, when you do find love, you'll be able to give yourself openly, honestly, and wholeheartedly.'" Hope held a deep breath for a long while. When she exhaled, Jo felt the long-buried feelings in the air on her skin. "She told me to be happy, then she'd be happy as well."

Hope was quiet for a little while. She gave a slight shake of her head and half sat up in bed.

Jo looked up at her. "What's wrong?"

"Don't the pups need to go out? They'll be about to explode."

"Yeah," Jo chuckled. "They'll be close to it, but I didn't want to stop you. I love hearing your story. I get the feeling I may be one of a very select few who have been lucky enough to hear all of this, and so I consider myself very privileged that you feel safe enough to talk to me about everything."

"What say we let Ruby and Oscar out for a wee? While they're out doing their business, we can both take the chance to relieve our own bladders. I'll finish the story over breakfast."

"Sounds like a plan to me."

***

The fluffy babies were happily curled between Jo and Hope as they settled on the couch to enjoy their raspberry jam on toast and strong coffee. As they ate, Hope began her story again. "It was in that same conversation when Aunt Em told me to be happy that I told her about my desire to travel and see the world. Aunt Em didn't hesitate; she told me there and then, 'If that's what ignites a passion inside you, then that's what you need to do.' We spent the rest of the night talking about where I'd like to go and what I'd like to see. I always knew I wanted to start my adventure in England, moving on from there."

"I headed to London with the desire to see as much of the UK and Europe as I could. I was happy to settle in different places, for short periods of time, finding whatever work I could and experiencing each place and its people. I didn't want to simply visit all the tourist destinations. I wanted to get a real feel for the countries. Know the essence of them."

"I'm fascinated. I couldn't imagine doing anything like that on my own. I think you're so brave to have done all of that."

"I didn't really think much about travelling alone. The truth is, I found making friends easy, so I never really felt I was on my own. When I got to London, my world was opened up in ways I'd never imagined."

"I bet it's worlds apart from here."

Hope shook her head. "You can say that again." The memories lit a smile across her face. "I saw an ad for a flatmate. When I went along to have a look and to meet the existing tenants, we all got on like a house on fire. Turned out to be a couple of lesbians, although they weren't a couple."

Hope drained the last of the coffee from her mug, then leaned forward to set it on the table in front of them. Jo continued to sip hers while she listened.

"Both were in their early twenties." Hope chuckled. "To be honest, it amazes me we all got on so well. I'd never thought about it or noticed it before now, but we're all so different. What we did have in common was a love of life and enjoying it to the fullest. They introduced me to a vast array of people and took great delight in showing me around the clubs." Hope's eyes widened. "I'd never been where I could meet other lesbians, so the club scene was quite an eye-opener to me."

Jo shifted on the couch. She'd finished her coffee and was running the backs of her fingers up and down Hope's forearm. Jo leaned in closer. "Tell me what the clubs were like."

"Oh my God, Jo, they were amazing. There were people from all walks of life, all together under one roof. Men in leather chaps, their butts bare to the world. Women in leathers with whips and chains. Women in men's clothing, and women in dresses and lipstick, alongside men in anything from suits and ties to skimpy shorts and tank tops. They all mingled together, loving life and not ashamed to be who they were within the safety of those walls." With a quick movement, Hope faced Jo full on, her eyes sparkling. "You'd have laughed at me if you'd seen my face the first time I went to the toilet in one of the clubs. I found the ladies' and went in. All the cubicles were full, so I waited. I was the only one waiting at that stage. A door opened and two guys came out, one doing up his fly and the other wiping his mouth. They looked at me and smiled. I went red and said I was sorry, I thought I was in the women's toilet. They laughed at me and said, 'Darling, you are, but around here we all just go where there is a free loo. If the line in here gets too long later, go to the men's. It's usually quicker.' I mumbled a thanks, still really embarrassed, and went into the cubicle. And *then*, when I came out, there was this seven-foot woman straightening her fishnets. I went to wash my hands, and this deep voice asks me if the seam at the back of the stockings was straight. I almost soaked the front of my pants as I quickly tried to turn the tap off. I checked and said the seam was fine. With a couple of exaggerated air kisses to each of my cheeks and a thanks darling, she was gone. That was my introduction to the world of drag queens."

Jo was laughing so hard there were tears flowing down her cheeks. "I wish I could have seen the look on your face. I bet it was priceless," Jo stammered trying to regain her breath.

"I reckon I looked like a possum caught in headlights. When I got back to the group I was with, they asked me if I was okay. I was too embarrassed to tell them about the encounters. I finally told my flatmates the next day, and they laughed so hard I thought they were going to pass out. By then I was laughing as well."

"As much as I'm laughing, I'd have been the same. I'd probably have run and grabbed the first flight home. Truth is, I couldn't even handle your bar. The one time I went in, before your birthday, I was overwhelmed by the large number of lesbians. I was terrified of half of them. They didn't do or say anything to make me that way—I was just so out of my comfort zone that I freaked out."

Hope had enjoyed the feel of Jo's fingers combing through her hair during the story, but now she felt the loss of that connection. Jo lowered her head, staring at her hands that were now tucked up in her lap. Hope could see the flush of red colour her cheeks. She should've guessed the bar at night would be too much for Jo who barely made eye contact or spoke to anyone during the day, and that was when everyone was sober and relatively well behaved.

Cradling Jo's face in her hands, Hope ran the pads of her thumbs over what were now very pink cheeks. "I can see how the bar would seem overwhelming to you. Some of the customers can be a little over the top, especially after a drink or two. That'd be intimidating for quieter people to be near, especially if you're on your own. Jo, simply going there on your own was a brave thing to do. I do understand how it'd seem loud and somewhat daunting for you. I'm ok with you not wanting to come back."

Jo leaned her face into Hope's touch, her mouth slowly curling upwards. "Thanks for understanding. It's nothing to do with your bar as such, it's just too far out of my comfort zone, I guess."

"I know." Hope kissed the tip of Jo's nose.

"Right then, back to your story, I want to hear more." Jo gave Hope's hand an encouraging squeeze.

Hope threaded her fingers with Jo's. "The three of us, my flatmates and I, are from very different backgrounds and are such a contrast to each other, but we shared enough similarities that we got on well. We laughed together a lot. Would you like me to share them with you? Although, I should warn you it may take a while."

Soft lips grazed over Hope's. "Yes, please, I'd love to hear all about them, and I don't care how long it takes."

"It's nice, remembering some of the times we shared. I fancy sharing my stories with you. How about we get fresh coffee before I tell you all about my crazy flatties?"

Jo reached for Hope's cup. "Good idea."

They made their way outside to enjoy the sunshine with the puppies and positioned their chairs under the big kauri so they could sit opposite one another. Hope went on to tell Jo all about the characters that had become her flatmates in London.

"Ang was from a small town in the south of Wales called Treharris. The town was originally developed to provide housing for the coal miners. It gave them somewhere to bring their families. The main source of work for the men in the village was the mining, and the women worked in the shops, or did cleaning or dressmaking, things like that. To us they would seem like very sexist roles, but it was all they'd known for generations and it worked for them.

"In 1991, the mine closed. Ang told me that the mine produced high quality steam coal and there was still a decent amount to be had. Unfortunately, due to years of water getting into the tunnels, the management of the Deep Navigation Colliery decided it wouldn't be financially viable to do the maintenance required. Ang said that, on the last working day, the Salvation Army band played and led a march of the final crew from the mine all the way to the town hall. It was a big deal to the town, this was their livelihood.

"Being the youngest of six kids, and with the closure of the mine, Ang couldn't wait to be old enough to leave. As soon as it was possible, she applied to train as a nurse and was accepted. The thing that always amazed me was that Ang wanted to be a nurse, yet she is really clever and could easily be a doctor. Her grades were good enough to have been accepted if she'd tried. However, when I asked her, she said it was simple. She wanted to help people, make a difference in their lives if possible. A doctor comes in and is gone again in a flash. A nurse takes time and is with the patient longer. She wanted to be there through the tough times.

"As a teen, Ang spent a lot of time studying and reading. She didn't want to be trapped in that town all her life. It wasn't a hardship though. Unlike the other girls her age, she had no desire to be attracting the boys of the village. She knew, early on, that she was a lesbian, and she also knew that if she stayed in her village she'd never be able to explore that and be true to herself. So, she got out as soon as she could."

Hope reached for her mug and downed half her coffee in one go. Stretching her leg out, she slid her foot up and down Jo's calves.

"She must be very determined and focused."

With a laugh, Hope agreed, "She's definitely both of those and so much more. Ang is the shortest of us all at about five foot one. She's curvy, with light brown hair and brown eyes, what a lot would consider plain to look at. But she grabs everyone's attention with her personality. She's happy more than not, and so full of life. She's kind and caring, sensitive to people's needs in a way I've never seen before. She seems to understand what they need from her, or just what they need in general, without having to be told. It always amazed me."

"She sounds lovely, Hope."

"She is. You'd like Ang a lot. The two of you are similar in a lot of ways." When Jo blushed again, Hope smiled. "As much as she's louder and loves gaining everyone's attention easily, and you're the opposite; you're alike in being able to read people and situations, and in caring about others."

Jo lowered her eyes to look at the grass between their legs. "Thank you."

Hope sprang to her feet, closing the small gap between them. As Jo looked up at the sudden movement, Hope planted a kiss on her lips. "You haven't been complimented often, have you?"

"No, not often."

"I hope to change that. I intend on complimenting you until you get used to it."

"How about you carry on and tell me more?"

Hope was aware Jo was changing the subject. She sat back down, not wanting to make Jo uncomfortable, but resolved to let Jo know just what she saw in her.

"PJ's story must wait. It's time for me to start thinking about heading home to shower and change."

"Not a problem. I'll look forward to hearing more."

Hope kissed Jo goodbye at the door and promised to be back as soon as she could leave the bar that night. "I'll text you later to let you know how busy we are and when I think I might be able to get away."

"I get that it's pretty hard to know what the night will be like. Don't worry about that. I'll be here when you finish, whenever that is."

Chapter Twenty-three

OLIVIA SQUEEZED THE ORANGES and poured fresh juice for herself and Jo. They sat in her kitchen to have a catch up. "Several of the neighbours have noticed a couple hanging around the street on and off over the last two weeks," Olivia said. "Apparently, they look like they may be homeless, but haven't done anything more than walk down one side, up the other, and out again. Some did notice that they seemed to hover around outside the house here, for a little while, but never looked like they were going to come on this property or any of the others. No one has seen them for a few days now, but please, promise me that you will be careful. Don't go out after dark on your own and make sure you keep your door locked at night and when you go out."

In the months that she'd been living in her cottage, Jo had overcome the strange and uncomfortable feelings when Olivia worried over her, and had grown to like the feeling of having someone care. She patted Olivia's hand reassuringly. "I will, I promise. I'll tell Hope to be safe as well. I know she has the car, but she still gets out and comes in through the gate in the middle of the night."

Olivia covered Jo's hand with her own. "Thank you for humouring an old lady, Jo. It's probably nothing, but with your place being separate from the main house, if they come on the property and wander around you never know. They may think it's an unused dwelling and try to get in for warmth. I'd hate for anything to happen to you."

A gentle smile lifted Jo's mouth. "I know. I feel the same about you, so let's do all we can to be safe and look after one another."

"It's lovely out now, if you don't have any plans, maybe we could take these three for a little walk?"

"Sounds like a good idea to me. Ruby and Oscar look nice and settled, but I say give it ten minutes and they'll be tearing around like mad dogs again."

By the time they finished their drinks, the puppies were ready for action. Olivia locked up, and the group headed off. The sky was a clear blue with just the slightest breeze, as they walked up the road at a leisurely pace.

"Where would you like to go?" Jo asked.

"How do you feel about heading down to the park? When we get there, we could sit for a minute before making our way back."

"I'm always happy to go to the park."

On the way there, the two chatted as they wandered and enjoyed the front gardens along their path. On the return, they walked most of the way in silence, commenting here and there about something that caught their eye. The three dogs were all tired out as they neared the house.

"You've done a fantastic job with Oscar and Ruby. They are doing so well on the lead. I knew you would be wonderful with them."

"I'm pretty happy with how they're doing. I've never raised puppies before, so I didn't have a clue what to do. The internet's a wonderful thing."

"You may have got the general information from others, but it's your patience and consistency that is helping these two scallywags learn good habits. You should be proud of yourself, Jo."

As Olivia patted her on the back, a growing sense of pride balanced the embarrassment that brushed Jo's cheeks with flames. Having someone care for her, see her, and acknowledge what she did was a strange feeling, but one Jo decided she liked.

The dogs were making a mess as they frantically lapped at their water bowls. Olivia chuckled at their silliness. "I need to go to the supermarket for a few things. Why don't you come with me? You can keep an old lady company."

"Sure, that sounds like a good idea to me. I'll just race and get my wallet."

***

Jo helped Olivia carry the grocery bags into the kitchen.

"I could whip up a salad to go with the chicken we just got while you put the groceries away," Jo said.

"That would be wonderful. It's so nice to have company." Stopping beside Jo, Olivia placed a hand on her shoulder. "Thanks, Jo."

Jo set down the knife and abandoned the tomato to turn and hug Olivia. "It's me who should be saying thanks. You've given me more than anyone. You've given me something even my own parents didn't. Family."

"You give me that as well, my dear, and something else I hadn't had for a very long time. You bring excitement back to my days. You bring life to this old house, and to these old bones."

"Can we agree that we're both lucky then?"

Olivia chuckled. "Yes, we can. Now, let's get a move on, I'm hungry. Would you like to eat outside this evening?"

"Yep, I sure would," Jo said, turning back to the tomatoes on the chopping board.

Timing everything perfectly, Olivia put the last of the groceries in the pantry as Jo put their dinner on trays to carry outside. Taking a tray each, they made their way to the Adirondack chairs and held their plates on their laps while they enjoyed their meal and the early summer evening.

"Jo dear, do you mind if I ask you something?"

"No, not at all, you can always ask me anything." Jo smiled her sincerity.

"Well, I was just wondering why it is that you never go to spend time with Hope at the café at night. The two of you seem to get along so well and enjoy one another's company. She's always keen to get back to you when she's able, from what I see. I would have thought that, being young and full of life, you might have gone to visit Hope at work on occasion."

"I did go in once, at night. Although, it was before I was seeing Hope. I felt out of my depth there, Olivia. The customers are drinking, and I really feel quite uncomfortable around people when they reach the point of being drunk. Added to that, a lot already knew one another, so there seemed to be little groups all over the place. The part that I struggled with the most, though, was the people who were loud and becoming obnoxious. It isn't my kind of place. I like the café at lunchtime, even though some of those same people may be there. The thing is, without the alcohol on board they're different. Even then, I always sit alone at the end of the counter, happy to eat and read in peace. I'm happy in my own company, I guess."

"I can understand how being around people who are drinking would be uncomfortable; I hadn't thought that through. I'm sorry, Jo, I should have been more aware."

"You have nothing to be sorry for, Olivia. It was a reasonable question. Most people my age would be happy to go. It's just not for me." Jo scrunched her face up, almost like she was in pain. "The funny thing is, you asked me that today when I'd just been thinking that maybe it would be nice for Hope to have a visit from me at some stage."

Olivia's amusement matched Jo's. "So, funny that we would both think about the same thing on the same day. What did you decide? Do you think you might one night?"

"I decided that Hope is always supportive of anything I'm interested in, so the least I could do is pop in for a short time one night. I thought maybe I'd wait a little and, in the next week or so, take some time to take myself back there in my mind, maybe get used to the memory of being in that environment and then give it a go."

"That sounds like a very wise idea. I'm very proud of you, my dear, you're prepared to challenge yourself for someone you care for and that's wonderful. I don't believe anyone should allow someone else's wants and interests to take over, but I think it's important to make room for some of the things that are important to them."

"Thanks Olivia. It's hard sometimes to know what to do. I've never been in a relationship before, and I sure as heck never had positive role models, so it's a lot of learning as I go."

"You're doing a wonderful job. The two of you always look so happy when you're together."

"Thanks, Olivia. Now, how about I come and do the dishes before I get my babies settled in for the night?"

Before she rose, Jo looked up at the tree sheltering her from above. She shook her head, barely able to believe how different her life was since meeting Olivia and Hope. She treasured the richness they brought her. Working together, they had the dishwasher running and the kitchen cleaned down in no time.

"It would be nice if both you and Hope could join me for dinner the next time she has a night off. Hope means a lot to you and so I would like very much to get to know her better. If she is important to you, then building a relationship with her is something I would like to work on."

Jo hugged Olivia, unsure of what to do with the emotions she felt. Olivia was the first adult in her life to care about her simply for who she was and not for what they might get from her. Olivia wanting to get to know Hope was the type of thing parents would do with their kids when they started dating.

Chapter Twenty-four

"I'D LOVE TO. I agree with Olivia, you care for us both and we both care a great deal for you, so getting to know each other is a good idea. When would Olivia like to have us over? I'll make arrangements for some cover that night."

Jo gave Hope a leisurely kiss. "Thank you, Hope. Olivia is the closest to family I've ever known, and that she wants to do this lets me know that she sees me in the same way. This means a great deal to me." Hope hadn't hesitated. Jo wasn't sure what emotions were stirring around, but she knew it was a big deal.

"I know, sweetie, I can see it in your eyes. That alone means it's important to me as well. I want you to have all the things you missed out on growing up. I know I can't replace what was taken from you, but I can give you this." Running her finger gently down Jo's cheek, Hope smiled.

They decided that Sunday night would work best for everyone. Olivia had no plans at all for the day so that would give her time for preparations, and *Jem's* was always a little slower on Sundays. Jo and Hope spent a lazy Sunday together. They took the dogs to the park. Hope lay on a blanket reading the paper, while Jo snapped shot after shot with her SLR. Stretched out with her face to the sun, Hope asked, "What's caught your line of vision today?"

"I'm playing with light at the moment. Capturing shadows, different angles, things like that." Jo sat next to Hope. "Here, look at the image on the screen."

Hope sat up to see the camera. The image in front of her was the park bench nearest them.

"I'm going to take a picture of that then we'll take the same image from a different angle." Snapping the image, Jo moved to lay on her stomach. "Now, join me down here and see what happens."

When Hope looked again, this time the bench was being viewed from below rather than at eye level. In the first image, the sun's rays warmed the wooden planks. From the lower position, those same planks were silhouetted making the seat look double its size.

"Wow, like that you'd never guess what the picture was even of."

"Light, or lack of, can make you see objects very differently. It's something I'm just playing with, but I like that it gets you to realise not everything is always like it might seem."

***

They'd made love in the afternoon light and finally lay spent and puffing on Jo's bed. With Jo's leg draped over her waist, Hope suddenly grumbled. "Damn."

"What's wrong?" Jo lifted her head in concern.

Pulling herself out from under Jo, Hope bent down and kissed the top of Jo's head. "Nothing that can't be fixed, my love. I wanted to get Olivia flowers and I forgot. More to the point, someone distracted me." Looking down at Jo, Hope raised her eyebrows at her.

"Ah, sorry." Jo looked up with the most innocent look she could manage. "But I don't think I can take all the blame. As they say, it takes two to tango."

Hope guffawed as she moved toward the bathroom. "I can still do this. If I take a quick shower then race to the shops while you shower, everything will work out." She turned sharply as she reached the ladder and pointed a finger at Jo. "But you need to stay right where you are if you want us to be on time."

Jo threw herself back on the mattress and sniggered. "I can't make any promises, but because this is for Olivia, I'll try my best."

While Hope showered and dressed, Jo filled in her time feeding the pups and making sure they got a little run around. She gave Hope a goodbye kiss at the door, a kiss that may have been mistaken for Hope leaving to serve her country rather than nipping out to get flowers. Jo stepped under the hot water of the shower with a grin on her face.

***

Hope was pleasantly surprised when she arrived at the flower stand in the local supermarket and discovered the florist was still there.

"I'm normally long gone by this time of the day, but I have a large order due to be collected first thing tomorrow morning that I need to get ready. I'm happy to make up whatever you like, seeing as I'm here."

The lady was very pleasant, chatting with Hope as she made up an arrangement of Hope's choosing.

"Thank you so much for this. I appreciate you going the extra mile. I own a little place up the road, called *Jem's*. Please call in at some stage so I can thank you properly. Just tell whoever serves you that you're the flower lady, and they'll make sure the meal is on me."

Pulling up outside Olivia's, Hope gathered the flowers into her arms and wandered through the gate. The fresh smells of roses, carnations, and freesia filled Hope's nostrils, as she almost skipped down the path. Something rustled beside her. A stick snapped, and she came to a halt.

"Oscar...Ruby, is that you? Your mum won't be happy if you two are in there getting messy when we're getting ready to go to dinner with Olivia," she said to the bushes that lined the fence along the driveway separating Olivia's property from the neighbour's.

The rustling stopped and Hope called again, "Oscar, Ruby, come on." When neither rascal appeared, she tried again. "Angel, is that you in there?"

Moving closer to the bushes, Hope heard another twig snap. "Come on guys," she called. "Oscar, come here boy. Ruby, baby, come on."

Still nothing. Stepping back, she turned toward the house. Carrying on back to the cottage, Hope was almost to the back door when suddenly before her, were two puppies peering through the gate and wagging their tails furiously at the sight of her nearing.

Chuckling to herself, Hope called out to them, "I'm pleased to see you're both in there and not getting up to any mischief."

Once inside, Hope placed the flowers on the bench so she had two free hands. She scooped up a pup under each arm and carried them to the living room. "I'm back, baby."

Putting Ruby and Oscar on the couch, she sat next to them. They clambered onto her, fighting to get to her first, and she giggled as Oscar climbed her chest trying to get to her nose.

"How'd you get on?" Jo called from the bathroom.

"Excellante!"

Jo joined Hope on the couch, and Hope told her the story of her good fortune in finding the florist still there, before they wandered through the yard to Olivia's back door. At the top of the back stairs, Jo tapped lightly on the door before turning the handle and walking in.

"Olivia, it's just Hope and I."

"I'm through in the lounge, dear."

Jo led the way, and as they entered the lounge Olivia sent them both a welcoming smile. "Hello girls, how has your day been?"

"It's been great; we got to spend a relaxing day together. We went to the park, and Hope read the paper while I played with my camera," Jo answered.

"Yes, it's been wonderful to get the entire day with Jo." Hope held out the bouquet. "Olivia I got these for you as a small thank you for having us over for dinner." Handing them over to Olivia, Hope worried when the older ladies eyes misted over.

"Thank you, Hope, it has been a very long time since I received the gift of flowers. My husband used to bring me a fresh bunch every Monday after work. He would tell me that I brought beauty to his world and so I deserved to have beauty in mine as well." Olivia grinned down at the flowers. Seemingly lost in her memories, she returned with a slight shake of her head. "He did this every week from the first week we were married."

"How long were you married?" Hope enquired.

"Freddy and I were married for forty-six years. We were young when we wed, but back then that wasn't so unusual. I was just sixteen, Freddy was almost eighteen. He passed away almost twelve years ago. In all that time, no one else has brought me flowers." Olivia gave Hope a brief hug. "Thank you, Hope, this is a very special moment."

"Wow, that's such a romantic thing for him to have done," Hope stated.

"I was very lucky; I was very much loved. Freddy was a true romantic, and he loved to get me little treats and spoil me in lots of ways. I would tell him, 'As long as I have your love, I have the world.' And he would tell me, 'When you have the love of a great woman, you make sure you treat her like the treasure she is.' That was just what he did."

Conversation continued to flow easily between the three women over dinner, with laughter being shared by all. Olivia asked Hope about her travels and she filled Olivia in on Ang, far more briefly than she had Jo, before getting to share PJ with them.

"PJ is really beautiful. She's got long, straight, blonde hair, big brown eyes, and a figure to die for. Whenever we went anywhere, everyone, I mean both men and women, would stop and watch her. I don't think I've ever met anyone with a bigger heart, either.

"But she is so unaware of her looks. She's also really intelligent, but again, unaware of just how much so. Constantly being told she's not as good as her brother has left her believing she is way less than she actually is. She's Penelope Jayne to her very wealthy, upper-class parents. She hated not only the name they insisted on calling her, but almost everything else about her family.

"Her parents met while studying law at Oxford University. PJ's dad was the top of their class. Her mum was only biding time until she married. Her family is very wealthy, and she learned very early on how to work the social scene. If PJ's father hadn't been such a hot shot on campus, with all the top law firms fighting to gain his attention, she would never have dated him. His family wasn't quite in her league.

"They married and had PJ then, two years later, Edward. It was always expected that Edward would become a lawyer and go into his father's firm, while PJ would find a suitably rich man to marry and be a happy housewife too.

"It was always very clear to PJ that she was never considered as important as Edward. He was a boy and would carry on the name as well as the practice. She was a girl and her only real job was to find a good husband.

"When PJ made it very clear that she wanted to study and gain a career, her parents told her she would have to do it herself; they would not support her financially. If she wanted to play silly games then it needed to be at her own expense, not theirs. Then when PJ was caught with a girl, her parents threatened to send her away and all sorts. The thing she knew she had over them was that they never wanted anyone to think they were anything but the perfect little family.

"They refused to let her leave home, despite not being prepared to cover her studies. I mean, what would people say if their daughter left home without finding a rich husband?"

"So how was it the three of you got to live together?" Olivia wondered, as she dished up apple pie and ice cream for dessert.

A smirk crept over Hope's face. "Ang and PJ met at uni, and the two of them actually had a relationship before I came along. It was Ang who helped PJ get out from her parent's house."

Hope giggled, then calmed herself enough to share the story. "The two brought out the best in one another. Ang is outgoing, forward, and more than happy to share her thoughts. But she can be selfish, spontaneous, and unyielding at times. PJ is giving, thoughtful, and sensible, but she can shortchange herself a lot of the time, be very timid and sometimes boring. The two help balance each other.

"PJ was worried about anyone finding out about the two of them; Ang didn't care who knew. One morning, PJ's mother came barging into her room, ranting and raving about something, only to discover the two of them in bed together. After screaming and running from the room like she'd just seen a dead body, she found her husband. Ang was told to leave and never come back. She was told she was never to see or speak to PJ again, and she was escorted from the house. PJ was told she was never to do anything to embarrass her family again and that it was time to stop playing games. It was time she found a husband and married.

"PJ tried to tell them she wasn't interested in a husband. She was a lesbian. At that point, her mother had an anxiety attack and her father told her she was never to see Ang again. PJ told them she was moving out and they said that was not going to happen. They would not have her do anything to cause people to talk badly of the family.

Jo leaned in close, her hands gripping the edge of the table. "So, what did they do?"

"Remember how I mentioned Ang sometimes acts without thinking?" Hope was grinning like a Cheshire cat.

Olivia and Jo nodded enthusiastically.

"Well, PJ told Ang what her parents had said. Ang didn't say a word for a while. When she did, she was very calm. She kissed PJ and said, 'It's okay babe, everything will work out, you wait and see.'

"PJ said she'd never been so surprised or relieved in her life that Ang was so calm. She figured they would be more discrete and not get caught again. That relief was short-lived. The following afternoon, when PJ got home from uni, Ang was sitting in the living room with her parents. PJ's mother was as white as a ghost which was in total contrast to her father. They both told me he was so red it looked like his head was about to explode.

"When PJ walked into the room, Ang got up and greeted her with a kiss, right there in front of PJ's parents and neither said or did a thing. PJ's father then told PJ that if she wanted to move out, they would cover her rent and a small allowance so she could dedicate more time to her studies.

"Turned out they had a bigger worry than their daughter being a lesbian. Seems their son liked to pay for sex, and he preferred those he paid to be of other cultures. Ang had seen him one night, when she was on her way home from a club. She wondered what he was doing in that part of town, so she followed him to make sure he was all right, and she saw him pick up a prostitute. Ang kept tracks on dearest Edward and managed to get a few different pictures that she knew would take the focus off her and PJ."

Olivia and Jo sat with their mouths open, speechless for a minute, before Olivia started cackling. Before long, all three were howling around the table.

"That Ang has a lot of spunk," Olivia said when they finally quieted.

"She sure does," Jo agreed, but a frown creased her forehead. "Are PJ and Ang still a couple?"

"No, they realised shortly after that they are better as friends than as partners. It wasn't long after that I met them. They'd decided to get a bigger place but still live together. That's when they advertised for a third flatmate and along I came. I was a little hesitant at first, because I didn't know how it would go between them. I mean, what if one decided she couldn't handle seeing the other with a date or something like that? But there were no issues. PJ has come out of her shell, and the two are still very close. I think they always will be. They know that in the end, if they had stayed together, they would have lost each other. Neither of them wanted to risk that. This way they still get to be there for each other."

"Oh my word, speaking of good friends, I almost forgot to tell you." Olivia looked so cute, raising her hands to cover her cheeks. "A friend of mine, in Australia, asked me if I'd like to join her on a cruise. I thought that was a wonderful idea. It goes around the Pacific islands, departing from Sydney in two weeks. So, I'll fly there, meet her, then we'll board the ship together. I was wondering if you'd be okay to look after Angel for me, rather than placing her in the kennel."

Jo reassured Olivia with a hug. "Of course, I can. It'll be nice to have the chance to do something to help for a change."

"Angel and I will both be much happier knowing she is with you," Olivia said, looking from Jo to Hope and back again. "I will write up the dates for you first thing in the morning and drop them in."

After dinner, the young lovers made their way across the garden to the cottage. As soon as Oscar and Ruby were settled, Jo and Hope climbed the ladder to the loft.

"Thank you for everything you did tonight, Hope."

"I had a wonderful time. Olivia's great company, but what I like the most is watching the way she looks at you so lovingly. You deserve that."

They each undressed the other, taking their time to savour the evening.

***

Most nights, they stayed at Jo's place to make things easier with the puppies. Today, Hope needed to be near the office and get some paperwork done.

Hope had taken the puppies to her place, and Jo made her way directly there as soon as she finished classes. Rather than take her bike, she'd gotten a ride from Hope that morning. As she walked briskly toward Hope's, Jo felt a sense of unease she couldn't quite pinpoint. It was a beautiful, sunny Friday afternoon. She was slowly developing a name amongst the world of photography in Auckland. She had a wonderful home and family with Olivia, and she was in a relationship with a sexy woman. *So why do I feel unsafe?*

She shrugged off the doubts before they could settle in and told herself it was just because she wasn't used to either family or having a girlfriend. Her life was changing and even good change was still going to feel a little unsettling. The instant Jo saw Hope on the couch, a puppy either side of her lap, the bad feelings disappeared. The pups sprang to their feet, tails wagging a hundred miles an hour. Following their lead, Hope laid her laptop on the floor and chased them across the room to Jo.

"Hi baby, I've missed you." Hope greeted Jo with a kiss that soon found tongues exploring and hands wandering.

When they parted, Jo rested her forehead on Hope's. "Wow, that's one heck of a welcome home. You'd better be careful; I could get used to that."

Hope pulled Jo to the couch and surprised her when she said, "I just might as well."

"Are you hungry?" she asked

"Is the Pope Catholic?"

Hope threw her head back laughing raucously. "In that case, how about you play with your babies while I nip next door and get something for us? Let me guess, a BLT for you?"

"You must be a mind reader." Jo played along, enjoying Hope's positive mood.

"I think maybe you're right. Let's see how good my talents are." Hope rubbed her temples, insinuating she was thinking hard. "Okay I'm getting more. With the BLT you're going to have a Coke."

Jo giggled. "Shit, we could make some serious money off these skills of yours." She wrapped her arms around Hope's neck and brought her in for a kiss.

While Hope was getting their food, Jo got on the floor to play with her little ones. Their clumsiness entertained her endlessly, while their devotion filled her with an unexpected sense of importance. By the time Hope returned, Jo had managed to tire the pups out enough that they could enjoy their lunch in relative peace.

"Did you manage to get much work done this morning with these two under foot?" Jo asked, taking another bite of her sandwich.

"I did." Hope nodded and smiled at Oscar and Ruby, curled up together between her and Jo. "Unfortunately, I still have more to do."

"I've got an essay I need to write, so we could work together this afternoon."

"I'd like that." Hope reached out, taking Jo's hand in her own. "What do you have to do the essay on?"

"We need to choose a photographer we believe made a difference in some way through their work. I've decided to do mine on Jerry Uelsmann and the work he does. His work intrigues me on several levels, and it ties in with where I am as well. I'm very interested in the lighting aspects as we discussed the other day, but I'd like to use that alongside the developing process—old school style—using negatives and a darkroom."

When Hope simply sat grinning at her, Jo wondered what she'd done.

"Have I got food on my face or something?"

"Nope, I just really enjoy seeing how animated you become when you talk about your photography."

Dipping her head, Jo mumbled, "Yeah...well...umm."

Hope reached out and hugged Jo, careful not to squash their two companions. "You're so cute."

Burying her face in Hope's chest, Jo squirmed in her seat before giving Hope a playful push. "I think it's time you got to work."

"All right, all right, man you're bossier than Andy."

They worked across from each other at the kitchen table in comfortable silence, each tapping away on their laptops. Hope stretched her foot out to nudge Jo's. "I was wondering how you'd feel about maybe spending another night here at my place. That way I'd be able to get fully caught up and not have to miss you."

"We can do that, I just need to nip home and grab some more dog food, I only brought enough for the one night."

"Maybe we should buy some to keep here. In the meantime, how about we all go for a walk to collect what we need for tonight?"

Jo came around the table and kissed the tip of Hope's nose. "Excellent idea. I'll pop in and say goodbye to Olivia and collect up Angel at the same time. Olivia's flight is early in the morning, so if I get Angel now, I won't have to get up and race home first thing tomorrow morning."

Hope stood to join Jo, wiggling her eyebrows suggestively. "I like the idea of you not having to get up and hurry off."

Jo laughed as she tapped Hope on her butt. "Good, I do too. I have plans for the morning that would require me to be here."

As they made their way out the driveway, they were laughing at their companions' tails wagging with excitement. The walk back to Jo's was easy and relaxed, the two meandering hand in hand. They found Olivia in the lounge and explained their plan. More than happy for Angel to stay with them at Hope's, Olivia gathered up Angel's lead.

"Jo, you know where her food is kept, and you already know her routine, so I didn't write instructions for you. I know she will be well looked after and happy with all of you while I'm away."

"She'll be fine, won't you Angel." Jo bent down and patted Angel who was already lying at her feet looking longingly at her lead hanging from Jo's hand. Jo gave Olivia a big hug. "Have a great time, Olivia."

Returning the hug, Olivia patted Jo's back. "I will and while I'm gone, you two promise me you'll look after each other."

"We will," Hope said.

After they said their goodbyes to Olivia, Jo ran into the cottage. She threw some more supplies into a bag, along with Angel's bowl, then rejoined Hope outside. Stepping onto the footpath in front of Olivia's house, they came face to face with a man and woman. Both wore tattered clothes that looked to be at least two sizes bigger than they needed. When the strangers got closer, a pungent odour filled Jo's nostrils. It was a mix of body odour, stale alcohol, and almost a chemical like smell. The pair seemed to be milling about.

The woman stood meekly behind the man as he spoke. "Can you tell us the time?"

Stepping slightly ahead of Jo, Hope pulled her in a little to stand just behind her. She raised her left arm. "Sure," she took note of the time on her watch, "it's just on four o'clock."

The man nodded with a toothless grin. "Thank you."

The woman bent to pat Oscar, as the couple made their way past Jo. The woman's hair was one huge, matted knot, and her voice was barely loud enough to be a whisper. "Very cute, I bet they're well loved." It was like she was trying to disguise her voice.

"Yes, they are," Jo agreed.

Hope and Jo watched as the two made their way to the top of the street before turning right and moving out of sight. They walked slowly enough to make sure they were aware of what the strangers were up to, yet tried not to stare. Hope and Jo had remained quiet. After the couple moved on, Jo said, "They must be the couple Olivia mentioned. They've been seen around here lately."

"When was this?"

"Oh, she mentioned it a while back. Apparently, they wander down one side of the street and up the other, then carry on just like they did today. The neighbours are aware of them and keep an eye out, but they haven't been any trouble."

"Why didn't you say anything about them earlier?"

"Honestly, I forgot about it. I meant to. That's the first time I've seen them."

Pulling Jo to a stop, Hope looked her in the eyes. "Please, if you see them again let me know. I got a strange feeling from them."

Jo nodded. "I will, I promise."

They continued in silence. As they approached Hope's driveway, Jo shook her head. "It's weird. That's the first time I've seen them, yet they seem familiar. I wonder if they've been at the park when I've been there taking pictures."

"Maybe, but as I said, I got a strange feeling from them. I need you to promise me you'll let me know if you see them on the street again, or anywhere."

Jo leaned in and placed a gentle kiss on Hope's cheek. "I promise."

Chapter Twenty-five

SATURDAY MORNING, AFTER A couple of hours spent first hungrily, then slowly savouring each other, they lay in each other's arms. "If it's all right with you, I thought the dogs and I could spend another night here. That way we could wander to the park in the morning and let them have a run around along that bush walk. I might be able to get some fun pictures of them playing,"

"That's a great idea. We might even be able to get Oscar and Ruby into the water, if we have Angel with us. I remember Olivia saying how much Angel loves to swim."

"That's right! I'd forgotten about that. Right, I will check that the battery in the camera is charged. I don't want to miss out, if they do go in."

The rest of the day went quickly. Hope made a chicken and kumara salad for their dinner, as they weren't overly hungry. Hope showered and dressed for work in her usual cargos and t-shirt. Jo was sitting on the couch reading, but very aware of Hope as she approached. *God, she's sexy.* When Hope bent down for a kiss, Jo pulled her in closer, moving the kiss from slow and smooth to very deep and heavy.

When both were out of breath, Hope stood and shook her head. "You definitely don't make it easy to leave, that's for sure."

"Good, that was the idea." Jo chuckled.

After Hope finally made it out the door, Jo picked up the book that she'd tossed when she saw Hope approaching her. *Definitely sexy.*

***

The dogs began to clamber over Jo and nudge against her hands. "It must be time to feed you guys." She checked her watch. "Nine thirty!" Engrossed in the lesbian romance that she'd found on Hope's bookcase, she'd lost all track of time.

"You guys must be starving, you poor babies. I'm sorry." Feeling bad that she'd left the dogs so long without their dinner, Jo added a treat to each dish before placing them down on the back patio. All three went straight to the treat, eating as fast as they could, just in case Jo would realise her mistake and take them back.

Giggling to herself, she went to the bedroom and pulled out a pair of cotton khakis from the bottom of her bag. Her one pair of good pants. Jo laid the khakis and a black, sleeveless, button-down shirt on the bed before going in search of an iron.

She was ready to try the club again. She figured if she made her way through the back and stayed off to the side, she could let Hope know she was there, while at the same time not having to be in the thick of everything. The iron was in clear view on a shelf in the laundry, and under the shelf was an ironing board to match. Jo took both back to the bedroom and plugged the iron in to heat up.

She collected the dog's dishes for a soak and a scrub, then headed back to the bedroom. With her clothes neatly pressed, Jo showered and washed her hair, then decided it would be a good idea to shave as well. She climbed from the shower and dried herself before slipping into her high-cut underwear and sports bra.

Knowing what Oscar and Ruby could be like, she threw on a t-shirt until she could secure them in their enclosure. She sat on the floor and played with the dogs for a while, making sure all three had some of her time and attention. She took them outside, encouraged them to have a drink, and waited until all had attended to business.

Angel and the pups settled in their beds quickly, and Jo went back to the bedroom to put on the clothes she'd pressed. In the bathroom, she spent what seemed like forever fixing her hair and getting it under control. Jo knew Hope liked her hair out, so she'd decided she wouldn't wear a beanie tonight.

Jo sighed. "That's as close to decent as I'm going to get," She mumbled, as she sprayed on some of her favourite ck one. Men's or unisex colognes were more to her liking than the sweet feminine scents.

The reflection in the mirror looked good. An unusual concept for her. Generally, she avoided her own reflection, and rarely did she find opportunity to think she looked even close to acceptable. This was an exceptional occasion.

She took a deep breath. "You can do this. Hope will appreciate the effort, and she deserves at least that much. Making Hope happy will make all of this worthwhile."

Jo turned out all the lights except for the lamp in the lounge, turned on the television to keep the dogs company, and went out the door and locked the place up. She made her way through the gate at the end of the garden and walked the short distance to the door at the rear of the bar. Sound hit her like a brick wall. Music. People yelling to be heard over one another. For a few seconds, she stood still in the doorway.

"You can do this." With a final deep inhale, Jo made her way through the corridors she now knew well.

Turning the corner, she came to a complete stop. Customers were four or five deep the length of the bar. This wasn't part of her plan. She couldn't even see her stool. Curiosity finally got the better of her, and she moved deeper into the bar to see what had everyone cheering.

Chapter Twenty-six

WHEN HOPE CALLED, TELLING Andy to get to the bar ASAP, he'd thought some major disaster must have struck. But when he arrived, he was surprised and delighted to find not only was everything fine, but Hope was on fire.

He'd seen her have fun with the customers often enough. Hope was fantastic at encouraging them to have a good time and in the process, spend more money over the bar than they might have. One of her favourite things was to supply a row of free shots. Often, the women in the bar would race to get there, hoping for the chance to join their host in tossing back the bourbon.

As soon as there was a person in front of each of the small thimble-like shot glasses, Hope would raise the nearest one to her lips, downing the amber liquid. The moment her glass touched back down on the bar, the next in line would down their shot, and so on. Only Andy knew that the contents of Hope's glass differed to that of the others. Where all the rest were filled to the brim with Jim Beam, hers was simple iced tea. If anyone had taken the time to look, they probably would have noticed the slight difference in colour, but no one ever did.

The shots had, on so many occasions, been a prelude to Hope's latest conquest coming forward. Over the course of a couple of hours, and a few such line-ups, there would always be one woman whose desire to be in Hope's company would show through. She'd inevitably position herself beside Hope, making her desires known.

Andy knew how it worked. The boss would take her break, grab the hand of her admirer, and lead her back to the office where some special customer care would be on offer. Just as soon as she'd satisfied the groupie's desires, Hope would use the excuse that her break was long over, leaving a half-naked woman alone to gather herself together, while Hope made her way back to the front.

Andy had watched Hope offer up polite words but little more, fending off her admirer for the remainder of the evening time and time again. When closing time neared, if the woman was still hovering, Hope would disappear out back, asking staff to call her when the bar was empty.

Since being with Jo, Hope had encouraged the other staff to take up her position in the shots line, happy to watch from the side. Some of the younger staff were more than eager to take on the customer satisfaction role. So, when Andy raced in through the door in response to Hope's ASAP call, he was more than shocked to discover a tall blonde draped over Hope. He was speechless.

The blonde proceeded to peel herself from Hope and climb on top of the bar. Facing the crowd, she removed her top, revealing a black lace bra struggling to contain her large breasts. She swung her shirt above her head, lasso style, before throwing it into the cheering crowd.

As two women jostled with one another in an attempt to claim rights to the now-discarded shirt, the blonde reclined along the length of Aunt Em's rimu bar. Hope balanced three shot glasses on the firm, flat stomach before her. Leaning over the shot glass nearest the woman's tummy button, Hope grabbed it between her teeth, flinging her head back and downing the contents. The crowd cheered, and Hope moved on to the second and the third.

Andy looked over to the end of the bar. Jo was standing at the very edge of the crowd. All colour had drained from her face, and tears filled her eyes. He tried to reach her, but she raced down the back corridor and out through the rear door.

Hope raised her hands in the air in celebration of her final shot. The blonde sat up and took Hope's face in her hands, pulling her in for a big kiss. The spectators let out a boisterous cheer, before the blonde called out, "Okay, who's next?"

As women stumbled over one another to be the next to experience this delight, Hope made her way through the throng to Andy. She was still laughing, as she approached and called over the noise, "Andy, man, am I glad you could make it."

"Yeah, well unfortunately, I wasn't the only one to make it tonight. Jo just took off before I could get to her. To say she didn't look happy would be an understatement."

The smile on Hope's face disappeared instantly. "What? Jo was here? Just now? Oh my God, did she see me doing the shots?"

Andy nodded. "Yes, yes, and yes."

Hope turned and ran, barging through the bar crowd at full speed. "Jo," Hope yelled, as she crashed through the back door. There was no reply and no sign of Jo. Hope ran through the back gate and up the path to a dark house.

The door was locked. She fumbled in her pockets to retrieve her keys and hurried to open the door. Flipping on the light, Hope could see the pups' spare enclosure was empty, and knew she wouldn't find Jo there. Hope ran out of the house, leaving everything open. At the end of the driveway, she made a right, running as fast as she could toward Jo's.

She reached the gate with no sign of Jo and followed the pathway toward the cottage. Darkness filled every nook and cranny of the well-established garden, as Hope relied on memory to make her way toward Jo's door. A twig snapped in the blackness.

"Jo, is that you? Please, let me explain."

No response. Figuring it must have been a cat, Hope continued down the path. She tapped on the door, calling out in a soft voice, not wanting to wake the neighbourhood.

"Jo, Jo, open the door. Sweetie, I can explain what you saw. I promise it was nothing like what I'm sure you must be imagining."

After five minutes of calling out and trying to encourage Jo to open the door, Hope made her way back up the road. She took out her mobile, and called Jo as she walked. When the answer phone kicked in, she left a message.

"Jo, it's me, Hope. If you would please come back to my house, or call me, I can explain everything. I promise you; I would never do anything to hurt you. What you saw is not at all what I imagine you think it was. Please, Jo, give me a chance to explain."

Chapter Twenty-seven

WATCHING HOPE TAKE SHOTS from the blonde's stomach left Jo feeling sick to her stomach. Hurtling through the back door into the darkness, she filled her lungs with deep breaths of night air, washing the nausea away. Unable to think clearly, all Jo knew was that she had to get the dogs and get out of there. She couldn't look at Hope, much less talk to her. That she was sure of. She grabbed her backpack and crammed in as much of her stuff as she could.

Jo scrambled to harness all three dogs, locked the door behind her, and made her way back into the night. At the end of the drive, rather than turn right toward home, she headed left. She needed to walk and clear her mind a little. They'd planned to visit the park together the next day. Now, Jo slumped onto the bench alone. The street light revealed her tears as images of the evening's show ran a constant replay in her mind. Eventually, the tears dried up, and Jo made her way back to the safety of her cottage. She wished Olivia was home. She'd have gone straight to her if she were. She knew Olivia truly cared for her.

Inside, Jo curled up on the couch. Oscar and Ruby snuggled into her, and Angel was on guard nearby. She needed the comfort of her babies tonight. Lying in the dark, Jo couldn't believe she'd been so foolish as to trust Hope. To believe her words and to think maybe Hope loved her.

How many nights had Hope had her fun with other women while Jo waited at home? Worse yet, how many of them had Hope had her way with before returning to Jo? The thought disgusted Jo and, again, she felt bile rise in her throat. She pushed it down but couldn't stop the tears that drained her until she could no longer keep her eyes open.

Jo woke the following morning, surprised she'd slept. The softness of Ruby and Oscar curled up beside her brought the memory of Hope's body tucked up against her in slumber. A fresh batch of salty humiliation gathered around the rims of her eyes, and Jo raised herself to take the dogs out for a much needed toilet break. As the three dogs sniffed the ground in search of just the right spot, Jo made her way to the bathroom, needing the relief as much as her companions.

The thought of eating didn't really appeal, but she knew she needed to. She wandered the garden with a piece of toast, trying to make sense of her thoughts. She had no idea what to do, how to deal with all of this. Not just the practical side of things, collecting the remainder of her belongings and returning any of Hope's that may still be in her place, but also the emotions running wild through her heart. A long time ago, Jo had taught herself to shut off emotions, to put up walls that would prevent her from being hurt. When you passed through so many homes, it was something you needed to do.

Without the walls others could, and would, chip away at you, bit by bit, eventually leaving you a hollow shell of a person. So many other fosters hadn't learned this skill, and Jo had seen even children turn to drugs and alcohol as substitutes.

Having seen the effects of both on so many around her, Jo had made a vow to never allow herself to do that. A drink here and there, socially, was the most she'd let herself have, and she never drank alone. She plucked a ripe plum from one of the many fruit trees in Olivia's yard. Jo knew she'd do her best to keep on as usual. She'd maintain her regular activities, beginning with her Sunday trip to a park with her camera.

Taking all three dogs was a bit much to handle. Instead, she'd play with them for a long while when she got back. The day was fine, so she moved their enclosure out under the shade of the tree, making sure there was plenty of water for all three, as well as a good supply of toys.

Jo gathered her camera along with both of her lenses and stored them safely in her backpack. She grabbed a bottle of water from the fridge and tucked it securely into one of the side pockets before swinging the pack into place on her back and walking her bike out the gate which she locked securely. Jo pushed off with her right foot on the pedal and swung her left leg over the seat.

Watching children at play always brought some peace to Jo. Seeing the families enjoying one another left her happy for them, while at the same time a little sad knowing that was something she'd never get to experience.

The fresh air helped clear her head, and she decided to work on a collection of black and whites to fill in time while Olivia was away. Using the morning light to her advantage, Jo snapped away, accumulating about three hundred images. She enjoyed putting together photo collections. She'd shown a number at the local gallery already, and had been lucky enough to sell a few prints. Maybe they'd show the black and whites.

The plan made Jo feel better about herself. She was even a little excited. Ideas were flowing rapidly through her mind, and she was keen to get home and make a start on them. Seeing as she liked to use both her digital and film cameras, she had several films at home waiting to be developed. An afternoon in the darkroom Olivia had set up for her in the attic would be perfect.

Coming around the corner of the house, Jo could see all three dogs sleeping peacefully. They came to life the second they heard her approach. Ruby and Oscar clambered over one another trying to climb the enclosure walls, while Angel simply whined quietly, her tail wagging frantically the entire time.

Jo opened the gate and they ran around the garden, chasing each other as well as Jo. By the time they'd tossed and tugged every toy, they were more than content to go back into the enclosure for a rest. Jo moved the pen around the other side of the tree before settling them in, making sure they were still protected from the heat of the sun.

Chapter Twenty-eight

HOPE MADE HER WAY back to the pub trying to make sense of everything, kicking herself every step of the way. She'd meant to go and tell Jo the news, but instead had allowed herself to get carried away in the moment. *What was Jo doing there anyway?* She'd made it crystal clear she didn't enjoy the club scene. Hope understood fully. *Didn't Jo know that?* "Oh, God. She was there for me; she wanted to do something for me. What have I done?"

The bar noise hit Hope like a slap in the face. The crowd was in top form tonight. As much as she'd been loving it earlier on, now she wanted to tell them all to just clear out. Knowing he'd be worried, Hope wove a path through the night's revelers to Andy. He saw her approach and moved to the side of the bar.

"Did you manage to sort everything out? Is Jo all right?"

"I couldn't find her. She was already gone. She must have raced in and grabbed the dogs and rushed off. I ran to her place, but she wouldn't open the door. I can't say I blame her. What she saw must have looked suspicious, and if I'd seen Jo behaving like that I'd be devastated."

"You need to try and fix this, Hope. Jo is the best thing to ever happen to you. Since being with her, you radiate a joy I've never seen in you. She's good for you in so many ways, my friend."

With a deep sigh, Hope nodded. "I know. She makes me happier than I thought possible. I can simply be me when I'm with her. I don't have to be the boss or the life of the party. I don't have to be perfect for her to be happy with me." Hope stopped talking when she saw Andy smirking at her. "What are you looking at me like that for?" The sudden realisation hit her. "Oh...my...God. I'm in love with Jo."

Andy's head tilted back, and a rough laugh escaped his throat. "Hallelujah." Taking Hope in his arms, he hugged her tight. He released her with a softer laugh. "Girl, you have been from the very beginning. I've bitten my tongue so many times, waiting, watching, to see when you'd make the discovery for yourself. Now that you have, what are you going to do about it?"

Hope walked past Andy, and poured herself a shot, a real shot, of bourbon, not tea. "I'm going to calm my nerves, and then..." She raised the glass to her lips, tipped her head back, and poured the contents down her throat. Slamming the empty glass on the bar, Hope turned back to Andy. "I'm going to do anything I can to fix this and get her back. Even if I fail, I should at least try, and then try again and again if need be. I'll go back to Jo's tomorrow and try to get her to at least listen to me."

Andy wrapped Hope in his arms again, bouncing up and down on the spot. "You have no idea how happy I am that I'm not going to have to hit you over the head with a blunt object to get you to see this. You know how I hate to break a nail, darling." When Hope smiled, Andy asked, "Will you be all right to lock up, or do you want me to stay and get that done for you?"

"No, the distraction will be good for me. You get going."

"Okay, but I want to hear some good news when I get here tomorrow." Andy started toward the door and turned. "I love you."

With tears already threatening, Hope smiled weakly. "I love you too, Andy." As he stepped away, Hope reached out to grasp his arm. "Thanks, Andy, for everything."

The energetic blonde kept the remainder of the night busy and lively, doing the rounds and spreading herself amongst the women. By the time Hope finally closed and made her way home, she was exhausted and her head was pounding. She needed to crawl into bed and get some rest, but as soon as her head hit the pillow, the events of the night played over and over in her mind.

Like pesky flies that dive-bomb your head, Hope's thoughts kept her awake, re-emerging every time sleep drew near. Rather than rehash what couldn't be changed, Hope decided she needed to plan for the next day.

Chapter Twenty-nine

SLEEP HAD NOT COME easily for Hope. When she did finally drift off, her night was very restless. After tossing and turning for a few hours, she flung the sheet back off herself. "That's about as good as I'm going to get."

It was still too early to turn up at Jo's. Besides, she wanted to make sure she didn't arrive empty handed. Jo deserved not only an apology and explanation, but to also be shown how special she is. *Jo. Bright, cheery, always enticing a smile. She lights me up from the inside out. What sort of flower looks like that?*

Hope would surely go insane before the florist opened, so she went over to her office to fill in time on paper work. Paying bills would occupy her mind for a little while, at least. An hour and a half later, the bills were paid and it was still too early. Hope made her way back home. She needed to calm down. A nice cup of chamomile would do the trick. As the water boiled, she popped a slice of Vogel's in the toaster. She hoped she could keep it down.

***

As Hope climbed out from behind the wheel, the shop assistant unlocked the front door and began pushing wheelbarrows, filled with brightly coloured flowers, out onto the path in front of the store. Hope stroked the flowers as she walked by them on the way to the counter where she found the florist.

Fifteen minutes later, she fumbled with the car keys. Her arms were full, but she managed to unlock the passenger side door. Gently, she settled twelve beautifully wrapped sunflowers on the front seat along with an oversized teddy bear holding a huge, red heart declaring *I Love You*. Hope went around and got in the driver's side.

She dug in the glove box to locate a pen and opened the card. Suddenly, her mind was blank. She ran a few sentences by in her head, but nothing was quite right. What did feel right, also felt scary. Before she chickened out, Hope quickly wrote *I Love You* before closing the card and shoving it in the envelope.

***

The shocking discovery of how much she needed Jo in her world threatened to beat her heart right out of her chest, as she walked through the front gate and along the path toward Jo's cottage. The dogs leapt all over each other, tails wagging. High pitched little barks seemed to signal they'd missed her after only one night. That meant a lot to Hope, and she shared their happiness.

"Hi guys, I can't pat you now, my hands are full. Let me see if I can go talk with Jo, and then I can come back and spend some time with you all."

Hope went to Jo's front door and knocked. She knew Jo must be home, because she didn't normally leave the dogs outside alone. When there was no reply to her knock, Hope tried again, this time a little harder, just in case Jo was upstairs having a nap. Still no response. Hope tried the door handle. Locked. Her only chance was to keep knocking.

After a good five minutes of knocking, not to mention calling out and begging for Jo to open the door so she could at least explain, Hope figured she wasn't going to get much further. She'd leave for now but vowed she'd come back and try again later, before the night shift.

Not wanting the flowers to wilt, or possibly even die off in the sun, Hope tucked them in the shade by the enclosure. Jo would find them when she came to get the pups. With her hands free at last, Hope made a big fuss of all three little ones.

***

From the darkroom, Jo could hear Oscar and Ruby's zealous yapping, along with Angel's slightly deeper voice. She wondered who'd earned their fervent barking, but she couldn't leave to see right now. If she did, the film would be ruined.

Standing next to the blackened-out window above the yard, Jo could just hear someone talking. She concentrated on the voice. *Hope.* Torn between wanting to race out and wrap her arms around Hope and wanting to never have to face her again, Jo concentrated on deep, measured breathing, an attempt to calm her now-shaky nerves.

Maybe it was a good thing she couldn't leave the darkroom just now. She needed more time to decide what she wanted to do. To figure out just what it was she was feeling. Her initial reaction had been based on shock, but now she was wondering if maybe she'd behaved a little too hastily. She focused on Hope's voice.

"I need you guys to look after your mummy for me. I love Jo, and I'm going to do everything I can to make sure she knows that. I promise you all, I won't give up; I'll be back again soon."

When Jo no longer heard any noise from outside, she went back to her pictures. Working in the darkroom had always been one of Jo's favourite pastimes. Seeing her pictures come to life around her usually generated an exuberance of creative ideas and energy, but today she was struggling. Today, her darkroom seemed big, cold, lonely.

The silver solution transformed negative to positive, as Hope floated out to greet her. Jo had forgotten she'd taken these photos. Hope had never told Jo she loved her, but these pictures told a different story. Eyes filled with love confirmed what she'd just overheard. She hung the last print to dry.

Jo was glad she hadn't given up on the developing. Those eyes helped her decide to give Hope a chance to explain. What she'd seen at the bar definitely didn't correspond with the tender affection staring back at her. Jo needed to know which was the real Hope and the only way to find out was to talk with her.

Just then, the dogs started up again. That couldn't be Hope again so soon. Jo still couldn't open the door to the darkroom. Five minutes later, she was done. Making her way to the back door, she was surprised to hear the barking hadn't stopped. That was unusual. Funny thing was, she could only hear two dogs barking. She recognised Angel's voice but was sure she could only hear one pup. How on earth could the other sleep through such a ruckus?

Chapter Thirty

JO PUSHED THE BUTTON on the back door to lock it as she walked out. Taking the steps two at a time, she heard the backdoor latch behind her. "Hey, hey, hey, that's enough now. Mummy's sorry she was so long," Jo called, heading toward the noise.

A beautiful bunch of stunning, bright-yellow sunflowers leaned against the enclosure, supported by a giant teddy bear. The bear held a pillow heart with the message *I Love You* on it. Maybe Jo was right to believe what the photos showed her in Hope's eyes.

Looking back to the pen she'd set up for the dogs, Jo halted abruptly. Angel and Ruby were barking and pawing the side of the cage, but there was no sign of Oscar. She ran the remaining steps, calling, "Oscar, Oscar, here boy. Oscar, where are you?"

How on earth could he have gotten himself out? Jo continued calling until she reached Ruby and Angel. When she reached the side of the pen, her eyes focused on a piece of paper up against the far side, poked into the corner. She hurried around and snatched up the sheet. The childlike scrawl delivered a chilling message.

If u want see ur dog agin
bring $500 to secind floor old
movee place on Queen Street
—— side door opens
NO COPS —— or we kill
ur mutt

The piece of paper slipped from Jo's hand, floating to the ground as she sank to her knees. *What am I going to do? I don't have five hundred dollars and, even if I did, going there could be dangerous. I have to get Oscar back though. Fuck, what will I do if anything happens to him?"*

Looking up, Jo spotted the flowers beside the tree. She knew what she needed to do now. Jo gathered up the flowers and bear and took them into her kitchen. She filled the sink with a little water and haphazardly deposited the stems in the cool liquid. "That'll work for the flowers, but am I ready for this?"

Angel and Ruby's little legs had to work overtime to keep up with Jo as she ran up the street. Jo pounded on the door. Her fist didn't stop beating on the wood until she felt it shift under her hammering. The door had only opened a crack. "Hope, please I need—"

The words came to a sudden halt, as Jo's eyes registered the blonde from the previous night, now standing in Hope's front doorway, dripping wet, with a towel wrapped around voluptuous breasts. Barely.

Jo could hear the shower still running, as Hope called out, "Who is it? Is that Andy?"

"I...I'm sorry to disturb you," Jo managed to stutter, before turning and walking aimlessly out Hope's driveway. The blonde was saying something, but Jo had no idea what. Her head was spinning, and the last thing she cared about was anything the blonde might have to say.

Jo made it to the corner and turned left, crossing the road without looking, stumbling along with Angel and Ruby in tow. Someone gripped her elbow and turned her body with their hand. Jo saw bare feet. She looked up. Shorts buttoned but not zipped. T-shirt inside out. Hair dripping wet. Hope stood in front of her.

"Jo, please come back with me so I can explain. It's nothing like what I know it must look like. Please," Hope begged.

Jo didn't answer. She continued her blank stare, not registering much of anything. But she did notice the deep lines that creased Hope's forehead.

"Jo, what's going on?" Hope looked around. "Jo, where's Oscar? Why do you only have the two girls?"

Tears slid over colourless cheeks, and she mumbled, "They took him."

"Who took him? Where?"

Jo pulled the crumpled note from her pocket. Hope whipped it from Jo's shaking hands and read the threatening demand.

"Shit. When did you find this?"

"Just a few minutes ago. I didn't know what to do. All I could think was to come to you." Lowering her head again, Jo mumbled, "Sorry to interrupt. You can go back now; I'll be fine." Jo turned her back and took a step away from Hope.

Hope engulfed her in strong arms. "You're coming with me. When we get home, the first thing I'll do is explain to you everything you've seen, both last night and today. Then, we'll figure out what to do."

Jo was too dazed to put up a fight, allowing Hope to lead them all back to her place. Jo knew she should be angry still, should shrug out of Hope's arm, but she didn't have the strength. Right there and then, the only strength she did have, was coming from Hope's embrace.

Hope removed her arm when they got to the house, moving slightly ahead of Jo to open the door. Jo let herself be guided to a seat on the couch and followed Hope with her eyes. She watched Hope remove Angel and Ruby's leads, then call them to the kitchen for a drink before joining Jo on the couch. Jo studied Hope, unsure how to react or behave. When Hope took her hand, she didn't resist.

"Jo, I know you just want to get to Oscar, but I really think we need to sort through last night before we do anything more. It'll make finding a solution much easier for us both, I think."

Jo nodded, her eyes never leaving Hope's. "I'm prepared to listen. Last night, I didn't respond so well, but now that I've had time to think I've realised I need to listen to what you have to say. I'd already made that decision and was about to come and see you when I found Oscar missing and the note in his place."

Hope ran her hands up and down her thighs. "Jo, I need you to know I never want to hurt you. Last night, I did make some mistakes, but not in the way you might be thinking. Yes, I did do shots off another woman's stomach, but that wasn't just any woman."

"Oh, I see," Jo said, her voice quiet, her manner calm. "So, it's okay to fuck around if the other person looks like a Playboy model?"

Jo had just finished her sentence when the model-like woman from the previous night meekly appeared from Hope's bedroom. Unable to believe what she was seeing, Jo's eyes almost bulged from her head.

Hope was quick. "Jo, I'd like you to meet my partner in crime. This is PJ."

Jo knew the name, but it took a few slow seconds to place the memory—London. The second she managed to join the dots, Jo's cheeks flushed like red-hot coals. "Oh God, I've been such a fool."

"No, you haven't Jo, I have," Hope assured her, backing up her words with a comforting arm around Jo's shoulders.

Jo looked at PJ. "I'm so sorry."

PJ smiled brightly at Jo. "You're very sweet when, in fact, it's me who owes you the apology. I turn up unannounced, stir everything up, then you tell me you're sorry for responding in a perfectly normal manner. Trust me, you have nothing to apologise for. I'm the one who's sorry."

Hope stood. "Neither of you need to say sorry about anything. PJ, you turned up and surprised the shit out of me in the best possible way. So, don't you dare be sorry for that." She knelt in front of Jo, speaking quietly. "You pushed yourself to do something I know was hard. You did that for me, so you definitely don't owe anyone an apology." Hope ran a finger lightly down Jo's cheek before standing again. "I'm the one who is very sorry. I planned to come and tell you PJ was here, then I allowed myself to get carried away with the excitement. I called Andy and told him to get here so he could join in the celebration as well. I was about to come see if you wanted to join us briefly, to meet PJ, but we got carried away before I had the chance."

Jo rose to her feet, moving closer to Hope. "I knew what I saw in the pictures couldn't be wrong." Extending her hand toward PJ, Jo attempted to start fresh. "Hi PJ, I'm Jo. I've heard lots about both you and Ang. It's wonderful to get the chance to meet you."

Rather than take Jo's hand, PJ threw her arms around Jo in a bear hug. "I'm very pleased to meet you as well, Jo, and I'm really glad we managed to work this out," PJ said, her voice filled with relief. When PJ released Jo, Hope took her place, sliding her arm around Jo's waist.

"Now, we need to figure out what we can do to get our boy back," Hope said. Jo didn't try to hide the fear in her eyes, and Hope held her close. "It's going to be okay. We'll get this sorted out and have him back here by tonight, I promise."

Chapter Thirty-one

"THEY SAID IF I bring the police they'll kill him. They want five hundred dollars, and I don't have that much money."

Jo found herself almost surplus to requirements while Hope and PJ rapidly threw ideas around, both keeping up with one another's thoughts. Before long, Hope explained what the two had come up with, asking Jo if she felt comfortable with everything. Jo, still in shock that this was happening at all, nodded and agreed. She was impressed with how quickly the others had come up with a plan of attack.

"So, we're going to stop at a money machine and get out the five hundred from my account on our way to Queen Street. We won't ring the police until we have Oscar, but we'll have PJ here as our back up. PJ, would you be willing to wait outside the building while we go in? If you don't hear from us within twenty minutes, then call the police and have them come in to look for us. Auckland Central is only a block over so if you tell them it's a kidnapping and possible hostage situation you'll have officers there in minutes."

PJ didn't hesitate. "Sure, I'm happy to do whatever it takes to get your little one back."

Hope made sure Angel and Ruby were taken out to go toilet before putting them both in the enclosure Jo had left behind. Taking Jo in her arms, Hope soothed, "We're going to get Oscar back and everything will be all right." With a quick kiss, Hope took Jo's hand in hers, making their way for the door.

The two walked hand in hand to the vacant building, stopping only to get the ransom money from the ATM. PJ walked a distance behind them, alone. This worked in their favour, allowing her to be their eyes as well as their safety net.

Reaching the heavy, wooden side door they were to enter, Hope checked, "Are you still okay to do this, sweetie? I can go in alone if you need to wait here."

Jo shook her head with determination. "No. Thanks to you and PJ coming up with a plan, giving me direction, I'm fine to do this. It was just, in the beginning, I couldn't get my mind around us, as well as Oscar being taken. I'm feeling stronger again now."

Hope squeezed Jo's arm. "That's my girl. So, I'm going to give you a hug, that's when you're going to snuggle your head in against my chest, slip your hand beneath the back of my shirt, and press the record button on the Dictaphone in my back pocket. Just make sure my shirt still covers the device." With a small smile, Hope asked, "All set?"

Jo gave one nod and Hope pulled her in close.

***

The lower level, where they entered, was brightly lit. Large glass doors allowed sunlight to filter through, bringing life to the empty space. Carpet that had once been a lush burgundy was now threadbare and covered in a layer of dust. As the two stood in the middle of the room looking around, Jo swore she could feel fleas feasting on her.

She recognised the smell of stale alcohol, but what was it mixed with? It was a smell she knew but couldn't put a name to. The hairs on the back of her neck twitched. *Knives stained with black dots.* Now, all too aware what the odour was, Jo pushed those memories aside. She concentrated, instead, on what needed to be done.

Hope pointed to the wide sweeping staircase to the right of the room. Not a word was spoken. They made their way in that direction, taking the steps hand in hand. Two steps before the top, Jo felt Hope grip her hand a little tighter. Jo returned the squeeze, letting Hope know she was all right. Slivers of light from downstairs filtered up to the second floor, managing to reach in about a metre before the room sunk into total darkness. Neither moved.

Out of the black came a gritty voice, "Do you have the money?"

They jumped, their hands gripping that bit tighter again. "Hope, I know that voice. That's the homeless guy from outside the house the other day." In a bold voice, Jo dared to challenge him, "You get no answers until I know my dog is safe."

Silence. Then rustling. A light came on, allowing Jo and Hope to see Oscar looking at them, his little tail wagging frantically. Hope held Jo back with a firm hand. "If we give you the money, how do we know you won't be back again in a day or two?"

The man laughed. A second laugh set the hair on the back of Jo's neck straight up. She knew that witch-like cackle. Memories flooded her mind. She fought hard to find her voice, and a shaky whisper managed to escape. "Oh. My. God."

***

Hope looked at Jo. "What is it? What's wrong?" Jo didn't respond, and Hope squeezed her hand. "Jo, what is it?"

"So, you haven't changed then. Still the same cruel, worthless addicts you always were."

Jo seethed with a venom to her voice Hope had never known before. Still unsure of what was going on, Hope remained silent beside her.

"How did you find me?"

Another sick laugh filled the room. "Luck. Saw ya one day gettin' on a fancy bike. Your mum thought it was her brat. Followed ya to the flash digs ya scored. Figured it's time ya pay us back."

"She is not my mother. I have no mother and no father. They died to me a very long time ago."

As the pieces fell into place, anger surged through Hope's veins and her fingers clenched around Jo's hand.

"I owe you nothing. You deserve the hellhole life you live."

Hope knew the bite to Jo's voice was warranted, but was surprised by it nonetheless.

"You owe us big, girly. If it wasn't for you we'd have money and be happy. Selfish brat. Whinin' 'bout bein' hungry all the time. Always needin' clothes. Take, take, take. All ya did."

"I was a small child who grew out of clothes and needed food to grow," Jo spat back.

One small, lone, cry entered the darkness.

Turning in a flash, Jo's so-called father yelled, "Shut that thing up, I'm sick of hearin' it all the bloody time."

Hope felt Jo sway slightly and heard her gasp before she whispered, "Oh no, not again." Darting toward the sound, Jo growled, "Where's the baby?"

"It's over there somewhere with ya mutt," he snapped, irritation obvious in his voice.

Jo grabbed the light from the floor and aimed it to where the noise had come from. There, under a plastic crate weighted down with a rock, was Oscar. His tail swished frantically when Jo came closer. By the look of him, he was thirsty. A newborn was lying, naked, on crumpled newspapers scattered over the floor.

"Who does he belong to?" Jo demanded.

"Us unfortunately," the man said. "I told the stupid bitch ta go ta the free clinic for a shot, but she got too high and passed out." Turning to the woman who'd given birth to both Jo and the baby, he kicked a can at her. The projectile hit its target. "Then I told her ta git rid of it, but she was too chickin ta go the clinic, case they locked us up agin, like they did when ya opened ya big mouth. Now we're stuck with it."

"How old is he?" Hope asked.

A pock-faced, scrawny woman, her hair oily, her body waif like, flailed her arms around as she spoke, her words barely coherent. "Yest...day, day fore maybe."

Jo scooped the infant up in her arms. "When did he last eat?"

The woman spoke again, "Dunno. Tried. Hurt me, lil bastard."

Not wanting to frighten the baby, Hope asked calmly, "So did you buy formula?"

"We got no money, we both need a fix fore it gits anythin'. That's why we took ya dog. Figured ya got lotsa money. Flash house. Fancy bike n all."

Facing the pathetic excuse for a human being, legally known as her father, Jo lowered her voice for the sake of the baby. "Well, you figured wrong. I had to borrow the money, and I can't believe your main concern is getting a fix before you feed this baby. You really are the scum of the earth, aren't you?" She turned to the woman who was attempting to get the last dregs from a wine bottle. "And you disgust me. You're so weak it's pathetic. For years, you let him beat me as you stood by cheering him on and then joined in. Now, you sit by, waiting for a fix, while your baby dies in a dark, dingy, flea-infested shit-hole."

Hope stepped over to Jo, placing an arm around her. "I'm going to get Oscar and then we're going to get them both the hell out of here."

"No one leaves here without handin' over the money."

Looking at the strung-out guy in front of her, Hope knew he could become violent at any time. He was desperate for a high. Because he saw them as a way to get that, Hope knew she needed to be wise. "I'm going to get some water for the dog and some formula for the baby." She tightened her hold on Jo. "Jo will stay here with you, so you know I'll be back. When I get back, if all three are safe and well, I'll hand over the money."

Hope felt Jo tense. When the pair agreed, she heard the anxiety in Jo's voice.

"Please, be as fast as you can. They're unpredictable, and I'm really worried about the baby."

"I know, sweetie. I'll be moving fast. I don't want any of you in here longer than need be." With a quick kiss, Hope ran for the stairs.

Chapter Thirty-two

HOPE TOOK THE STAIRS three at a time, running through the downstairs foyer and bursting into the city's bustle. The bright rays of the sun blinded her momentarily, but didn't slow her down. PJ was waiting and watching from across the road. Hope waved her over.

PJ sprinted across the busy inner city road, causing drivers to honk their horns in frustration and anger. Taking no notice of the abusive blaring, PJ gripped Hope's upper arm. "Where's Jo? What's going on Hope?"

"Jo's okay. I need your help and don't have time to explain."

"Sure, what?"

"I need you to go up the road a little; there's a dairy there. I need a baby's bottle, two bottles of water, but not from the fridge, and a small bowl of some sort. Meet me back here."

"Got it, baby's bottle, water not from the fridge, small bowl," PJ repeated back, letting Hope know she had it.

"Great PJ, thanks. We need to go fast. I'll meet you here ASAP." Hope turned at the last minute, calling out, "And a blanket or towel, anything like that."

Not stopping, PJ gave Hope a thumbs up.

Hope ran through people as quickly as she could, while at the same time trying not to knock into anyone. She knew exactly where she was headed.

***

Jo studied the scene in front of her. These p-freak losers were much thinner than her childhood abusers had been. Their faces and arms were marred with scars and festering sores. Disgusted by what she saw, Jo wondered how they could share the same genes.

The baby stirred in her arms, and Oscar whimpered from the dark corner. She stepped toward the crate. She heard a quick rustle followed by a sharp click, and turned to see a knife in his hand. The teeth on the ten-centimetre blade looked jagged and dirty. Nicotine stained fingers fiercely gripped the molded handle.

"Stay back. You git nothin' till I git my money."

Cold steel. Warm blood. Hot blade. Blistering skin. Memories rushed back. Jo couldn't stop shaking as adrenaline bombarded her system. The sweat running down her back had nothing to do with the stuffy room. She looked down at the floor.

One. Two. Three...Ten boards from his foot to hers. Four nails in each board. Ten times four is forty. She shook her head. She had to get to Oscar, but there were two of them and only one of her, and she was holding the baby. The woman was a soulless shell, had always been weak willed. Always did his bidding. Now, she had two masters, him and meth. She'd do nothing to help and might even hurt the baby or Oscar, if Jo tried to tackle him.

Oscar yipped. "It's okay, boy."

"Shut up!"

Jo looked into his sunken eyes and saw the evil laughter she knew so well in her nightmares. *How could I have come from these people? Oh, Hope, where are you?*

***

Hope ran a hundred metres or so up a side alley, until she reached the dark-grey, metal door she was after. Rust and paint flaked away as she banged on the door. Her fist pounded hard, over and over, until a bleary-eyed young man in his late teens opened the door.

The teen seemed less than happy to be disturbed during daylight hours. "What the hell are you doing, ya crazy bitch?"

Not fazed by his aggression, Hope pushed him aside, barging past. Moving down the murky, dingy hall, Hope entered a large room. There were no windows. Dull bulbs, some flickering, attempted to bounce light off the brick walls, revealing the paint peeling off in strips. Scattered around the room, bodies sprawled on couches and the floor. Some draped over others, some alone. All of them were asleep and heavily so.

Hope briskly stepped over the bodies. The old, stained carpet may have been cream at one time in its life, but now was a dull grey in the cleanest spots. Reaching a door to the right of the room Hope strode straight in.

The translucent-skinned guy that had been following Hope finally caught up to her. "Who the fuck do ya think you are, barging in here?" he barked at her in his best attempt at sounding tough.

"None of your business." Hope's tone caused him to take a step back.

Before he could do or say anything more, a deep voice came from the bed in front of them. "It's ok, Casper, I've got this." The blankets moved, and out from under them lumbered a mammoth bundle of muscles in the form of a man. Standing up slowly, he finally reached his full height of just over six foot six.

"Sorry, Tiny, she just stormed in," Casper attempted to soothe.

Keeping his eyes fixed on Hope, Tiny's voice was a deep rumble. "Shut the door and make sure no one else comes in."

Keen to please, Casper ran for the door. "Sure, Tiny, I got it."

The second the door shut, Tiny trudged over to Hope. She was dwarfed by his size and lost in his bear hug. "Hope, what are you doing here and why are you banging down my door so early in the day?"

"Tiny, I don't have much time to explain, but I need your help. I need some of your specialty baked goods, and I need it now. If you come to the bar tonight, I can explain then, but I really need to get what I came for and run."

"It's not for you, is it?"

"Tiny, you know me and so you know it's not for me."

"I just needed to check, Hope." From the second Hope had told him what she needed, Tiny had looked concerned. Now, he smiled. "I do know you and that means I can trust you know what you're doing. Wait here. I'll get you what you asked for."

Reaching the door, Tiny asked over his shoulder, "Is that all you need?"

"Shit, no, I probably need a needle as well. I don't know."

"I'll get together a kit and be right back."

As soon as the door closed behind Tiny, Hope began pacing the room. She hated that Tiny lived like this, but right now, she was also relieved that she could count on him. It's something they both could always do. Count on each other.

The door opened again, and Tiny handed Hope a black backpack. "Everything you need is in here. I need you to promise me you'll be careful, though. Do you need me to send someone with you?"

Hope took the bag and slung it over her back. "No, I'm all right." Hope took the two steps to Tiny and did her best to stretch her arms all the way around him, not succeeding. "Thanks, Tiny, I love you."

Slipping out of his arms, she heard Tiny as she opened the door. "Love you too, Hope."

Pulling the bedroom door behind her, Hope hurried to the one she'd entered. Casper was right behind her. Making her way back outside, she began to run again.

Her legs moved as fast as she could force them to go, and her lungs burned as she reached the cinema. PJ was already there waiting.

"I got all you wanted, now what?"

"I need you to come in with me this time, PJ. Are you all right with that?"

"Anything you need, Hope."

Hope climbed the stairs as fast as she could, leading the way. At the top, she ran to Jo. "Are you all right? I went as fast as I could. PJ helped."

Jo looked past Hope. "Thanks, PJ."

PJ stood motionless, her mouth gaping open. She looked from Jo to the baby in her arms to their surroundings. She closed her mouth and nodded.

"Where's my money?"

Hope turned to face the man who should have loved Jo, but instead had inflicted years of abuse on her. Hope had to use all the self-control she possessed to not take to him with her own fists.

"I've got your money, and I went and got you a little treat, as well." She threw the backpack at him. "It's in there; knock yourself out."

Opening the bag slowly, a smirk crept its way over his craggly face when he discovered what was in the backpack. As he pulled out the foil-wrapped package, his snigger reverberated down Hope's spine like crackling ice.

"Git over 'ere bitch, this'll make ya happy."

Dragging herself up, she shuffled over to her husband. Her grin was almost toothless. "Hurry up an' light it," she ordered impatiently.

Holding a shaking flame beneath the glass bowl, the sad excuse for a man took a few big hits before passing the pipe over to his wife. While she greedily drew on the smoke, time and time again, he withdrew a can of beer from the bag, popping the top and gulping the liquid like he was at an oasis in the desert.

Hope quietly drew the others aside. "I was able to get enough dope to keep them busy for a while, as well as a dozen cans of beer. By the time they finish that we'll be able to do what we have to." She rested a hand on Jo's arm. "You make sure you keep hold of this little one, and PJ and I will do the rest. PJ, take as many pictures as you can, quickly, then grab Oscar. I'll keep my hands free in case they decide to try and make things difficult."

When all three agreed, Hope opened a bottle of water, pouring some into the baby bottle PJ had gotten at the dairy. She passed the baby bottle to Jo.

"I know he needs milk, but this will do for now. At least it will hydrate the poor, wee guy. We'll get milk very soon." She looked into Jo's worried eyes before leaning forward to seal the words with a kiss to her forehead. "I promise," she whispered.

Hope carefully stepped near PJ and discretely nodded her head in the direction of the two who had found the rest of the kit. "Make sure you take pictures of them, as well as Oscar and all the rest of this. Where the baby has been, what they have had him in, and anything else you think will be useful."

"Oh, I'm more than happy to do that," PJ assured Hope.

"I don't think it will be long before the pair are out cold. That stuff will be really strong shit. As soon as they pass out, we move."

As Hope had predicted, the pair were near/y unconscious five minutes later. PJ took pictures of Oscar under the crate and where both he and the baby had been kept. The dusty old newspapers were covered in new filth. Blood, afterbirth, pee, and poo were added to the dried mouse turds. While PJ snapped away, Hope filled the bowl with water, released a whining Oscar, and made sure he had a good drink. Then she picked him up, holding him close. "It's okay, buddy, we're here now, and we'll have you home with the others very soon."

Hope took Oscar to stand beside Jo. "PJ's just getting some pictures we can use, then we'll get out of here."

"I can't leave him here, Hope." She felt the hungry mouth grab hold of the nipple and breathed a sigh of relief. "You're a fighter, aren't you, little man."

Hope stroked Jo's cheek with her thumb before looking down at the suckling infant. "I know, baby, that's why I got them a fix. We'll be able to leave with him safely, now." Hope placed her arm around Jo's shoulders. "I can't walk away from him either, Jo."

"What are we going to do?"

"We're going to get him to my place and then, while I make some phone calls, you can try and get some milk into him and get him cleaned up. We can talk about the rest later."

Jo nodded then looked down at the still listless infant in her arms. Although his reflex to suck seemed normal, he made no other efforts to move. "He's so little."

"He is." Hope watched Jo cradling the filth-covered infant close, providing comfort and warmth without thought to herself. Hope was worried too, but she needed to be strong for Jo. "He'll be okay, Jo, we'll get him home. From there, I can make sure we do for him what he needs. Now, let's see if PJ is ready to head off."

Chapter Thirty-three

PJ COLLECTED ALL THE supplies and their wrappers, shoving them into the backpack before taking the towel to Jo. She helped wrap the towel around the baby in Jo's arms. She threw on the backpack before picking up Oscar, holding him snug against her chest. Hope kept her arm around Jo, as she led them out.

Jo paused briefly at the top of the stairs, looking back over her shoulder, and Hope pulled her in closer. "I've got you."

Hope grabbed a taxi. She asked the driver to take them to the supermarket, where she collected everything she thought they might need. The others stayed in the car with the driver. Hope raced through the self-serve checkout and back to the taxi. Thankfully, the driver turned up his radio, paying them no interest.

As soon as they reached Hope's driveway, PJ spoke up. "You two go on in; I'll pay the driver."

Neither Hope nor Jo argued, both wanting to get in the house as soon as they could. Hope carried the bags in one hand and Oscar in the other. As soon as they were behind the closed gate, she let Oscar down, freeing up a hand to open the door. In the house, Hope let Ruby and Angel out of the enclosure. All three were over the moon to be reunited, barking and chasing each other round and round the house.

"Jo, do you know what to do with the formula? I got one that says it's for newborns, so it should be okay, but seriously, there were like a million to choose from!"

"I'm sure whatever you got will be better than what he's had. I'll go and make some for him now." Jo walked to Hope and laid the baby in her arms. "You can do this, just hold him close to you, so he feels safe."

"Maybe it's better if you just tell me what to do and then you can hold him."

"Come with me to the kitchen and watch. Then you'll know for next time, and if he gets unsettled we can swap."

Jo didn't give Hope a chance to argue. She walked to the kitchen and filled the jug. While it was boiling, Hope sat at the table and watched as Jo had suggested. As the jug heated, Jo filled a pot with water and dropped in the new bottles Hope had bought, along with the newborn teats and a dummy. She turned the stovetop on and placed the pot over the heat.

As soon as the kettle boiled, Jo filled a small Pyrex bowl with water and left it to the side. She found the chamomile tea and poured three cups. Placing the tea in front of Hope, Jo leaned down and kissed the top of the baby's head. She raised her head and kissed Hope gently on the lips.

Without a word, Jo moved back to the stovetop, removed the teats and pacifier from the now boiling water with a fork, and placed them on a tea towel on the bench. While the bottles and lids continued to sterilise, Jo opened the can of baby formula, and then took the pot off the heat. She carefully selected a bottle from the boiling water and filled it to the 100-ml mark with the cooled water from the Pyrex bowl. After reading the instructions on the can, Jo added the formula, secured the lid, and shook the contents, making sure everything was mixed in well.

Jo tipped the bottle up, watching as two small drops made their way from the teat to the inside of her wrist. "This is still too hot for him, so while it cools some more I think I'll give him a bath and clean him up."

***

Hope looked at the new life in her arms. His eyes were open, but he was very still. She hoped that with some nourishment he'd become a little more alert. She couldn't understand how any human being could treat an infant with such disregard. She couldn't understand that any more than she could the abuse they had dished out to Jo as a small child.

"Okay a bath it is. What do you need me to do?"

"You could either continue holding him or I could take him and you could run some water in the sink for me."

Hope thought for a moment before answering, "I think while he's happy here, he should stay put until you have the water ready. Besides, I wouldn't know how hot to make the water or how much to use."

"Would you like to learn?"

"Yes, very much," Hope replied without hesitation, surprising herself.

Jo rinsed the sink and began filling it as she spoke over her shoulder to Hope. "Cause he's still so small we can bathe him in the sink. A big bath would be frightening for him. Babies usually don't like bath time when they're small. If you think about it, they've been in a small cosy space for nine months, so to be stripped down naked and dumped in a big bath, must be scary as hell."

"I've never thought about it, but when you say that, I can imagine how it would be." Hope had been watching Jo's back as she moved from one task to the next so efficiently. She imagined Jo as a young child having to be responsible for so much, for the care of babies when she was still a child herself. She wanted to hold Jo in her arms and keep her safe, always.

Jo turned the water off and made her way over to Hope. "Do you mind if I use the kitchen table to lie him on when I dry him off?"

"Jo, use whatever you need to." Timidly reaching a hand out, Hope took one of Jo's and slowly brought her closer. "Jo, you don't need to ask permission to do anything in this house. I want you here." She looked down at the baby. "I want you all here, you, the puppies, and this little guy."

Jo smiled down at her before leaning over and brushing her lips lightly over Hope's. Hope responded as Jo deepened the kiss and slid her hand to the back of Hope's head, her fingers weaving their way through Hope's hair. Her lips felt soft and warm on Hope's. Their mouths slowly parted, and Jo whispered, "Thank you." Stepping back a little, she cleared her throat. "Okay, I'm just going to get some towels and a blanket, then I can clean this little guy up."

While Jo was collecting what she needed, Hope took the time to think. She knew what she would do next as far as the practical side of things. Making sure Jo and the baby were safe was her first and top priority. She had friends she could call who would be able to help with that. *What about the rest though? I have no idea what to do with these emotions. I'm going to need to learn, and fast.*

"Right. I think I've got everything I'll need." Jo breezed back into the kitchen and began laying out the goodies she'd collected from around Hope's place. She placed one towel down on the counter, beside the sink, before laying another out on the table. This one she left folded in half. Beside the towel on the table, Jo placed a container of baby powder and a small blanket.

"Where did you find the powder?"

Jo laughed, tilting her head to look at Hope. "It was in the back of the cupboard under the sink in the bathroom. I gather it's not something you use."

"No, I'd forgotten Aunt Em liked to use baby powder," she said softly.

"Well, I'm glad she did. It will be nice to put on his little tush." Jo walked over to the sink. "If you come on over you can see how much water I have in the sink for him."

Hope moved slowly over next to the sink, not wanting to wake the baby.

"What I want is enough water to cover him and keep him warm. If he is fairly well covered then when he moves his arms and legs about, his limbs will move easily through the water, floating, like what he is used to."

"Wow that's not something I'd ever have thought of."

"Not many parents do. Most are terrified they'll drop their squirmy baby in the water, so they put just a little water in the tub. This often makes the baby even wigglier, and the experience is pretty awful for all involved." Jo dipped her elbow in the water. "What I'm doing now is checking the temperature of the water. What we're after is for it to feel tepid on my elbow. That way it'll be warm enough for him, but not so hot as to burn."

* * *

Jo opened the towel the infant was wrapped in. Tears formed in her eyes, as she saw the newspaper, blood, and feces clinging to his tiny form. Lifting him to her, she kissed his head and spoke quietly to him, "Hey, little man, I know you were really happy in Hope's arms, but I need to clean you up a little bit. I also need to look you over. I'll do my best to get this over with as quickly as I can, and then we have some milk for you. I think you'll like that."

The baby squirmed a little but remained quiet. Jo lowered him slowly into the water, one hand under his bottom, the other safely cradling his head. As his little body entered the water, he opened his eyes, but still not a sound. With one hand holding his head out of the water, Jo scooped water into her other hand and poured it gently over his head. He turned his head with a little gasp, eyes wide open.

"Look, Jo, he's got blue eyes."

Jo looked at Hope and her eyes were soft when she spoke. "Nearly all newborns have blue eyes. When they're about six weeks old, they start to change."

Hope lowered her eyes, her cheeks flushed. "Oh."

Jo leaned over to Hope so their shoulders were touching, "Don't be thinking you're foolish or anything like that. It's nice that you're interested in his eyes."

While Hope watched, Jo ran soapy fingers over and through tiny folds of skin. Every movement was gentle and loving, like a silk scarf caressing soft, new skin. Jo was in awe of this new life in front of her.

"So now, I'm going to lift him from the water and wrap him in the towel beside us. If he's going to cry, it'll be now. He may not like being removed from the comfort of the water, so I just want to warn you that if he gets upset it's all right."

Hope nodded. "Right, thanks, now I'm prepared and won't panic." She laughed, "Well, not as much."

Jo laughed with Hope as she lifted the baby from the water, wrapping him quickly, before raising him up and bringing him close in to her chest. He began what sounded like an attempt at a cry, but as soon as he was up against Jo that stopped.

Jo walked to the table with him, Hope close behind. Laying the baby on the second towel, Jo carefully exposed the little boy limb by limb, drying him thoroughly as she did so. "It's important to make sure you dry in between all the little folds. Otherwise sores will develop and that's not nice for little ones." When he was dry and freshly powdered, Jo wrapped him in the blanket.

"Hang on!" Hope raced out of the kitchen, calling behind her, "Just a second, hang on, hang on. I'll be right back."

Rushing back to the kitchen, Hope carried another supermarket bag. She pulled out a packet of nappies. "I figured these would be a good idea." She beamed triumphantly.

"Oh, you were so right." Jo gave Hope a big, warm smile.

"I got the newborn. Do you have any idea how many choices there are in nappies? Man, I couldn't believe it. I got these, because I remembered seeing this packet at Jane's."

"Hope, they're perfect. I can't believe you managed to think of everything when you were only in there for such a short time. You not only got milk, but a good newborn one, as well as bottles and teats for new babies. On top of that you thought to get newborn nappies. Wow, you sure have surprised me!"

"Ah, but wait, that's not all." Hope grinned.

Jo had just succeeded in securing the nappy on a slightly squirmier baby. Dipping her hand back into the bag, Hope pulled out an all-in-one sleepsuit. It was white, with a cute little bear playing with a ball on the top left.

"Oh my God Hope, that is so cute. You thought to get him that?"

Keeping one hand on the baby, Jo moved closer, wrapping her free arm around Hope. She pulled her in close for a kiss.

"Hey, hey, hey, there's a baby in the room." Both Hope and Jo laughed as PJ entered the room. "How's he doing?"

"He's still really lethargic, but he seems okay," Hope informed her friend. "We had to wait for the milk to cool down, so Jo gave him a bath. He was so good."

Jo watched Hope's face light up as she talked about this little being that they hadn't known existed until a few hours ago. In that very brief time, he'd managed to make himself completely at home amongst them, and Jo was suddenly scared.

"Ohhh, he is so cute," PJ added.

Jo picked up her new charge. "Hope, would you like to feed him?"

The question brought Hope to a sudden halt. Shaking her head, she backed up a little. "Umm no, you should do that, I need to make some phone calls."

Both Jo and PJ laughed at the look on Hope's face. "You should see the fear in your eyes right now," PJ teased.

"Well, he's so small. I'd probably choke him!"

"You would not," Jo stated firmly. "I'll let you off the hook this time, because those phone calls are important. But next time, it's your job. In the meantime, I'll show you how to test the milk."

"I think I can handle that."

"I know you can, after this morning I'm sure you can handle anything." Hope blushed as Jo laughed softly. "Right then, this bottle. What I need you to do is tip it up and let a couple of drips land on the inside of your wrist. Again, we're looking for tepid. Ideally, if you can't feel the drops at all then it's the right temperature."

Hope followed Jo's instructions, and with a grin, informed both Jo and PJ, "It's perfect now."

"Great, then let's see if we can get this little one to drink some." As she took the bottle from Hope, Jo had one more request, "PJ, would you be able to pour some hot water into a smaller jug, so I can use it to keep the milk warm while I wind him?"

"Sure, anything to help."

Jo made her way to the couch, grabbing a tea towel on her way. She'd need that when it came time to get up his wind. Hope followed closely, watching as Jo sat and ran the tip of the teat over the baby's lips. Instinctively, he opened his mouth, and Jo let the teat slip in. Jo and Hope shared a smile when the little guy began to suck.

Hope was still staring at the baby when PJ came in with the hot water. Sitting next to Jo, PJ ran her hand lightly over the fine, dark hair covering the small boy's head. Hope went outside to start making her calls.

Chapter Thirty-four

AS MUCH AS HOPE may have denied admirers what they wanted, she'd always done her best to treat them with honesty and kindness. In doing so she'd managed to remain on friendly terms with most and, today, she was very grateful for this.

With the phone calls out of the way, she made her way back to Jo and PJ. The woman who had managed to capture her heart was nursing the infant who was making his way into all their hearts. The enormity of the morning's events brought her to a sudden halt. *Oh my God, if I'm feeling a bond grow between this gorgeous little boy and myself, what on earth must Jo be feeling? This is her brother, and those sad excuses for human beings are her parents. What sort of emotions must this be stirring up for her?* She gave herself a mental shake away from that troublesome path and knelt in front of Jo and the baby.

"I've made those calls. We'll be getting a few visitors shortly. Helene is a social worker; Kim's a lawyer; and Kath's a cop. I gave them all a basic run down, and they'll be here as soon as they can."

Hope ran her hand gently over the infant's tiny hand. With her free hand, she stroked Jo's cheek with the same gentleness. "Are you all right?"

Lifting her gaze from the baby to Hope, Jo was honest. "I'm scared about what might happen to us. We kidnapped a baby, Hope."

"I know. We could be in trouble, but I believe the reasons for our actions will be legitimate enough to allow some leeway." Leaning forward, Hope kissed Jo lightly. "Besides, I'd do it again if I had to. There's no way I could leave him there. I don't think he'd have survived much longer." Looking to the now sleeping child, Hope asked, "How did he do with the milk?"

PJ said, "He did really well. He drank a bit then, when he started to fall asleep, Jo picked him up. She rubbed and patted his back, and he did an enormous burp. I'm still in shock that something so small could make such a noise."

Jo laughed. "That's nothing, wait till it needs to come out the other end."

At the suggestion of what might be on its way, PJ's eyes almost bulged out of her head, and Jo's laughter turned into a giggle. Grateful for the distraction, Hope joined in. A knock on the front door silenced them all.

Hope rose. "Everything will be fine."

Hope returned, accompanied by three women. She stood beside Jo, resting a hand on her shoulder while she made the introductions. "Despite the circumstances, I'm very proud to introduce you all to my girlfriend, Jo, and one of my best friends, PJ."

Stepping back to the newcomers, Hope continued. "This is Helene." Hope placed a casual arm around the back of an extremely attractive woman with large, kind eyes. "Helene works for CYFs. PJ, that's Children, Youth and Family."

Helene's pale-blue eyes sparkled with a smile that was welcoming and soothing all in one. Jo began to release the breath she'd subconsciously been holding. "I'm really sorry I have to meet you both under these circumstances."

Helene looked Jo firmly in her eyes. "I'm especially happy to meet the woman who seems to have captured Hope's heart, something, I might add, I never thought I'd see." Helene moved her gaze to PJ and smirked. "And to meet the whirlwind that had the bar alive last night is indeed a treat."

With everything that had happened, it was hard to believe all of that had taken place only the night before. Hope wasn't surprised to see PJ's face blazing crimson. The PJ in the bar was by no means the PJ Hope knew. The woman who had, without question, stood by Hope and Jo all day, the PJ who was loyal and caring, sensible and levelheaded. That was the PJ she knew.

"Please, don't judge me based on first impressions."

"I never do. In my line of work, you learn, early on, that things, and more so people, are often nothing like they initially appear."

Hope's eyes flicked from PJ to Helene, intrigued by the very faint smirk still playing at the edges of Helene's eyes and lips. Hope placed a hand on the shoulder of the woman standing beside Helene. "This is Kath. Kath's a detective, and much to my surprise, is now going out with Sarah." Hope turned to their remaining visitor. "Thanks for coming along, we really appreciate you all taking time out from your days to help us with this mess."

Kath's voice was deep and smooth, like satin sliding over soft skin. "You were lucky; you caught both Sarah and I on a day off. When I told her about your call, Sarah insisted on coming along to check the little one over." Kath addressed Jo and PJ. "Sarah's an ER doctor, so she can look the baby over and make sure he isn't hurt in any way. If that's all right with everyone."

"That'd be wonderful, I'm worried about dehydration and heaven knows what else may have happened to him while he was with them." Jo seemed to consider her words, as she looked back to the baby who slept on in her arms. Returning her eyes to Sarah, she was honest, "Another concern is that both my parents are drug addicts. I'm sure our mother would have continued to get high throughout the pregnancy, so he may well have that to contend with. He's been very listless since we found him."

Sarah knelt before Jo. "How about I look him over now and see what I find. We can decide what we may want or need to do after that. I'll just get my bag from the front door."

Sarah moved away, and Jo stood waiting with the baby in her arms. When Sarah returned, Jo kept the infant snuggled in her arms as she led Sarah to the bedroom, leaving Hope and PJ with the others.

***

By the time Jo and Sarah rejoined the group, there was a new face to greet them. The newcomer stood and met them halfway, extending her hand. "Hi, I'm Nicole."

Jo returned the vigorous handshake. "Hi, I'm Jo, nice to meet you. Thanks for coming over."

"When Hope rang and explained to me your situation, I was more than happy to pass a couple of files over to my colleagues to clear my schedule."

Jo looked around the room at everyone gathered. "I can't thank you all enough." Remembering her manners, Jo turned to Nicole. "Sorry, this is Sarah, I'm not sure if the two of you know one another."

Nicole reached out to shake Sarah's hand. "Not officially, but I've seen you at the bar a couple of times with Kath. It's nice to actually get the chance to meet you properly."

"Yeah, the bar's fun, but not really the easiest place to get to meet and know new people," Sarah agreed.

While they greeted one another, Hope worked her way around the room to stand beside Jo, her arm resting around her waist. "How is he?"

Watching Hope tenderly stroke the baby's cheek, Jo relayed Sarah's findings. "He seems to be well enough. Although, Sarah's weighed and measured him, and she believes he's probably only about thirty-seven weeks' gestation, based on his size. It's hard to be sure though, seeing as we don't know what drugs she may have taken while pregnant, or if she was eating enough."

"So, how old do you think he is? I mean, when do you think he might have been born? Sarah, is there any way to know that?"

"I'm not able to say for certain, but I've done a general examination and, as Jo mentioned, I believe he's probably about three weeks premature. I agree with Jo, he is a little less energetic than I'd expect, but again, agree that it's probably more to do with a lack of nourishment since he was born. Other than that, he seems to be doing well. I'd say that by the time he gets some sleep and a couple more bottles into him, we'll see a huge improvement in his energy levels. The good news is I'm not seeing any of the tell-tale signs of a baby born addicted. "

Concern was evident in the creases across Hope's forehead. "Will he be able to stay with us for now or do we have to take him to the hospital?"

Sarah placed an arm around Hope's tense shoulders. "It's okay, Hope. I will have to register his birth but will do so as a home birth and at this stage he can stay where he is. I can monitor him closely, and if he continues to improve then there's no need for him to be admitted."

"Sarah does think, though, that he's probably less than twenty-four hours old." Jo touched those tiny fingertips, as she shared what she'd learned.

As the reality sank in, both Jo and Hope lowered onto the couch. Hope mumbled. "She must have, virtually, just had him, cleaned herself up, and then left him alone in that dark, dingy shit-hole, where anything could have happened to him, to go and take Oscar." Her voice rose in volume as she stood. "They'd have to be the lowest forms of life I've ever had the misfortune to stumble across. Not only did they abuse Jo throughout her childhood, but years later feel she needs to suffer some more along with making this new life suffer." Hope faced the group, her jaw tense. "We have to do whatever it takes to make sure this little guy never has to go through what Jo endured, or worse."

Rummaging through her briefcase, Sarah emerged with pad and pen. "I agree, and I'll be doing everything I can to make sure he's safe from now on." She turned to her partner. "Kath, I need to make a few phone calls; would you be able to execute an s42?" She explained to the others, "An s42 is a Search without Warrant."

"Yeah, I'll get that under way and have a couple of patrol cars swing by the movie theatre to see if Jo's parents are still there. I'm guessing they will be, based on what you've told us. I'd say their only desire today is to continue getting high. I'd also put money on it that they haven't even noticed their baby isn't there."

Sarah shook her head. "Sadly, I'd have to say I'm with you on that." She eased back her take-charge approach and sat next to Jo. "I realise the two of you will be reeling from all of this, and you will hear lots of terms that will be foreign to you both. The s42 is one rule. There are two others that we will work with immediately. An s39 is a Place of Safety Warrant, which we use when we feel a child is in danger for several different reasons, neglect being one which we have evidence of here. This one we'll need to have before the courts within five days. Then there is the s40, a Warrant to Remove a Child or Young Person. As much as we have already removed him, we need to file this in order to keep him from them. I'll take care of these, and we'll aim to have them before a judge as soon as we can." Sarah took a hand each of Jo and Hope's and held them tightly. "Are you both okay? I know this is all a huge shock and will seem overwhelming."

Neither spoke, but both nodded.

"We'll do this together. We're all here for you both." With notepad in hand, Sarah was a woman on a mission. "Let's get moving then, folks. Hope, I need you to send the pictures you and PJ took to Kath, Helene, and myself. We can all put them in our files and use them as evidence, not only to keep this adorable, wee boy safe and out of their care, but also to prosecute them."

"I can do that. If you all write your email addresses down, I'll do that straight away."

Feeling lost, and overwhelmed, but most of all embarrassed that her so-called parents were the reason for all of this. Jo wanted to run and hide before the commotion could drown her in its whirlpool. She felt a gentle pressure and looked down at Hope's protective hand on her knee. Jo was grateful for the lifeline. She met Hope's gaze and, in that minute, Jo knew she wanted to grab on to that lifeline with all she had and never let go.

Looking around the room at the diverse group of women, Jo was taken aback. These women were not only gorgeous in their own very different ways, but they were also extremely intelligent and successful. They'd all managed to gain Hope's attention at one time or another. Jo was stumped as to what it was Hope saw in her. *I'm a student with no money, no assets, and a fucked-up past that is coming back to grab hold of me again. What the hell does she see in me when she could have had any one of these women as well as many more?*

A squirming baby dragged Jo from her thoughts. He looked like he might wake soon, so Jo asked PJ to hold the little guy so she could get another bottle ready. Safely alone in the kitchen, Jo took a minute to catch her breath. As she tapped the scoop of milk powder into the bottle, Hope came from behind and rested her arms around Jo's waist.

Leaning down, Hope whispered in her ear, "I love you, and I'm not going anywhere."

Turning in Hope's arms, Jo looked up in wonder. "How did you know what I was thinking?"

"Because as busy as this house is right now, and as important as all we're doing is, you're my priority. I've been making sure to keep an eye on you, and I've seen the fear and anger in your eyes. I saw you look around the room at the women in there, and I'm sure I know what must have been going through your mind. As well hidden as it's been, I've seen your reaction to those people being called your parents. I've also seen the way you look at your brother."

As a lone tear slowly carved a path in Jo's cheek, she rested her head against Hope's chest. "You amaze me more and more every day. Hell, more and more every minute."

Gently placing fingertips under her chin, Hope raised Jo's face until they were eye to eye. "I love you, Jo. I can't change my past any more than you can yours. Yes, I've known other women; I've never hidden that or lied to you about it. Jo, I've never lied to you about anything, and I'm not about to start now. From the first time I saw you in the café, I was mesmerised by you. I wanted to know you, be around you. When I got that chance, I wanted to have more time and then more and more. No one else has ever made me want that. I love the way you see the world. Despite your upbringing, you're positive and see the best in people. You want to make something of your life, but not at the risk of selling out to what you're passionate about." Placing a hand on either side of Jo's cheeks, Hope kissed her gently. "Jo, you're one of the most amazing women I've ever met, and I'm very much in love with you."

Before Jo had the chance to respond, a cry from the lounge reminded her why she was in the kitchen. Both women laughed, their foreheads resting together. "Hope, I'm in love with you, too." Hope's lips brushed over Jo's gently. As the kiss began to deepen, another cry bought them back to the here and now. "You're all doing so much, what can I do to help?"

"You're already doing the most important job, sweetheart. You're looking after that angel in there. If you can keep doing that, we can get the other bits sorted. There isn't a lot I can do to help, but I'll get those pictures sent through to everyone. Then, I can help you with whatever you need."

Chapter Thirty-five

HOPE FINISHED EMAILING THE pictures to her friends. It was only when she walked into the office that she'd thought about work. Getting the pictures sent off had been her priority, but now she needed to try and get ahold of Andy. As she dialed the number, Hope sat back in her desk chair, head resting on the soft leather behind her. On the fifth ring, her office door flew open. Andy raced through, with PJ right behind him.

"Oh, my God! Why didn't you ring me?" Andy demanded as he rounded the desk.

Waving the phone in front of her, Hope laughed. "I was trying to. Why didn't you answer?"

Gathering her up into his arms, Andy held Hope tight before stepping back to look at her. "I was rushing here to see you, so I wasn't about to waste time answering my phone."

PJ laughed from the other side of the desk, and Hope and Andy joined in. "PJ, I gather I have you to thank for this overgrown whirlwind blowing through the door."

"Guilty as charged. While you were all busy, I snuck over here and called Andy. I knew you'd want him to know what was happening and figured you might need his help."

"You were right." Hope turned to Andy. "This is the first chance I've had to call. From the second Jo knocked on the door this morning we've barely had a chance to breathe."

"So, what can I do?"

"I'd really like to be able to stay with Jo. Would you be okay to work tonight?"

Wrapping his arms around Hope again, Andy kissed her head. "I can work tonight and any other night you need. I'm here for you both, in any way I can be."

"I can help out here, as well. I'm not much use at the house," PJ offered.

"Christ, Andy, you should have seen PJ this morning. She was amazing," Hope gushed.

As she sat on the couch, PJ snorted. "I hardly think so. I just did without really even thinking."

Hope went on to tell Andy about all that had taken place, making sure she didn't let PJ sell herself short. The more she told Andy, the more she became aware of how brave and clear thinking PJ had been. Without her, Hope didn't know if she would have been able to remain so in control herself.

She wrapped her arm around PJ's shoulders. "I couldn't have gotten through today without you, but I'm not sure if I should be relieved or terrified about the thought of the two of you taking control of the bar."

As Hope was about to walk out the door, Andy called, "Oh, I made a mad call to Jane after PJ told me what was happening. She's gathering up some clothes that Ben no longer fits and will drop them in as soon as she can."

***

Silence greeted Hope when she walked into her house. Wondering where Jo and the baby were, she wandered toward her bedroom. At the door, Hope took the opportunity to just watch. Jo was in the centre of Hope's bed, on her side, arm wrapped protectively around her infant brother.

Hope moved closer, her heart missing a beat, as she saw the similarities in the two siblings. In their peaceful state of sleep, Hope could see that they shared the same chin and nose. It was too early to tell if the baby would also have the same incredibly green eyes of his older sister, but Hope was pretty sure from the little hair he did have that he, too, was destined for curls.

Hope was almost at the bed, ready to curl up behind Jo, when there was a knock at the door. Hope quickly and quietly closed the bedroom door behind her. Running as fast as she could on tiptoes, Hope found Jane at the door, laden down with bags.

"I hear the two of you could use these." Jane offered the bags to Hope.

Relieving Jane of some of her load, Hope turned back into the house, and Jane followed.

"How are you doing?" Jane asked, as she deposited the remaining bags next to those Hope had set down beside the couch.

"Honestly?"

With a firm nod, Jane said, "Yep."

Hope sat, letting her hands land with a slight slap on her knees. "I don't know."

"You know, that's understandable. This is a lot to take in."

Moving her hands to her head, Hope ran her fingers through her hair. "Shit, two days ago, I was down and out because I thought I'd stuffed everything up with Jo. I couldn't get her to talk to me and thought I had well and truly stuffed up, and I was miserable. Then this morning, Jo knocks on the door, needing my help to get Oscar back. I was so happy it was me she came to and didn't hesitate to help. I want to be there for her. Then we not only find Oscar, but a baby. Not just any baby, but Jo's brother."

Jane reached out and gently squeezed Hope's hand. "It's okay to be freaked. Hell, it's a lot for me to take in, and I'm a bystander."

Hope looked at Jane with weary eyes. "Thanks, Jane. For the clothes and for letting me unload."

Jane patted Hope's hand. "It's what friends do." She pulled up a couple of bags. "I've got clothes in some and these here have bottles and some newborn nappies that Ben's outgrown already. If you rummage through, there are a few blankets and other bits and pieces I thought might be handy. Out on the doorstep is a bassinet as well."

"I can't thank you enough. I did stop on the way here and grabbed a few nappies and one outfit for him, but haven't had a chance to even think about what else we might need."

"Hey, I felt overwhelmed when Ben arrived, and I knew he was on the way. I can only imagine what this must be like." Jane put the bags back on the floor and stood. "How 'bout a cuppa?"

"Oh God, yes please." Hope spread her arms in a big stretch.

Jane walked into the kitchen. "Where are Jo and the baby?"

"They're out cold on my bed. I was just watching them before you got here. He looks like her, just a smaller version."

Jane placed two teabags into cups. "How is she doing?"

"Okay, I think, but we haven't even had a chance to really talk. I'm worried what all of this may stir up for Jo."

"Do you think Jo will want to keep the baby?"

Before Hope had time to admit she hadn't even thought of that, there was another knock at the door. Hope raced again to get there before Jo and the baby woke.

***

The commotion of people in the house was enough to wake Jo. Jane took orders and made everyone a drink, while Kath informed everyone that her team had found Jo's parents at the theatre. As they had suspected, neither had a clue the baby was gone. They were both arrested on child abuse charges and for kidnapping Oscar. At this very minute, they were in cells at the local station.

Sarah and Helene let the group know that they had filed all the papers with the courts. Sarah's were to have the baby placed in care. "Jo, at this stage I've put down that he is in the care of a family member. I thought if he stayed with you tonight, seeing as you have a feeding pattern starting and he's content and safe here, you and Hope can decide what you want to do. We can talk more tomorrow."

Jo looked to Hope who nodded. "Thanks Sarah, tomorrow would be good."

Hope called over to Andy and arranged for some food to be sent over for everyone. She figured after everything they'd all done to help her and Jo, the least she could do was make sure they all had a decent meal.

PJ brought the dinners over, taking them into the kitchen. Hope made the most of the chance and followed her. "PJ, how are you doing? I haven't had a chance to ask before now, and I'm so sorry about that."

PJ didn't hesitate to wrap Hope in a huge hug. "I'm fine. I was a little shaken earlier on, the adrenaline pumping, but being with Andy has been good for me. He's had me laughing and we're having a good time together."

Returning PJ's hug, Hope spoke sincerely, "I'm so blessed to have such incredible friends. We wouldn't have been able to get through this mess without your help. You were amazing, PJ."

"Amazing is one word for her, I'm sure I could find a few more," Sarah declared, coming up behind them.

PJ went bright red, and Hope laughed. She gave Sarah a playful slap. "I'd be interested to see what other words you could come up with."

"Oh my God, I'm never going to live that night down, am I?" PJ headed for the door. "I think I can hear Andy calling, sorry ladies, gotta go." As PJ made a hasty retreat to the bar, Hope and Sarah enjoyed some much needed laughter.

Chapter Thirty-six

JO WAS IN THE bedroom putting the baby in the little bassinet Jane had lent them. She'd just fed him again, and both she and Hope were happy to see the baby taking more milk now. He appeared to be livelier. When Jo last changed his nappy, he'd kept his focus on her while she spoke to him. Hope came closer and called to Jo and he had been startled by the added noise. As much as neither of them liked the idea of their guest being upset, both smiled at one another when he began to cry. His normal actions were a relief to Jo. They let her know the love and nourishment they were giving him was working.

She was exhausted, despite the nap she'd taken in the late afternoon. It was now ten, everyone had gone home, and all Jo wanted to do was sleep. She knew she'd have to fit this in with the little guy and the best way to get any rest was to sleep when he did. Looking at her brother sleeping peacefully, the significance of the recent events began to settle in. She had a brother. She had a chance at having a family.

Jo thought back to the theatre they'd found him in and shivered. Thankful they'd found him when they did, she headed back to Hope. Jo sat next to her on the couch and sank into the safety of her warm hug.

"Is he all right?"

"He's fine. Sound asleep with a full tummy." She rested her cheek against Hope's chest. "I was just watching him sleep. Imagine if we hadn't found him when we did."

Stroking Jo's back, Hope soothed her. "I think it's better if we don't think about the what-ifs. Instead, let's think about the positives, like we did find him, and in time." Hope kissed Jo's head. "We can think about how lucky we are to be surrounded by incredible people who are there to support us and do all they can for an adorable little boy to make sure he's in safe hands."

Jo lifted her head. She smiled a tired, crooked smile. "You're right. We need to stay positive. He's safe now, and we're doing all we can to make sure he never has to go back to people who don't deserve him."

They sat in silence for a minute before Jo quietly added, "It was hard having everyone discover just what I came from, and knowing that they're my parents, but saving my brother from them makes it worth it in the end."

"Jo, no one thinks any less of you because of who your parents are. If anything, that just makes you an even more amazing woman. That you have been through all you have and come out of it the strong, caring, supportive, thoughtful woman you are is credit to you and your strength of character."

Hope leaned into Jo, the kiss she deposited soft and tender. When their lips parted, Hope whispered, "I love the woman you are."

Too tired to fight the tears that wanted to break free, Jo gave in. As the first of them made their way over the rim of her eyes, tracking down her cheek, she whispered back, "I love you, too, Hope."

***

Hope sent Jo to bed, while she went around the house locking up and turning out lights. By the time she climbed between the sheets, Jo was fast asleep. Hope snuggled in beside the woman she loved and closed her eyes, but even as tired as she was, sleep wouldn't come.

The baby's snuffles and grunts could be heard from the bassinet beside the bed. These weren't enough to keep Hope from sleep; it was the gaps between them that had her lying awake for hours. Every time she started to relax, thinking she might nod off, he would sound as though he'd stopped breathing. She'd be wide awake again, listening for the snuffles. Inevitably they would follow and sleep would again be lost.

Hope thought it sounded like he was more restless in his sleep as she looked at the clock beside the bed. Counting back, Hope realised it had been three hours since Jo had fed him. Figuring he must be getting ready to wake, she decided to see if she could save Jo from having to get up.

Sliding gently from the bed, Hope made her way to the kitchen. The bright light left her blinking, briefly, before she could walk to the bench where the formula was. Hope followed the instructions to make the bottle.

While the jug boiled, she tiptoed to the toilet, she'd needed to go for over an hour and was busting. Feeling much better, she retraced her steps and filled a jug with hot water then placed the baby's bottle in to keep warm, like she'd seen Jo do. Feeling very pleased with herself, she went to gather up the baby.

She held the blanketed bundle in her arms, set the jug and bottle beside the couch, and eased into the embrace of the soft fabric. She tested the milk on her wrist as Jo had taught her. Not really knowing what it should feel like, though, she took the bottle from the hot water and placed it beside her while she quickly checked out what the internet could tell her.

Thanking the universe for the wonder of the World Wide Web, she tested the milk again, discovering it was perfect just as the first sign of a cry made its way from the baby's lungs. Popping the teat in his mouth, Hope couldn't help but grin at him when he immediately began sucking.

The sucking slowed and his lips softened, Hope took the teat from the infant's mouth and lifted him slowly to her shoulder. After a few pats, she was rewarded with a very loud burp. A few more pats and two more burps later, Hope laid the little bundle back and offered him more milk.

She gave herself a mental pat on the back. *Look at you go. You've got this. Maybe you could be a mum.* That brought her back to earth. *What the hell are you thinking? You've only just grown up enough to have a girlfriend!* Lifting the baby to her shoulder again, she was rewarded with a wet trail down her back. "See, even he agrees."

After a small fight with a baby Gro-suit and its little snaps, Hope managed to change the little guy's nappy, grateful it was only wet. She gently deposited him, fed and dry, back in his bed and tucked him in carefully. She was happy she'd managed to not wake Jo. Hope climbed back in beside her girlfriend and eventually drifted off, her mind as tired as her body.

***

Jo bolted upright in bed. The sun was just trying to push its way around the edge of the curtains.

"Oh my God! Is he all right? He didn't wake up!"

As Jo scrambled for the side of the bed, a sleepy Hope reached out and gently took hold of her arm. "Everything's fine. He did wake, but I got to him before he could wake you. I wanted you to get as much sleep as you could. I'd say he must be due to wake again any minute now."

Hope opened her eyes, Jo was sitting, mouth open, staring down at her.

221

"What's wrong? Did I forget to do something? Is he okay?" Now panicked herself, Hope sat up.

"Umm, I don't think anything's wrong. I haven't actually looked at the baby yet," Jo admitted.

Collapsing back against her pillow, Hope groaned. "Ohhh, you had me worried." One arm lay across her eyes, blocking out the sun. "Then why are you looking at me like that?"

Jo's lips touched Hope's gently at first, then with more pressure. Hope responded as Jo deepened the kiss, drawing a moan from Hope.

"I was looking at you like that in surprise. You did that for me so I could sleep?" Jo nestled on her chest.

"Aha." Hope ran her hand over Jo's bare arm. "I couldn't sleep. Every time he would stop snuffling, I was terrified he'd stopped breathing. Seemed silly to let him wake you when I was already awake. You were exhausted and needed some sleep."

As Jo stretched herself along the length of Hope, a small cry came from the bed beside them. Smiling at Hope, Jo declared, "I do believe that's my call."

Both laughed, before Jo made her way off the bed. "Try and get a little more sleep sweetheart, you must be exhausted."

"I'm fine. I'll get up in a minute and make you some breakfast."

Jo picked up her brother and looked over at Hope, "I love you. Thank you for last night."

Hope laughed. "Not usually what I get thanked for the morning after, but you're welcome, baby."

***

Hope stretched her arms and legs as far and wide as they could go, blinking as she slowly stirred and opened her eyes. The room was bathed in sunlight. Realising she must have fallen asleep again after Jo got up to feed the baby, she rubbed her eyes before shuffling to the edge of the bed. Her shuffle continued into the lounge, where she was greeted by the welcoming smiles of two beautiful women.

"Good morning, sleepyhead," Jo teased. Hope leaned over kissing Jo's forehead then bent farther placing a kiss on the baby's nose. Jo claimed a real kiss.

"Look, sweetheart, Olivia just got back this morning." Jo's excitement was obvious.

The older woman's return brought a sense of comfort, and Hope smiled. "Hi Olivia, it's really good to see you. Did you enjoy your trip?"

"Yes dear, I had a wonderful time, but I'm happy to be home."

"I'm so pleased to have you back. I missed you," Jo said.

Olivia held Jo's hand. "I missed you, as well." Raising her head, she addressed Hope, "Seems I've missed out on a lot of excitement in my absence."

Suspecting Olivia wasn't simply referring to the more obvious baby in Jo's arms, Hope blushed. "Umm, yeah, there have been a few things to deal with."

"Well, I'm glad the two of you were able to figure things out together."

Hope nodded. "So am I." She smiled at Jo. "Very happy." Rubbing her hand over her eyes, Hope headed toward the kitchen. "I need coffee. Can I get anyone anything?"

Both replied they were fine, and Hope returned to her mission of finding caffeine. She wandered back through the lounge, returning to the bedroom with her cup of hot, black goodness.

"I'm just going to take my coffee and grab a shower. The mix of hot water and caffeine should revive me." Hope giggled. Despite the lack of sleep, she was in a good mood. She gathered up fresh clothes and made a beeline for the bathroom.

The hot water running over her shoulders felt wonderful, and Hope was happy to stand there as long as the water remained hot. As her muscles slowly relaxed, her mind wandered. Seeing Olivia had been a pleasant surprise. In all the pandemonium, she'd totally forgotten about Olivia being due to return. Seeing the joy in Jo's eyes at having Olivia home was nice. Jo may have been without family for many years, but she now had what she deserved in Olivia. As she dried herself, Hope remembered greeting Jo and the baby in the lounge. That kiss had nearly melted her.

***

Hope found the lounge empty, but could hear the faint sounds of voices from the bedroom. She stopped in the doorway. Olivia had her arm around Jo as they stood over the bassinet.

Hope couldn't see Jo's face, but she could tell she was crying. Hope could hear the small cracking in her lover's quiet voice, and her heart felt like it would break. Seeing the woman she loved in pain tore Hope apart. She knew it was rude to listen, but at the same time she couldn't walk away.

"I don't know what to do, Olivia. I'm in love with Hope. When I'm with her, I feel more alive than I ever knew possible. She brings out things in me I didn't even know existed before she came into my life. I don't want to lose her, or what we have, but the thought of this little guy growing up in homes like I did makes me want to be sick. I want to keep him with me where I know he is safe and will grow up with love, but that would mean losing Hope and who's to say I would be a better choice for him, anyway."

Coming up behind Jo quietly, Hope wrapped her arm around Jo's waist and pulled Jo back into her. "I say you'd be a better choice for him; I think you'd be the perfect choice for him. I'd also say you wouldn't lose anything. You'd gain a family almost overnight, and so would Olivia and I. Now seems to be the perfect time for new beginnings."

***

Hope watched as Asher chased Ruby and Oscar, his crawling still wobbly, but his determination strong. Just when he was within reach of them, the two little dogs would move a few steps along before sitting and watching the baby again. Jo's laughter floated through the air, settling around Hope and reminding her again that she was a very lucky woman.

They had named the baby Asher. The name meant 'blessed one', and they both agreed that he was, indeed, blessed to have come through all he had, unscathed. Tests had been able to confirm that despite drug and alcohol use during the pregnancy, he was one of the lucky ones who didn't have residual effects. Their mother had admitted to using, but not often. Apparently, their father had not let her have any during most of the pregnancy. This had nothing to do with him caring about the baby and everything to do with him seeing it as his chance to get the lot himself. Hope and Jo were grateful for his selfishness. It had allowed Asher to come through the pregnancy without harm.

They were convinced that having Asher in their lives left them even more blessed. He brought them together as a family, and neither could imagine life any other way. Hope could hardly believe it had been nine months since they'd found their little gift. In that time, they'd all moved into the main house with Olivia, bringing life back into the large house and adding to the tales it already held. Tales of love and laughter, of family.

Recalling the night she'd laid on the hospital bed, curled up in Aunt Em's arms as she had when she was a small girl, Hope remembered her aunt's final words to her. *'It's very important you know how much joy you've given me. You have been the greatest gift. I've been so lucky to have had you. You have always been, and always will be, my greatest pride. You're an amazing woman, and you need to let someone special share in that one day. Don't be afraid to love, and don't be afraid to be loved.'* I know that pride myself now, Aunt Em, and I'm not afraid anymore.

Hope made her way over to the blanket that was spread out on the back lawn. She bent and swooped the little boy into the air. "Hi rascal, have you been a good boy for Mummy while I was at work?"

Hope received a treasure of giggles, as she kissed her son's chubby cheeks. Depositing him back on the blanket beside Jo, Hope sat and kicked her shoes off before leaning over to her partner. She took her time kissing Jo, enjoying the softness of her lips while the sun's late afternoon rays settled over them.

As their lips parted, Jo whispered, "I love the way you come home to us."

"I love coming home to you both."

Jo laughed. "We need to make the most of the time we have for kisses like that. Before we know it, Asher will be moaning about his mums kissing."

"In that case, we need to get in as many as we can." Hope was smiling, as she covered Jo's mouth with her own. Sitting back up, Hope's face grew serious as she took Jo's hand in her own. "I've been thinking about something."

Jo sat herself up as well. "What is it, sweetheart? Is everything okay?"

"There's nothing to worry about. I have come to realise something, though."

Jo raised a cautious eyebrow. "And what might that be?"

Hope turned to face the woman she loved. "Not so long ago, I found myself excited every day to see the stool at the end of the counter at *Jem's* occupied by a beautiful and intriguing woman. I'd look out for its regular patron, and if she didn't show, I'd be filled with disappointment. An empty stool was something I dreaded. Now, when I look and find an empty stool I fill with a light I thought would never shine in me again, a light that was switched on because the woman who once filled that stool now fills every other part of my life. She fills it with love and laughter, and she fills it with family." Asher pulled himself up on Jo's shoulder, and Hope grinned at the smiling face. She stroked his cheek gently before doing the same to Jo. "Jo, I can live with an empty stool, but I don't ever want to live with an empty life. You and Asher fill my days and my heart. I love you, Jo. Will you marry me?"

As the tears began to flow, Jo reached up, stroking Hope's cheek in return. "I love you, too, Hope. Yes, a thousand times, I will marry you."

The End

About TJ Whittle

TJ Whittle sees herself as many things and happily puts being a mother at the top of her list. With three teenagers, there is never a dull moment but she wouldn't have it any other way. Being a mum is not simply something she does, but is a role she cherishes, believing that it is not only the most challenging role she will ever take on, but hands down the most rewarding.

For TJ 2013 and 2014 bought some tough times. During these she rediscovered her love of reading. Picking up AJ Adaire's Sunset Island, TJ was able to lose herself in these characters and the love that developed between them. This led to more books and before long TJ found she had stories of her own she wanted to share. This led to her first novel, *Without Your Courage*. There are plenty more to come.

Having been born and raised in Auckland, New Zealand, TJ is very proud to be a Kiwi. She grew up in a society where everyone knew their neighbour's and kids played out till after dark. Where kids roamed freely between houses and everyone looked out for one another.

TJ loves to spend time in nature, the beach being one of her favourite places. Regardless the season, the beach is somewhere TJ is always sure to come away from feeling calm and refreshed. A day by the water's edge with her family, laughing, playing, exploring, is a day of making memories.

Contact Information
Email: treezr345@hotmail.com
Facebook: TJ Whittle

Other Books from Desert Palm Press

TJ Whittle

Without Your Courage

ISBN: 9781310147548

What does courage look like to you? Is it a young girl facing an unwanted marriage? Does it echo the fears of a spouse exposing their secret? Is it the strength of a young woman protecting her unborn child? Perhaps it's as simple as a first kiss. Without Your Courage takes us to Auckland, New Zealand and the surrounding countryside, to join the lives of four strong women.

1940s. Violet and Charlotte form a beautiful friendship while John is away at war. What will happen when he returns?

Present Day. An accident introduces Ella and Gemma, who struggle to define their new friendship across the barrier of age. Four women with their lives entwined. Will they find the love they seek?

Desert Palm Press

AJ Adaire

Friends Series

Sunset Island

ISBN: 9781301136629

Ren Madison is certain her life couldn't be more perfect. She owns a private island with an Inn off the coast of Maine. She treasures her loving relationship with her older brother Jack, his wife, Marie, and dotes on her niece Laura. She has a passionate and supportive relationship with her partner, Brooke, and a successful business that doesn't require her undivided attention allowing her ample time to pursue her true passion, painting.

Ren's idyllic world crumbles when Brooke dies. Friends and family worry that Ren may never fully recover from her loss.

Dr. Lindy Caprini, a multi-lingual professor, is looking for an artist to illustrate the book she is writing comparing fairy tales from around the world. To make working together on the book easier, Lindy takes a year sabbatical and leaves friends, home, and boyfriend in Pennsylvania and moves to Ren's island. Ren soon discovers that the beautiful and mischievous Lindy is a talented author and a witty conversationalist. Their collaboration on the book leads to a close, light hearted, and flirtatious friendship. Will their collaboration end there?

The Interim (a novelette)
ISBN: 9781311099051
Devastated that her partner cheated, Melanie flees to a new job in Maine, where she meets Ren Madison. Ren is dealing with issues of her own after losing her partner Brooke in a plane crash

What happens in the interim after one relationship ends and you're really ready to love again? For Ren Madison, Melanie was what happened.

The Interim fills in the details of Ren Madison's life on Sunset Island after Brooke but before Lindy.

Awaiting My Assignment
ISBN: 9781310825248
Bernie was a liar. Amanda learned that much when she caught her lover cheating the first time. Upon discovering a second indiscretion, Amanda vows there will never be another. She leaves the relationship, fleeing to her friend Dana in New York State. While staying at Dana's home, Amanda meets and falls in love with a wonderful woman named Mallory.

Amanda is ready to move on. However, the consistently surprising Bernie isn't finished yet. Amanda learns of Bernie's rudest betrayal yet when she receives a package from her recently deceased ex-lover. A very surprising revelation and one final request are contained therein. The favor comes with a gift that delivers dramatic and life-altering changes, not only to Amanda's life, but to the lives of her closest friends and new partner as well.

Anything Your Heart Desires
ISBN: 978131163912
"Whoa—lesbians!" That was Stacy Alexander's first thought as she observes the group of women in the new shop across the street kiss each other in greeting. Stacy had been staring out her apartment window trying to think of a motive for the death of the character she'd killed off in her mystery novel. Ah ha—extortion! What could be a better reason for the murder of my heroine than being blackmailed

because she's a lesbian? Now all I need is a lesbian to teach me about the 'lesbian lifestyle.'

That's where policewoman Jo Martin enters the picture. Jo has two rules by which she religiously lives her life: never get involved with someone already in a relationship and never, ever date a straight woman. As Jo and Stacy collaborate on the novel, will Stacy want to gain a more intimate knowledge of the topic, and will Jo hold steadfastly to her rules?

One Day Longer Than Forever
ISBN: 9781310847738

Dr. Kate Martin needs a vacation after a failed romance with her business partner nearly ruins her. Lee Foster is recovering from her first lesbian relationship that self-destructed when her partner moved several states away, leaving her behind.

Two failed romances, a double booked vacation cabin, and a blizzard—will fate intervene again and turn a passionate affair with a stranger, into something more?

It's Complicated
ISBN: 9781311122964

Victoria Brannigham had a guilty pleasure. Every day she would take a detour, sit on the boardwalk, and wait. She tried not to covet what could never be hers. Beverly McMannis was lonely, until she discovered another lesbian on the island. Bev eagerly embraced the growing friendship with her neighbor. Victoria was honest with Bev right from the start; explaining that she wasn't free to explore their attraction. Bev promised to honor the boundaries. Love isn't always easy, sometimes it's complicated...especially when she doesn't know you're still being faithful.

I Love My Life
ISBN: 9781311310002

Betrayal by her former partner sends Chris Baxter fleeing to Maine. To escape the monotony of staring at the four walls of her isolated cabin, she enrolls in a sailing class. A chance pairing with Stephanie Kincaid and her cohorts, Tina and Terry, offers an opportunity for new friendship. Their shared homework assignment might offer Chris the potential for more than just knowledge of navigation.

An urgent message interrupts the classmates' sailing vacation along the coast of Maine. While Chris rushes back to her twin's bedside, the others remain onboard to sail back to their homeport. Will the revelations from her ex, her sister, and her family, change everything in the new life that Chris has rebuilt?

Journey to You
ISBN: 9781311571854

What do you do if you are one of the few who remain alive after a mysterious, flu-like virus claims most of the global population? This is a question Kim Robins and Peri Henderson have to answer when the world changes and society falls apart.

Violent gangs of looters make it unsafe to remain in the city. Hoping to improve their chances for survival, Kim and Peri decide to hike into the remote forest area of Maine.

Dangerous circumstances along the trail cause the women to join forces with another hiker and her dog. The longtime friends and their new companions set off on a daunting trek filled with both menacing and kindhearted survivors.

In this romantic adventure, the real question to be answered is, will this journey bring each of the women the happiness and safety she seeks?

S.L. Kassidy

Please Baby
ISBN: 9781311485137

Jayce Newton's life is going downhill after she rescues her little niece from an awful situation. She plans to hold onto her niece and gain custody of her, but there are some factors against her. Her girlfriend doesn't want the baby around. Her mother wants to take the baby from her, and her brother has disappeared. Things only seem to get worse when Gus Tucker comes into her life.

Gus Tucker's life isn't going much better. She recently divorced her wife and moved into a new home. She's looking forward to a new start and spending time with her sister. Before she can do that, though, she ends up causing trouble for Jayce Newton, getting her fired from her job and kicked out of her home. She tries to make it up to Jayce by taking her in during her time of need. Now, it's just a struggle to see if they're able to coexist in the same house with a baby between them.

Desert Palm Press

Scarred for Life Series

Scarred for Life
ISBN: 9781310171352

Dane Wolfe is a loner. Forsaken by her family and betrayed by people close to her, she has lost all faith in people and spends her days wandering the streets with no direction or meaning. She drifts through life, existing and nothing more. Nicole Cardell is a successful attorney. She has too much faith in people and is being taken advantage of by her boyfriend, Tyler, Dane's cousin. She's tired of his selfish ways and tosses him out. The bad relationship leaves her questioning her judgment. Circumstances bring Dane and Nicole together and a friendship brings them closer. They're able to heal each other and bring balance to each other's lives. Their peace is shattered when family causes trouble and tears them apart. Will they find their path back to each other and to the love that was slowly growing?

New Cuts, Old Wounds

ISBN: 9781310217289

In this sequel to *Scarred for Life*, Nicole Cardell and Dane Wolfe have been together for a year. They are doing their best to move forward with their relationship and open up to each other. It's time to meet family members. Dane's nervous about meeting Nicole's family, but she's even more nervous about Nicole meeting her family. Nicole is eager for both. Nicole thinks Dane should bond with her family while Dane thinks she needs to get as far away from them as possible. The Wolfe family seems to agree with Dane, but keep inviting her to things and Nicole keeps accepting the invites. Will family make or break Dane and Nicole?

Bandages

ISBN: 9781942976103

Nicole and Dane return in the third installment of the *Scarred* series. Life is good. The musician gave the lawyer a ring, a not-engagement ring, a promise; this is forever. But, they both still had some growing and healing to work through.

Healing is strange. There are those days when the bandage falls off on its own and you think you're good to go. Days when laughter comes easy and you forget the past. And there are days when the past doesn't want to be forgotten; you still need a stitch or a cast to hold yourself together. There are even relapses when the poisonous past needs release.

Share their journey through eighteen short stories of play, passion, and a deepening partnership. You'll enjoy the journey as much as where it leads.

Desert Palm Press

BJ Phillips

Hurricane Season

ISBN: 9781942976

Shawn Richards (aka S.K. Richardson) is a romance author. She's had her heart broken badly again and is done with love. Ditching San Francisco, she moves back home to Southwest Florida to get her feet back under her and finish her latest novel.

Carrie Alexander is a huge S.K. Richardson fan, but has no idea what she looks like. She does, however, like the looks of the new neighbor down the street, Shawn Richards.

Drawn to each other as friends, Shawn still tries to keep some distance in spite of what she's beginning to feel for Carrie. Carrie isn't the kind of woman you just have a fun night with and then move on. Carrie's the kind you fall in love with and make love to, and live happily ever after with—but she just can't let herself trust her heart yet. After all, the last time she fell for one of her fans, it ended badly.

Carrie is looking for 'happy ever after' just like in all those romance novels she reads. Shawn could be the one, or maybe Carrie's fooling herself and there's really no such thing as all that romantic stuff in Shawn's books.

Shawn is afraid she can't deliver on that 'happy ever after' she knows Carrie wants—and she wants, too, truth be told. Destiny might have given them a push when Carrie tripped at the local grocery store and literally fell into Shawn's arms. But fear could cost Shawn the woman of her dreams.

Note to Readers: